DURHAM ACADEMY
50TH ANNIVERSARY

Design by Ann Kenan

Max's Gang

Frank Baer

Max's Gang

TRANSLATION BY IVANKA ROBERTS

LITTLE, BROWN AND COMPANY

BOSTON   TORONTO

GERMAN LANGUAGE EDITION COPYRIGHT © BY ALBRECHT KNAUS VERLAG,
HAMBURG, 1979

ENGLISH LANGUAGE TRANSLATION COPYRIGHT © 1983
BY LITTLE, BROWN AND COMPANY

FIRST AMERICAN EDITION

This book was first published by
Albrecht Knaus Verlag, Hamburg, in 1979
under the title *Die Magermilch-Bande.*

Library of Congress Cataloging in Publication Data

Baer, Frank.
  Max's gang.

  Translation of: Die Magermilchbande.
  Summary: Five German children make their way home
from Czechoslovakia across the war-torn countryside of
1945, enduring hardship and danger in the desperate hope
of being reunited with their families in Berlin.
  1. World War, 1939–1945—Juvenile fiction.
[1. World War, 1939–1945—Germany—Fiction.
2. Germany—History—Allied occupation, 1945
—Fiction. 3. Survival—Fiction] I. Title.
PZ7.B1389Max 1982   [Fic]   82–24918
ISBN 0–316–07517–5

BP

Published simultaneously in Canada
by Little, Brown & Company (Canada) Limited

PRINTED IN THE UNITED STATES OF AMERICA

Contents

Introduction

This book tells of the adventures of a group of children from Berlin who made their way home from Czechoslovakia after the end of World War II — between April and October 1945. The story of Max's gang is based on contemporary history.

In Germany, during the last years of the war, hundreds of thousands of schoolchildren and their teachers were evacuated from bomb-threatened cities and placed in so-called Children's Evacuation Camps, CEC. The children from Berlin were taken to Western Poland and Czechoslovakia. As the war was ending they were hastily shipped to the west. Most of them ended up in the Bavarian Forest. During the chaos of the final days of the war they were put up in makeshift quarters, badly fed, and sometimes deserted by their teachers or separated from their classmates. Having had no news of their parents for months, many children took matters into their own hands and tried to get to Berlin on their own.

Younger readers may find it difficult to imagine a time when there was no mail service, no telephones; when you could not travel without a special permit, and could only buy things in shops with ration cards; a time in which tens of thousands of children in Germany and elsewhere in Europe were wandering around, fending for themselves, searching for their parents, for their relatives, for a home.

This book is the result of journalistic research. The five children of Max's gang are fictional. But their adventures are based on facts.

Among other things, I analyzed over four hundred interviews for this book, including forty with former Berlin schoolchildren who had experiences similar to those of the children of Max's gang. I could not have written this story without them.

My thanks especially to:

Frau Susanne Schwettke, Berlin

Frau Ursula Stross, Berlin

Herr Arno Dudschus, Berlin

Herr Wolfgang Janssen, Berlin

Herr Gunther Lang, Steinbach

Herr Alfred Lemke, Berlin

Herr Hanns Pannier, Berlin

Herr Hans Potthoff, Berlin

Herr Udo Rossow, Berlin

Herr Peter Stein, Roedermarkt-Urberach

and particularly Frau Marga Ullrich.

Max's Gang

1

Departure

For days rumors had been circulating like wildfire through the boys' annex of the Kusice Children's Evacuation Camp: Hitler was launching a powerful new counteroffensive; the Americans were coming; the Russians were coming. No one knew what to believe.

But this morning one thing had become clear — the camp itself was going to be evacuated. From their windows the boys had seen the girls gather in front of their quarters in the "old castle," surrounded by huge heaps of luggage: knapsacks, boxes tied with string, suitcases, hampers, everything jumbled together. The girls had huddled there all morning in the chill April drizzle. Apparently there was some sort of problem about transportation, but finally a horsecart had come and the luggage was piled on, reaching precarious heights.

Max Milk had missed the girls' actual departure. He had

been summoned to the camp commandant's office: another infraction of the rules; another punishment. But The Emperor (as everyone called Dr. Kayser behind his back) had not exhibited his usual severity. He seemed preoccupied. The office too was not as usual — files and loose papers were piled every which way on the commandant's normally immaculate desktop. The Emperor had barely launched into his scolding and had not even reached for his cane when they were interrupted by a group of teachers and Wald, the camp team leader.

"You may leave, Milk, but I'll get back to you later, young man!" The Emperor snapped, and Max had wasted no time making his escape.

Max walked very slowly around the camp, delaying as long as possible his return to the annex and savoring being alone for a change. The other boys were all right, but he had only one real friend, Adolf. Sometimes he just couldn't stand always being surrounded by other people, listening to fat Heini's constant bragging, the two Hermans' endless arguing. Occasionally he would walk to the nearby village to get away from them all, but there was nothing to do there and he could sense the hostility of the Czech villagers — they hadn't been pleased to have a boys' school and a girls' school full of Germans take over the "old castle" and the buildings and fields around it. They'd be happy to see the camp moving out.

All in all, Max was glad it was happening also. The camp had been his home for almost four years, ever since his parents had decided that Berlin was too dangerous and that he'd be better off in the countryside, but he hadn't grown fond of it. He hated the strict discipline. The teachers were bad enough, but the business of team leaders and group leaders and room seniors was worse: a bunch of bullies always pulling rank, acting as though they were in the real army. Max was a room senior himself, but he refused to take it seriously and was frequently in trouble as a result. Dangerous or not, he wanted to be back with his family in Berlin.

"How'd it go?" Max was startled. He hadn't heard Adolf come up. "I've been looking all over for you. I called, but I guess you didn't hear me — I had to run to catch up." Adolf looked a bit embarrassed by the last admission — although he was almost Max's age, he looked several years younger because he was so small.

"It was nothing," Max said.

"The girls' school left finally. Did The Emperor say anything about us while you were there?"

"No," Max replied, "but I'm sure we'll be going soon."

"Where do you think we'll go?"

Max walked on without answering. He had no idea. "Come on," he said finally; "we better get back to the annex."

The others in the room were in the middle of packing. The room seniors had been called to the camp commandant. Peter had gone in place of Max; he was his deputy. When Max and Adolf entered the room he was reading everything they were to put in their field packs from a slip of paper: "Wash kit, cleaning things, bandages, sewing kit, mess kit, sheath knife, spare underwear, spare pants, two shirts, sweater, a pair of shoes, two pairs of socks." The rest of the luggage would be taken to the railroad station by car.

Fat Heini was hopping around shouting: "There y'are, that's what I've been saying all along." Peter threw him a mean glance, and continued to read from the note. After lunch field rations for three days would be distributed. They had to leave enough room for them in their knapsacks. And they were to wear their warmest and sturdiest clothing for the journey, civilian clothing or winter uniform and, most important, sturdy shoes.

Then Peter folded the paper, put it away, and with a sideways glance at Heini said: "The field pack mustn't be too heavy, because we may have to go part of the way on foot."

"How come? Who said so?" asked fat Heini in dismay. He looked around at his cherished accordion, his piles of toys and clothes. Heini had more of everything than anyone else in the room.

"The Emperor, who else!" said Peter.

"But how come? I mean, since we're going by train anyhow," asked fat Heini in a quiet voice.

"Because the train may be shot at," said Peter maliciously, "because the fighters can't know that *you're* sitting in it with your stupid squeeze-box!" It sounded as though he had gleefully thought up this sentence on his way back to the room. He was annoyed because he had hoped to trade for Heini's toy soldiers which he had had his eye on for a long time. If they had been allowed to take along only a field pack, he was sure he could have managed something. But the way it looked now, fat Heini would naturally not want to part with them. So let him keep his dumb soldiers.

They sorted their belongings and spread them out on their

beds and the floor, snatched the neatly stacked piles of clothes out of the lockers, arranged them, rearranged them. Luckily, before Easter, they had had a general clean-out. They had given the things they had grown out of to the refugee camp, so they did not have much left. They stuffed their suitcases, knapsacks, briefcases, satchels and field bags. What about the blankets? Peter had forgotten to check them off his list. The blankets were to be strapped to the knapsacks. That made Heini happy again, because he was the only one with a real knapsack, trimmed with fur and leather thongs, so the blanket could be strapped on from the outside. He put it on right away, and turned his back to the mirror, almost dislocating his neck as he tried to admire himself in it. He was terribly proud, because the knapsack with the strapped-on blanket made him look as though he were in full battle dress. Adolf packed all his books in one case, which was then so heavy he could hardly lift it. He wanted to take *Ben Hur* along, because he was right in the middle of reading it. But he could not get it into the outside pocket of his knapsack, so he tore off the cover and the part he had already read. Then it fit.

Max's knapsack didn't hold very much. Whatever did not fit inside, he tied to the outside: washbag, shoes, rolled-up pants, blanket — everything dangling down at the back. No one but he and Adolf had finished packing by the time the lunch bell sounded.

The only teacher present was old Klettmann — The Barnacle — who taught them math and geometry. They tried to get him to tell them where they were going, and for how long, and when they would get back to Berlin, and whether he had heard the *Wehrmacht* report. But he either did not know anything, or he did not want to say anything. He probably did not know anything. He never did.

In the afternoon they sprawled around on their beds and were bored. Time crawled by as slowly as in a waiting room. Adolf pulled his crystal receiver out of his suitcase, lay down on his stomach on his bed, and put his ear against the headphones, with the pillow over his head. He was the only one in the room who owned a radio. He had often rented it to the others for twenty pfennigs an hour.

He stayed under the pillow for quite a while, looking for a station. The others had just about forgotten him when he sat bolt upright and said that they had just announced that the Russians had already reached the outskirts of Berlin.

The others all stared at the receiver in Adolf's hands, as though it were a poisonous insect that had crept into their room unnoticed. Peter, Christo, and skinny Tjaden shouted at Adolf that he should keep his trap shut, that it must have been an enemy station — he could end up in concentration camp for that — it was all merely enemy propaganda.

Adolf replied that the *Wehrmacht* report also had said that the Russians had broken through the Oder Line.

The others said the Führer was sure to have a reason why he had let them come so far: let them all come in, then shut the trap, and they would be caught in the snare, and none of them would get away.

Adolf said no more, and did not resist when they took the receiver from him. Peter held the headphone to his ear. But Christo wanted to listen, too, and the headphone broke off. So they threw the receiver at Adolf's feet and Adolf packed it away again.

Shortly after four o'clock the corporal in charge bellowed down the corridor that they should bring the heavy luggage to the school door. After that they were to get potatoes. Everyone's mess tin was filled to the top, then they had their evening meal, potatoes with white sauce and caraway seeds.

It was almost eight when they finally marched off, class by class, two abreast. The fifth class led, then came the youngest ones; in the middle was the cart with the luggage, and they themselves brought up the rear with The Barnacle. They marched down the castle avenue. The only sounds were the steady whining squeak of the cart's wheels and the noise of their boots on the asphalt, sometimes loud and in step, then monotonously pattering when they fell out of step. The boys at the front began to sing, but The Emperor, who was walking next to the cart, called to them that they should be quiet. It had turned so dark in the meantime that they could hardly make out the head of the column.

They marched silently into the town and across the market place. No one looked back. Although some of them had lived here for almost four years, they weren't sad to be leaving. Behind them a woman began to scream something in Czech, shrill and scolding, almost hysterical. Then there was silence again, just the reassuring marching rhythm of their boots.

The knapsacks felt light, although they had stuffed so much into them that they could only just get the buckle into the last hole. Mess tins and canteens dangled on their belts, and sacks and bags hung on shoulder straps. They marched out of the town and farther down the valley. A wet fog hung in the air and felt sticky on their skin. They could only sense the railroad station down in the valley. Everything was hidden in darkness.

They followed the cart, which drove to the right around the station and stopped alongside the fence that closed off the platform.

Then they heard Wald's voice up front: "Co-o-ompany halt!"

Gathered in a large group between the cart and the building, they huddled together in the darkness and pricked their ears to catch what was going on. Then they heard Wald's commanding voice as he directed the fifth class to unload, and the voice of The Emperor, calm and resolute, every word clear and distinct.

"Listen, lads!" He did not have to wait for silence — No one had dared to say a word anyway.

"The first and second classes will come with me into the station hall. Everyone else will wait here until I return and then look for a spot on the platform. Each boy will look after his own luggage; no one will leave his place. When the train comes in, you will all line up in twos, just as you came here. I will then call the individual classes. First One-A, then One-B, and so on. Each class will wait in place until called. No pushing or shoving! Anyone who doesn't get the message will be in deep trouble!"

They waited in silence until the little ones had disappeared into the station. They heard the fifth class heaving the luggage over the fence and stacking it on the platform.

When The Emperor came out, he gave them a sign and they followed him through the station hall. A frosted yellow bulb spread a dim glow. Boards had been nailed across the windows. The little ones were sitting huddled together on the benches along the walls and on the ground among their luggage. Only a narrow passage had been left free. The older boys shuffled forward in single file. There was an open door to the right of the exit. A railroad man in a Czech uniform was sitting in the room beyond. He had a telephone receiver pressed to his ear and was cranking the handle. A round iron stove pushed a flood of warm air out of the room.

The swinging door leading to the platform was slightly ajar. One by one, they squeezed through it, keeping close to each other so as not to have to let go of the knapsack of the boy in front. They groped their way forward, looked for a spot where they could lean against the wall, and took off their knapsacks.

Slowly their eyes became accustomed to the darkness again. They knew where they were. They were familiar with the station, the narrow cast-iron pillars holding up the roof, the double rail tracks, and beyond, in the black darkness, the indistinct outlines of the bombed storage shed.

The cold slowly crept through their clothes as they waited, but no one dared unstrap his blanket from his knapsack because the train could arrive at any moment. They strained their ears for a sound in the night, knowing the direction from which it would come. Though no trains had passed through Kusice for days, they had no doubt that the train would come. If The Emperor said it would come, it would.

An hour later when they heard the quiet pounding of an approaching steam engine, they did not get particularly excited. They put on their knapsacks, picked up their luggage, and calmly waited, each in his place.

The steam engine slowly edged its way past them, a black shadow that made the night under the roof even darker. Then car after car, endlessly, the rhythmic sound of the wheels on the tracks becoming imperceptibly slower, until finally there came the long-drawn-out muffled squealing of the brakes. In the black wall in front of them narrow, glinting, blue slits opened up, something moved, people were looking out. Farther forward doors slammed and a cone of light from a flashlight, hopping around restlessly, quickly came closer, right to the edge of the platform in front of them. And then more flashlights, quiet calls, soft commands. Wald's voice came from somewhere ahead: "Quick, quick, everything into the baggage car!" They waited until The Emperor called them, shuffled slowly forward, foot by foot. They pushed their way forward, silent, grim; suddenly they were afraid that the train would leave without them.

Inside the car were pale-blue flickering lights, emergency lights, blackout screens across the windows, wooden benches. Instantly the shouting and arguing began, just as on a school outing. "I want to be next to the window! That's my place, beat it! Move it! Don't stand around in the corridor! Why don't you watch what you're doing!" Knapsacks into the luggage rack, the clatter of mess tins, jostling, more and more crowding in. The last ones to enter had to sit on the floor because every space was already taken; piles of luggage were all over the place. Finally The Barnacle

climbed in, and fat Heini had to vacate his window seat.
When he grumbled The Barnacle suddenly became severe
and gave him a resounding slap. At that very moment the
train started with a jolt, and for a second there was silence.
Then they all started to shout, yell, and shriek, the same way
they did at the movies when the lights slowly dimmed and
the film flashed onto the screen.

Peter had memorized the route. Twenty-five miles to Pilsen,
then Klattau, Bayrisch Eisenstein, and then the border. They
had left shortly before ten. If the train traveled at twenty
miles an hour, they could be over the border by two o'clock.
And then? They wondered where they would go from there
and studied the map. They asked The Barnacle again, but he
just told them to leave him in peace. In the blue light he
looked very tired and absolutely ancient, and he was the first
to fall asleep. He crumpled up, his head fell onto his shoulder, and little bubbles of saliva formed in the corner of his
mouth when he breathed out. They pointed it out to each
other and giggled, but soon it became boring, and with the
regular pounding of the wheels, they dozed off one by one.

Max awoke when the train rumbled over some switches
with a hard jolt and then over some more. All the others
were asleep. He walked along the corridor to the rear platform and raised the blackout screen on the window until
there was a small slit to see through.

At first he could see only his own face reflected in the
glass. He made a mask with his hands to shut out the light,
and then he could see outside a dark-red, flickering glow in
the sky and the black outlines of houses, trees, and telegraph

poles. Was this Pilsen? Was something that the planes had bombed that morning still burning? How long had they been on the train? He did not have a watch. On his way back he looked at the watch of a boy whose sleeve had slid up his arm. Half past two. Did that mean they were over the border already? He fell asleep again.

When he awoke the second time, the train had stopped. Farther forward they had rolled up one of the screens, and broad daylight flooded in. It was cold. Adolf's head was resting on his shoulder; the little boy was still asleep. Max carefully pushed him away and stood up. The Barnacle's seat was empty.

He went along to the exit. A boy from the fifth class blocked his way. "No one's allowed out. By order of the camp commandant," he said pompously.

"Where are we? In Bavaria already?" asked Max.

The other boy threw him a disdainful glance. "We're just a little way past Pilsen, you fool," he said haughtily. Max was still too sleepy to feel insulted. He looked out of the window.

Three railroad tracks next to each other. On the third one a row of tank cars, the tanks torn to pieces, full of holes, ragged. Behind them the charred skeleton of a shed, and a steep embankment with scorched shrub and black burn marks in the parched grass, a delicate down of young green over it.

Max went back into the car. The others had awoken and were crowding to the windows. A boy from 4A had some binoculars and was scanning the scene. Two figures appeared next to the sandbag barrier, steel helmets on their heads, *Wehrmacht* coats reaching to their ankles, carbines over their shoulders.

"Hey, they're some of ours; they're boys from the fifth!" the boy with the binoculars cried suddenly. "The one on the right looks like Schilling! It *is* Schilling!" They tried to pull down the window, but it was stuck. They waved their arms around behind the windowpane and snatched the binoculars from each other's hands.

The two figures on the embankment were beating their arms against their chests. They did not wave back. Maybe they had not noticed that the boys in the train below them were waving at them; maybe, as soldiers, they were not allowed to wave.

The Barnacle returned to the car. He stood at the end of the middle gangway and tried to make himself heard above the noise. "Be quiet, children, be quiet!" It took some time before he got their attention. "I just want to tell you what's happening!" That finally quieted them. "We've had to stop because the tracks are obstructed. For the time being we will stay here in the train. We may have to wait until night. So behave decently, and be particularly careful to leave the toilets clean!"

"When are we going to get something to eat?" one of the boys called from the other end of the car, and at once everyone began to shout again.

"You'll have to eat from your rations for the time being," said The Barnacle.

They took their rations out of the knapsacks and dug in.

Several of them opened up their cans of liver sausage — after all, they were sure to be in Bavaria by the following night, so why let the stuff go moldy?

The day wore on. Some of them played blackjack on the floor of the car. Skinny Tjaden made an attempt to break the farting record, but only made it last for seven seconds. Other than that, nothing special happened all morning. They did not even see The Barnacle again.

The toilet stank like cat shit. The water was not running anymore, and there had not been any toilet paper from the very beginning. Adolf handed out pages from *Ben Hur* that he had already read. Later they stood next to him and tore the pages from his hands as he read them. He was the only one in the whole car who had packed a book in his knapsack.

In time they became restless, and that afternoon when skinny Tjaden started preparing for another attempt to break the record, three of them jumped on him and pounded on him so hard that Max and Peter had to haul him out.

The Barnacle did not return until about six o'clock in the evening. The Emperor came with him. He was angrier than they had ever seen him. "Has the camp team leader been here?" he barked.

They stared at him; no one said a word.

"When did you last see him?"

They conferred with each other in whispers. Most had seen him running alongside the train, but that had been in the morning, absolute ages ago. Christo reported that it had been at nine o'clock.

"No one's seen him since then? Are you quite sure?" The Emperor asked insistently.

They shook their heads, anxiously waiting for an explanation, but The Emperor just said something softly to The Barnacle, then they both turned and left the car.

The only one who had heard anything was Adolf. They all crowded around him, and he had to repeat it at least a dozen times. Each boy wanted to hear it with his own ears. "That bastard! If I ever lay my hands on him again!" That's what The Emperor had said, word for word. And Adolf took pains to give an exact imitation of the intonation. "That *bastard!* If I *ever* lay my hands on him again!"

They wanted more, but Adolf had heard only that. So they chewed on this one sentence.

Apparently Wald had gone. Had he taken off? Why? After all, everything was organized perfectly, everything was going without a hitch. Their means of transport was assured, and they would be in Bavaria tomorrow. Wouldn't they? Did Wald know something? Had this skunk simply run off because he knew that they were stuck here?

At last, around seven o'clock, as it was beginning to get dark, The Barnacle returned.

Yes, no one had seen the camp team leader since morning. No, no one could say he'd skipped out. No, of course they were not stuck here. Yes, they would be continuing the journey tonight.

Darkness fell quickly, and since not even the blue emergency lights were on, they were soon sitting in pitch blackness. From time to time a flashlight clicked on, quiet whispers were heard when one of them tried to get more comfortable in his sleeping place, subdued swearing when two boys got in each other's way, and in between the deep breathing of those who were asleep, muffled snoring, sighing, wheezing. Soon they were all asleep.

Max woke up abruptly. His eyes flew open; black night surrounded him, and silence. A scream echoed in his ears. Someone had screamed in his dream, a dream he had remembered clearly just a moment ago but which now was becoming hazy. He strained his ears. There was something outside that had not been there in the evening. Voices, noises: indistinct, indistinguishable.

And then suddenly that scream again. No dream—it came from outside. Someone was screaming. Not really screaming, but moaning—a hideous screaming moan that rose agonizingly slowly, reared up, hung suspended for an unbearably long time, and finally rattled away and died.

Then other screams, as though the first one had awoken them. Max sat up, rigid, listening. The screams ebbed away again, became quiet, lost themselves.

Max groped his way forward to the car door. The boy from the fifth class who had been given guard duty was asleep. Max quietly pressed the doorhandle down and pushed the door open. Compared to the darkness inside the car, outside it was almost light. Gray night. Or was it day already?

A train was standing on the second tracks, with long express train cars, black against the night sky. It must have pulled in quite quietly during the night. The moaning and screaming were coming from it. The sounds ran the length of the train, sometimes almost inaudible, but then increasing again to a scream of pain.

Suddenly Max heard footsteps on the gravel. A dark shadow detached itself from the blackness of the cars and came toward him across the tracks. The click of metal. It was a sentry. Max started to close the door very slowly, but the sentry did not let him get that far.

"Wait!" he called quietly and urgently, as though he were afraid that the door would be shut in his face. He was small. And he seemed to be old. His voice sounded old. His breath stank of tobacco.

"Listen," he whispered, "have you got something to eat?"

Max was so surprised that at first he could not say a word.

"Don't you have anything to eat?" the sentry repeated. It almost sounded like pleading. "Just a piece of bread, anything."

"We only have a few field rations ourselves," said Max hesitantly. The man in front of him was a *Wehrmacht* corporal — he recognized the stripes. It could not be true that a *Wehrmacht* soldier was begging for something to eat. There had to be another reason. He was probably testing him.

He heard someone crawling closer to him and felt a hand on his shoulder. Someone asked in a whisper: "What's the matter?" It was Peter.

"He wants something to eat," Max whispered back.

"If you have anything, I'll pay for it," said the sentry. "I don't want it for free."

"I'll get something," whispered Peter.

"Where d'you come from?" the sentry asked. "What're you doing here?"

"We're from Berlin, CEC," said Max. "We're on our way to Bavaria."

"You're lucky then," said the sentry. The moaning came from the black train across the tracks again. It did not just hit your ear, it went through your skin, it made your hair stand on end.

"Poor bastards," said the sentry, "yet they're not all that badly off."

"What d'you mean?" asked Max. His voice was hoarse, toneless.

"At least they're in a train," said the sentry. "They'll be home soon. First class to the military hospital."

"Where did they come from?" asked Max.

"From the Oder Front," said the sentry.

Peter returned with two slices of bread. It was getting lighter outside.

"Don't you have a bit more?" asked the sentry. He rummaged around in his coat pocket. "Just a minute. I've got something I can give you for it." He held a decoration under their noses.

"Lord! That's an Iron Cross First Class!" said Peter, dumbfounded. They stared at the dimly glittering object. "Is it yours? Was it awarded to *you*?" Peter asked in awe.

"It's yours for a loaf of bread," said the sentry.

They held their breath. Had the man gone crazy? Had he been hit on the head? It simply could not be true that he would give away his Iron Cross First Class. That was not just any old medal that anyone could get; it was only one step lower than the Knight's Cross. To get it you had to do something exceptional in the face of the enemy. He could not just throw it away for a piece of bread.

"Well, what's the matter?" the sentry asked urgently. "Don't you want it?" They were still speechless. "Okay, half a loaf," he said. "Surely you can give me half a loaf for it." He was standing in the door like a beggar.

"Each of us has only a couple of slices left . . . two or three slices, that's all," said Max uncertainly.

"Then give me a couple more slices — that'll do," said the sentry. He chewed and chewed, making each bite last as long as possible.

The boy from the fifth class woke up suddenly and scrambled up. "Have you gone crazy?" he whispered angrily. The sentry disappeared instantly, and the door clicked shut.

Then suddenly, a long way away, they heard the pounding of a steam engine. It came from the head of the train and got louder and louder. And outside they could hear steps, hurried steps on the gravel, and shouts and whistles. Then a jolt ran through the train and the buffers crashed. A steam engine had been coupled on. The door was thrown open and a shaft of light glared in, forcing them to squint. They recognized The Barnacle laboriously hauling himself up into the train, and behind him was another man holding a flashlight. Its cone of light was directed at them as they stood up and pressed against the wall.

"What're you doing here?!"

The Emperor.

Peter edged around the corner. The cone of light stayed

on Max, who was nearest the door. The Barnacle pushed Max ahead of him.

"Take away the blackout screens," The Emperor called after them. Then the door slammed shut.

Max grasped for a screen. "Shall I open it?" he asked over his shoulder. The Barnacle held onto his shoulders with both hands. "Yes, open it." Max let the screen roll up. "Are we leaving?" he asked.

"Yes, we're leaving," said The Barnacle.

"But it's daylight already," said Max.

"Sit down in your place," said The Barnacle.

Then the train started off with a jolt. Slowly it gained speed and crept out of the station. Car by car the hospital train receded past the windows. Meanwhile it was so light that they could clearly see the red cross painted on the roof of the cars. The engine at the front was getting up steam, but the train was still moving so slowly that you could have walked alongside of it. And it did not get much faster.

"Crawling," said Peter. "It's just crawling." But at least they were moving, they were going forward.

Imperceptibly the sky got lighter, the contours of the countryside became distinguishable. A valley, a river between trees, a bleak avenue of poplars. Then forest, tall, dark forest to the right and left, right up to the tracks. The eternally monotonous up-and-down of the telegraph wires. And then a broad plain with scattered islands of trees. A swarm of crows flew up from a field and landed on a solitary tree. Low, crouching farms between trees, simple villages far away, a little town which they skirted. And forest again, almost endless, monotonous. Sad, gloomy fir forest.

They watched the sky. Eight spotters at each window, searching the horizon for suspicious black dots. Each time the train entered a wooded area they breathed a sigh of relief, as though the woods could hide them from the eyes of a plane. The only one asleep was The Barnacle. He had crumpled up in his corner, his arms hanging limply between his legs. He looked gray. Like a dead man.

They were still in the woods when an antiaircraft gun suddenly started to bark. A long burst of fire drowned out the pounding of the steam engine. At the front of the car someone was screaming his head off: "Take cover! Fighters!" But they sat as though turned to stone and went on gaping out of the windows. The forest had ended, there were broad fields, a road with a row of low trees, chimney stacks in the distance, and over them a black speck in the white sky, flying upward. Suddenly it pitched down and quickly became larger.

Here it came — so close to the ground that it almost shaved the row of trees. The boy up front was still screaming "Take cover! Fighters!" and over that, the squealing of brakes, and the barking of the antiaircraft gun. Finally they leaped up and tripped over each other toward the exit, became wedged in the narrow corridor in front of the door.

A face in the cockpit was so close they could make it out.

And over their heads bullets ripped through the roof of the car, and then the snarl above their heads again, and smoke, and the smell of burning, and screams through the smoke, and one boy hitting wildly around him, and then they were out of the door, jumped down, hit the ground hard, tumbled down the embankment, away, away from the train. Heavy wet earth, in which their shoes got stuck, and deep furrows, into which they let themselves fall, cold sticky earth. And far away the buzzing of the airplane engine and the wail of the steam whistle of the engine like a cry for help.

Max raised his head. The train was standing in the middle of an open field. No cover. Far in front of them, the engine, very small. Right behind the engine, on a long, low-sided freight car, was the antiaircraft gun, which started to bark again. A toy AA gun in a gray concrete ring, much too small on the low flat car. It fell silent again and three figures jumped from the car, deserted the toy, threw themselves onto the ground. Some more figures leaped out of the cars behind, crawled between the wheels, ran away from the train into the open field. Those from the last car raced toward the woods that the train had just left, hopping over the furrows like rabbits.

They pressed down into the furrows, made themselves as small and flat as possible. Heard the plane coming. The sharp sawing sound of the engine that raced at top speed toward them and turned into a thunderous howl over their heads. It passed over them, disappeared above the woods, close to the treetops. The pilot had not fired. Why hadn't he fired?

They listened to the receding buzz of the engine. No howl. The plane did not make a loop; it flew on.

"He's gone, he won't be back," whispered Max, as though he were afraid that a loud word would bring him back. "I don't think he'll be back."

Next to him Adolf got up, wet earth on his face and coat. And after him Peter. His face was white under the crust of dirt, and he swallowed convulsively, swallowed something that kept coming back up.

All over the field they now started to get up, wiping the dirt from their faces and clothes. "Did ya see the steam coming from the engine! Boy-oh-boy, he could've picked us off one by one! Those dimwits with the AA gun! They ran away even before he'd come!" All of them had seen it. "Those assholes! They could've brought him down with a hand grenade!"

The Emperor appeared next to the last car, gesticulating wildly. "Camp annex! Come here!" he roared. "Move-move-move! Get a move on!"

They hurried to get over to him. The others were gathering in front of the cars closer to the front. Now, at last, they could see how many of them there were. At least a thousand, maybe two thousand. They were swarming all over. Next to them was a girls' school, in front of them boys again. And masses of teachers. It was impossible that they could all have been in one train.

"Silence!" roared The Emperor. "You've got five minutes to get your luggage out of the car!"

They raced off, got wedged in the doors, pushed and shoved, squeezed up over the running board.

"Children, that's not the way to do it!" scolded The Barnacle. "Form a line! Stand in line!"

No one listened to him. You just had to get in. The most important thing was to get inside. Five minutes! He must have gone crazy — they'd never make it. At last they were inside. Some boys were pushing in the opposite direction, wanting to get out with their luggage. "Break the windows!" shouted the boys outside. "Break the windows!"

Max climbed up between two benches, caught hold of the luggage racks on the left and right, hung there like an ape, swung to and fro with his knees bent, kicked with both feet together, hit the glass full with his heels. The pane shattered into pieces.

They gathered their things together. Everything was just lying around, the knapsacks open, the blankets spread out. They threw everything out of the window, climbed after it, jumped down, collected their pieces of luggage. The others were already traipsing around on top of their belongings, trampling them into the sticky, yellow-brown clay earth. Five minutes! Had they made it? Where was The Emperor?

He was farther forward, about the middle of the train, waving and shouting. What was he shouting? He looked as though he were waving them to come to him. Again they raced off, throwing their knapsacks over their shoulders, dragging their blankets behind them. The girls in the next car were still busy packing, and the boys behind had not got much further, either.

"Over here! Over here!" yelled The Emperor. He was standing in front of the baggage car. The sliding door was open, and cases, boxes, packages, tied-up bundles were flying out through it. Their luggage. Their heavy luggage. They had got in last, so their luggage had been at the front and came out first. What luck.

"Collect your things!" roared The Emperor. "Get going! Move it! Watch out that you don't get hit in the head! Take everything over there to the dirt road!" The first ones were already on their way, dragging suitcases across the field; then they came back, stood there exhausted. "Go on — move along!" roared The Emperor. "No lagging! Move-move-move! You big boys help the little ones!"

They ran to and fro between the piles of luggage by the train and the dirt road, tripping over the furrows, thick clumps of dirt sticking to their shoes, which became heavier and heavier. Then it dawned on them why The Emperor was making them hurry — because now the others from the other cars were arriving and the pushing and shoving around the luggage became greater. But by then they had taken most of it away and could watch the others scrabbling.

2

Three Are Left Behind

They were standing in a long line by the dirt road waiting for The Emperor, who was herding the last stragglers over. The Barnacle was excitedly scuttling to and fro like an old, lame sheepdog. "Line up in classes!" he shouted in a thin voice. Then, at last, The Emperor came.

"First clean the mud from your clothes, you little pigs. Just look at yourselves, you're a sight!" he roared. And while they hastily scrubbed their jackets and pants, trying to scratch off the brown muck with their fingernails, he continued in a calmer voice: "Well, boys, you must have realized by now that we'll have to go on on foot. First we'll head for Klattau. That's about thirty miles. We'll try to cover the distance in two days. Therefore take only the most necessary things from your heavy luggage: valuables, food, warm clothing. Have you got that?" He ran his eye over the line of schoolboys as though he wanted to take in each of them individually. "By the time I return, you'll all be set and ready to leave. Line up in classes, two abreast, One-A at the front, the fifth last. Any questions?"

No one had any questions. Silently they watched The Emperor stride across the field to the train, where a small group of teachers had gathered. Two men in uniform were with them; one looked like a regional leader.

"On foot!" wailed fat Heini. "Thirty miles!" He sat on his thick leather suitcase, holding his accordion in his arms the way a mother holds a baby. He looked as if he would burst into tears any minute.

"So what?" said Peter. "We could do that on one leg!"

Max was sitting on his heels in front of his cardboard box and took out a stack of textbooks and notebooks. He stood up, looked around grinning, and slowly began casually to toss the books and notebooks, one by one, as far across the field as possible. They sailed through the air, opened up so the pages fluttered, and fell to the ground like birds with broken wings. It was a signal to them all. They copied him, tossed their school things all over the place. Then followed the underwear, coats and shoes. Soon the whole field was covered with them.

When The Emperor returned they were standing in a line as they had been told. He brought the fifth class to the front and placed them among the little ones from 1A and 1B. Then he gave the sign to leave. They were the first school to go. That was because they had The Emperor as camp commandant. As long as he was with them, nothing could happen to them.

Behind them the other schools were beginning to get into formation, but they had quite a large lead. That was important, because if they were in front, they would be the first to reach the new quarters and the first to eat, and they would get the best places and the largest portions.

They turned onto a wide dirt road that led away from the railroad embankment at a sharp angle toward the highway. It was cold, and a cutting wind blew into their faces and made them bow their heads. But by the time they reached the highway, they were so warm from walking that they unbuttoned their jackets and coats.

Ahead of them The Emperor struck up a song, and they bawled along with him, fell into step, and strode along vigorously, as though they wanted to cover the thirty miles to Klattau in one go. The mess tins clattered in harmony, and the straps creaked, and their heels clicked dully on the asphalt, and for a while it was just like being on a day's hike.

Gradually the mood had grown more somber. They now trudged along in single file, and had slowed down noticeably. The little ones at the front were tired, their legs were beginning to ache.

The wind had strengthened and now came from directly in front. The road ran straight as an arrow ahead of them. Glittering cart tracks on the asphalt, long, intertwining wavy lines. From time to time cars came up behind them, large limousines with blinds across the windows, passenger cars in small groups of three or four with crates and hampers strapped onto them, small trucks piled high, and once, five heavy *Wehrmacht* trucks in convoy, all of them empty except for well-muffled lookout posts with binoculars on the first and last ones. None stopped to offer a lift.

Max counted the trees along the side of the road. How long had they been walking? At the snail's pace they were going they could not be doing more than two miles an hour. They had left the train at half past six. What was the time now? He asked Peter, who was walking in front of him. It was nine, so they had been marching for two and a half hours. Five miles. It was high time they took a rest. The little ones could not take this. His own belongings seemed to be getting heavier and heavier. Maybe The Emperor wanted to wait till they reached a village. But there was no village in sight, just solitary farms off to the side of the road.

Finally, in a wood, the command came from ahead: "Division halt! Rest!"

They slipped the straps off their shoulders where they stood, let their knapsacks plump to the ground, dragged them behind them through the ditch, threw themselves down at the edge of the trees. They had not realized until now just how heavy their luggage was.

Adolf was still standing on the road, his head lowered, his arms hanging at his sides, as though he no longer had the strength to take off his knapsack. Max went to get him. "Come on," he said so quietly that the others could not hear him. "Are you sick?"

Adolf silently shook his head and dropped to the ground, stiff-legged.

"What's the matter with him?" asked Peter casually. He did not expect an answer. He was sitting with his back against a tree trunk, his feet stretched out in front of him. He chewed on his bread and kept his eye on fat Heini.

Heini had collapsed between his two packs, puffing and panting, his shoulders twitching, tears streaming from his eyes. The accordion was lying in front of him, the keys and mother-of-pearl glittering dully. The case had broken open when he had dropped it on the ground, and the instrument had burst out, but he did not seem to notice. He stared at it with glazed eyes.

He had never been good at walking, always one of the last on marches. And this time he was carrying twice as much. It was no surprise that he had collapsed. It was a miracle that he had got this far.

Adolf strapped up his knapsack. He had taken out his spare pair of shoes, a pair of longs pants, a jacket, a set of underwear, his writing things, his cleaning kit, and finally even the binoculars he had been given for his tenth birthday. Everything lay in a neat pile next to the tree stump on which he was sitting, the binoculars hidden under the underwear. At first he had planned to give them to Max, but he knew Max would not accept them. Max would insist on returning them when they arrived. He could not let that happen.

At least his knapsack was quite a bit lighter now. He stepped across the ditch and fell into line. He was one of the last; the ones at the front were beginning to march off. Only fat Heini was still standing at the edge of the wood. He had his knapsack on his back and the accordion in his arms, just the instrument, without the case. Suddenly he gave out a howl of rage and misery, lifted it over his head, and slammed it onto the ground. The accordion spread out, and he jumped into the middle of it, trampled around on it, kicked at it with his boots, kicked at the keys until they flew off. He gave out a howl with every kick and tears ran down his cheeks.

When they left the woods a village came into sight. They walked faster, encouraged by the sight of the houses. It was a little village. Low houses with gray plaster, high tile roofs, standing in a row on either side of the road, joined by walls with wide gates in between. All the gates and doors were shut, and the ground-floor shutters were closed. Dogs were barking behind the walls and closed gates. Other than that, not a sound. Not a soul in sight.

They watched as The Emperor walked past the houses, heard him calling and hammering on the doors. Then suddenly he started running and turned into a side street.

They could hear a violent exchange of words coming from the side street, and when they arrived at the junction they saw an ox pulling an empty haycart, and a farmer leading the ox, and next to him The Emperor, who was aiming a revolver at the farmer.

"Stop!" he yelled at them. "Division halt!" They stopped dead in their tracks, and no one moved as the oxcart turned into the main road and moved forward between the rows.

A window opened above them, and a woman leaned out and shouted something in Czech. The farmer next to the ox turned around and called something to her. And everywhere the dogs began to bark again with twice the fury, and the woman railed and screamed until the cart reached the head of the column and stopped.

The windows and doors now began to open in the other houses as well, and men came out and stood at the sides of the road, their arms crossed, and formed small groups. The farmer called out again, and some of the men answered.

One by one the little boys at the front began to load their luggage onto the cart. They lifted their knapsacks in from both sides, and then marched on. Those behind advanced, moving slowly forward in single file. But the cart was soon full. The knapsacks towered into the air even before it was the second class's turn, and after 3A it was absolutely full.

The dirty farmer, why didn't he have a larger cart? And why didn't The Emperor get hold of a second one since he had a revolver? But then they were moving on again. The Emperor hurried them along, and they silently marched past the men standing at the side of the road watching them with hostility.

The sky had clouded over and the wind lashed a fine drizzle into their faces. They pulled the visors of their caps low over their foreheads, braced themselves against the wind, bent forward, their heads lowered, so the only thing each could see were the heels of the boy directly in front.

More and more cars passed them now, whirling long trails of spray behind them, soaking them in a fine drizzle that seeped deeper and deeper into their clothes. The asphalt was broken up by deep cracks caused by freezing and filled with yellow-brown water. Sometimes they were so deep that the muck ran in over the tops of their shoes.

Far ahead of them rose forested hills with softly rounded, black summits. They did not seem to come any closer. And there was no town in sight, no village, not even a church spire which would have announced a village.

It had to be long after midday. In the meantime the dampness had soaked through to the skin on their shoulders; the straps were rubbing them raw, and they had to hold them away with their thumbs. And the water in their shoes squelched with every step.

Then suddenly they were going downhill, down into the valley through which a river and railroad tracks ran. Cyclists came toward them, and down by the river were small fenced gardens in which people were working. Farther along the valley they saw a church spire and houses spread out on the slopes above the river.

Just after they entered the town they stopped in front of a tall, dirty-red brick building with windows only on the ground floor and a wide door in the middle with an outdoor staircase leading to it. The Emperor disappeared through the door with the Czech farmer.

They waited outside in silence with the patience of exhaustion.

At last The Emperor came out and took them into the building. Behind the door was a small lobby, where The Barnacle was standing with a laundry basket into which each boy had to throw half of his potato ration. A roomy restaurant adjoined the lobby.

The boys shuffled forward slowly, up some stairs and through a large double door into a large room that took up the whole upper floor of the building.

They sat down on the floor. Peter pulled out his map and looked for the town. At last they knew where they were, and that was worth something. They worked out the distance to Klattau using the scale and found it was a bit over twenty miles. There was even a shortcut using secondary roads, where they could save two or three miles. It really was not all that much farther. They took off their damp jackets, shoes, their wet socks. Rubbed their cold feet with their hands; rubbed the red indented marks made by the knitted pattern of their socks. They got fresh socks out of their knapsacks, and spare shirts and sweaters, changed, and wrapped themselves in their blankets. There was a smell of wet wool and floor polish. They stretched out their legs and dozed a bit.

An hour and a half later they were called to eat, and stood in an endless line. Each one received two ladlefuls in his mess tin. It was not much, just a watery potato soup, not even vegetables in it, but at least it was warm. They spooned it slowly and with deliberation, and what they could not get with their spoons they got with their fingers.

They had hardly finished eating when the command came to leave, and they marched off again. Through the town and across the river, and up the hill on the other side. Adolf gritted his teeth. A twinge of pain went through his feet with every step, as though he had thumbtacks in his shoes. He had hardly been able to get his shoes back on after the meal, his feet had swollen so badly during the short break. If only he had put on his old, worn shoes and not his new boots! But they were lying next to the road some miles back. There was nothing he could do anymore. He wondered what else he could throw away to lighten the knapsack. And late that afternoon, when they reached another range of hills, and a long climb lay ahead of them again, he threw the whole knapsack into the ditch, keeping only his field bag.

Max and Peter were the only ones who did not show any signs of exhaustion. Peter had picked up a stamp collection that one of the boys from 3B had thrown away, and a camera in a leather case, which he was carrying on his belt like an ammunition pouch. As far as he was concerned the march could go on for a long time yet. The more boys who collapsed, the greater his choice. Fantastic treasures were sure to be waiting for him yet, — all he had to do was pick them up when the others threw them away. He was not worried about carrying them. He could handle a lot. Up to now his knapsack was nowhere near too heavy. He kept his eyes peeled, but he did not find anything else of value for the rest of the day.

Shortly before darkness fell they came to a palatial building, which seemed to be uninhabited and deserted. Next to the door hung the triangular CEC camp sign. The Emperor shouted and rattled the door. Then the fifth class broke off the flagpost standing in front of the building, and broke down the door with it.

There was no light inside and they had to find their sleeping places in the dark. On the upper floor they found a room furnished exactly the same way as the one they had left in Kusice: two-tiered bunks, metal lockers, and a mirror on the door. Even the bed linen was still there, neatly folded. They threw themselves on the beds just as they were, taking off only their shoes.

Adolf, however, slept with his boots on; he just loosened the laces. He was afraid that he would not be able to get them on in the morning if he took them off. He felt the blood throbbing in his heels.

In the morning, when the door was thrown open and someone bellowed: "Time to get up!" they were still so exhausted that they could barely wake up. They thought they could take their time, but The Emperor roared loudly from below and tried to hurry them up. He made them go through everything — morning roll call, morning gymnastics, washing — exactly according to the rules of the camp. For breakfast they got only a slice of bread, and as if that weren't bad enough, he told them not to eat all of it at once, but to keep some for later. Then he sent them to the cellar to look for food. They found three sacks of sugar, and the bigger boys filled their mess tins. Max found a box of vitamin tablets in a cupboard in the dining room, the same kind as they had received at breakfast in Kusice, and stuffed them into his pockets.

Up in the room Max found Adolf lying on the bed. No one had even noticed that he had been missing the whole time. Max asked him if anything was wrong. Adolf said no, silently put his things away, placed his feet gingerly on the ground, and stood up.

A sharp stab of pain shot up his legs. It felt as though his heels had grown onto his boots overnight, and the skin had now been torn off with a jerk. He pressed his lips together and screwed up his eyes. With every step the pain shot up his legs. He knew he could not stand it much longer, but he mustered all his strength. He did not want to be the first to collapse.

They stood in marching formation in front of the house and listened to The Emperor consulting with the other teachers. The Czech farmer with his cart was no longer there. For that reason the third and fourth classes were to go ahead with The Barnacle and with Spidersleg, another of the teachers. The Emperor wanted to try to get hold of another cart and would then follow with the little ones and the fifth class. They agreed on the railroad station in Klattau as their meeting place.

At exactly eight they marched off. Adolf walked as if in a trance, leaning forward, dragging his feet behind him, putting his soles down flat. With every step he thought he could not stand it anymore, but nevertheless took another step, and yet another, until the pain in his heels receded more and more, as though it were not his feet that hurt, as though the pain had nothing to do with him anymore.

After a long climb the command finally came from up front for the first rest. Adolf did not seem to hear it. He ran into Peter who had stopped dead, and when Peter turned around and grabbed his shoulders, he still went on moving his legs like a robot. He did not stop until Peter shouted at him.

Long after the others had thrown themselves down at the edge of the forest; he was still standing completely alone on the road, not moving.

"Adolf, come here," called Max. "Come over here!"

Adolf took one step toward Max, tried to take another

step, and collapsed like a puppet whose strings have been cut.

In three bounds Max was at his side. He shook him, slapped his face with his open palm, carried him across the ditch with Peter's help, laid him down on the ground. Skinny Tjaden ran to get The Barnacle. But Adolf had regained consciousness before he arrived, and looked around in surprise, as though he could not understand why he was suddenly lying on the ground and the others were standing round him, staring down at him. He moved his lips, wanted to say something. The others saw the effort he was making to get out a word, but he could not get his jaws apart; it was as though they were locked.

Max started to take off Adolf's shoes. He worked carefully, first untying the laces and pushing the flaps apart. He already suspected what he would find. But it was even worse than he had thought. The socks were wet with blood, rubbed through, bloodsoaked rags he had to cut apart before he could pull them off. He turned Adolf onto his stomach and sat so he had Adolf's feet in his lap. The heels were raw. There were no more blisters, not even broken blisters. The skin under the blisters had been rubbed away. He could see the raw flesh.

Max poured medicinal powder onto the raw spots, took a bandage for burns from his first-aid kit, and wound it around Adolf's feet, wound his boxing bandages around that, and pulled a pair of thick ski socks over them.

The Barnacle stood next to him, flapping his arms and wailing: "Good God, boy, why didn't you say something?" and ran forward again to fetch help. He returned with Spidersleg, and The Barnacle said that maybe they could build a kind of stretcher and take turns carrying it. But Spidersleg said that that was absolutely impossible, if they did that, they would not cover any ground at all. The only thing they could do was to bind thick footcloths around Adolf's feet, and he would have to try to walk like that. They discussed what they should use for the footcloths and asked around to see who still had anything useable in his knapsack.

While they were talking, Max stowed away his first-aid kit and buckled up his knapsack. When he had finished he stood up and quietly said: "He can't walk. He can't walk with those feet!"

At first everyone was silent; then Spidersleg asked, slightly superciliously: "What would you suggest, Milk?"

And Max said: "I'd wait till the camp commandant comes with the cart."

"With the cart," repeated Spidersleg, "Of course, with the cart." He kept running his fingers through his hair. "What do you think, Mr. Klettmann? Naturally we could all wait here. But we would lose a lot of time." He paused, waiting for confirmation, but The Barnacle helplessly shrugged his shoulders and put on a sullen expression that revealed nothing.

"I think he really would be better off in Kayser's group," Spidersleg continued. "Even if Mr. Kayser didn't find a cart, he still has the fifth class with him, and the bigger ones are in a better position to help transport an injured person, wouldn't you say?" The Barnacle shrugged his shoulders again.

Max said: "I can wait with him. Then you can go on with the others."

Spidersleg stared at him, swallowed hard, and said: "It probably would be the best solution if Milk stays with him." He went over to Max and showed signs of wanting to put his hand on his shoulder. He hesitated when he saw Max stiffen, and let his raised arm fall on Peter's shoulder. "Or let's say Milk and Reuther. Would you agree to that, Mr. Klettmann?"

"If you think so," said The Barnacle halfheartedly. Spidersleg raised both hands defensively. "But, my dear Mr. Klettmann, I don't want to interfere in any way. After all, it's your class."

Max thought that if they continued to blather much longer, they would not have to bother anymore, because The Emperor would have already arrived. He bent down to Adolf and asked softly: "How're you doing?" And Adolf stuck out his lower lip and raised his eyebrows. "Don't you think I could walk?" he whispered back. It sounded like a plea, as though he found it embarrassing to be the center of attention, as though he wanted to put an end to it as quickly as possible.

Max shook his head and said close to Adolf's ear: "You'd be crazy! If we wait, you'll get a ride. The Emperor'll have found a cart, you can be sure of that."

"D'you think so?" Adolf asked hopefully.

"Sure," said Max.

The others left and the three of them began to wait. They expected to wait for half an hour. Max and Peter cut some twigs from the trees, stacked them on the ground, spread a blanket over them and laid Adolf on top.

After an hour Adolf began to freeze despite the blanket

they had wrapped around him. He did not say anything, but Max saw how he was shivering, and rubbed him with his hands to warm him up. Peter had run down to the bend so he could see farther down the road. He stood there, his hand raised, shading his eyes. He did not seem to see anything.

"They'll be here," said Max; "the little ones are just slower, that's all. The march yesterday took more out of them than anyone else." Adolf looked at him doubtfully, but did not say anything. Peter did not say anything, either, when he came back. He just stared sulkily down the road.

They waited until almost midday, then Peter went down to the bend again and Max followed him. Nothing. That was not possible; something was wrong.

"What if they took the shortcut?" suggested Max.

Peter had already thought of that, but had pushed the unsettling idea from his mind. Now Max's question re-awakened his worry. He stared at the clearing where the road came out of the forest, as if willing The Emperor and the others to appear. He closed his eyes and counted slowly, "One, two, two and a half, two and three-quarters . . . three," and opened his eyes again. Nothing.

"What should we do?" he asked.

"We'll stop a car. We know where the meeting place is. It'll be okay," said Max.

"What if they come after all?"

"I don't think they will."

"We can wait another half hour." Peter had regained his confidence. "There're only three of us, someone's bound to pick us up. Don't you think so?"

They went back to Adolf. Stared at the road. Adolf did

not dare look at them. He also did not dare suggest that they open the last can of liver sausage which he had in his field pack, although he was so hungry he was getting cramps. It was his fault that they were sitting here. He felt awful.

"They've got a two-and-a-half-hour start, that means six miles at most," said Max. "If we stop a car we'll catch up with them in a quarter of an hour."

Peter looked at him in surprise. "D'you think so?" And when Max nodded, he got very excited and said: "But then it would be stupid to stop. It'd be better to drive on to Klattau, be taken straight to the railroad station." He was thrilled with his idea. And when a car appeared around the bend, he jumped into the road and shouted and waved his arms around like a puppet.

The car drove by without slowing down. As far as they could see, it was full. Then others came with plenty of room, large limousines in which there were only two people. They, too, zoomed by, and the people sitting inside just stared straight ahead.

The two of them stood in the middle of the road and tried to force the cars to stop by standing in their way, but the drivers were not about to step on the brakes; they just honked their horns continually, shook their fists, wound down the windows and yelled at them.

Max and Peter laid Adolf on the side of the road so that his bandaged feet were visible. That did not help, either. Not a single car stopped.

Late in the afternoon a refugee cart rumbled up the hill-side. It was heavy boxcart drawn by two horses. Its towering load was covered with canvas. A cow trotted along behind it, and next to the horses walked a tall, thin man in a short gray coat with a fur collar, a cap on his head, his pantlegs stuffed into his boots. He stopped even before they asked him.

"Well, you three, I guess you want to come along," he said. He had a hard accent, like a Polish worker. They nodded hesitantly.

Max pointed to Adolf and said: "He can't walk anymore."

The man got hold of Adolf under his shoulders and lifted him onto the board that served as a driver's seat. "You two'll have to walk," he said to Max and Peter. "I'm sorry."

A boy about their age came around the back of the cart. He was wearing the same kind of coat and cap as the man. He looked at them curiously. A woman who was sitting bundled up, half under the canvas, took their knapsacks and stowed them away in the cart. She looked ill, and had a scarf wrapped around her head as though she had toothache.

Max and Peter walked along behind the cart, next to the cow and the boy in the cap, who untiringly spurred the cow on with a stick. The boy ignored them.

Adolf sat huddled up on the box, his feet hanging down, and when the cart hit a pothole he supported himself on his hands to soften the jolts. He tried to make himself as small as possible so that he would not weigh so much and the horses would not have to pull so hard. He felt very unhappy. He knew he was a burden to everyone.

"So tell us where you're from," asked the man. "What're you doing alone here?"

Adolf told him about the camp, the train journey, the

fighter plane attack, and explained why they had stayed behind.

"You think you can still catch up with your school?" the man asked.

"Yes!" said Adolf. And, as though he were trying to give himself courage, he added with confidence: "Yes, of course!"

Several cars drove up behind them, honking loudly and impatiently. The man led the horses to the edge of the road, held the sorrel, which was on the left, by its halter, and talked to it reassuringly. The cars raced by, still honking, three black limousines, one after another. The man raised his whip threateningly and called a bad-tempered curse after them, which was drowned by the noise of their engines.

After a while he turned to Adolf and said calmly: "We come from Zabsche." And when he saw Adolf's blank expression he explained: "From Hindenburg." Adolf nodded, though neither name was familiar.

"We've been on the road since January," the man said.

"Where are you heading?" asked Adolf, just to say something. He did not want to seem rude.

The man raised his shoulders imperceptibly. "Wherever we find something," he said. He walked with measured steps next to the horses, like a farmer bringing in the harvest.

Adolf crumpled up under the jolting of the cart. There was something soft under the canvas behind him, like a mattress, or a rolled-up down comforter, which gave way when he leaned back, and let him sink into it. He felt the tiredness spreading through him, and desperately fought to stay upright. But soon everything blurred before his eyes.

The gently swaying backs of the horses and the nodding tips of their collars, the monotonous grating of the wheels and the dull clopping of the hooves on the asphalt, all lulled him to sleep. He crumpled up again and slowly sank backward.

When Adolf awoke it was dark and the cart was standing still. It took a while before he realized where he was. There were houses on both sides. They were in a town. Had they reached Klattau already? Had they arrived? He wanted to call for Max, but did not dare. Then he heard voices, the deep, throaty voice of the man who had taken them along and a high-pitched woman's voice. They were behind him. He slid as far as he could to the right on the board, and looked round. A weak ray of light shone from a door. In the light he saw the man, a woman, and Max and Peter standing next to them. Then, as he was straining to hear what they were saying, less than a yard away, in the cart behind him, he suddenly discovered the face of a small girl, bundled up to her nose in blankets. He saw only her eyes, watching him intently. He smiled shyly, but the girl did not bat an eyelid, just stared at him until he turned away in embarrassment. Then the man came over and lifted him off the box, holding him in his arms like a small child; he carried him to the house and along a dark corridor into a large, gloomy room. Hot, stifling air came surging toward him and almost took his breath away. Many indistinct voices caught his ear. When he was put down on the floor, his heels hit hard. The pain jolted him wide awake.

There were masses of girls around him, inquisitive faces

gaping at him. At last he saw Max bending down to him. He held his breath and swallowed and made a tremendous effort to make his voice sound quite calm. "Have we reached Klattau already?" he asked.

He saw Max shake his head, and then he heard the man. "Well, I'll wish you luck, boys! Get home safely!" The man was standing by the door and waved to them, and while Adolf followed him with his eyes, he heard Max's voice in his ear: "The swine simply dumped us here!"

"What d'you mean 'dumped'?" asked Adolf.

"We're still a long way from Klattau," said Max grimly.

Adolf felt a wall at his back. He was sitting against a counter. Now, at last, he noticed where they were. The room was a restaurant, full of tables and chairs, wood-paneled walls with stag antlers on them, tall clothes racks packed so full that they looked like trees. In the middle, next to a cast-iron pillar, was a round iron stove and around the stove were two rows of chairs on which coats and dresses had been spread out. They were steaming from the heat. Girls were sitting all over the place, on the chairs, on the benches along the wall, on the suitcases. Everything was full of girls. Several were standing in a circle around them, whispering to each other and giggling furtively.

Suddenly the girls fell silent and stepped aside to form a path, and through this path came a thin old lady who planted herself in front of them. She was wearing a dark ski skirt and a short jacket over it. She had a mouth without lips, and eyes without brows, and, perched at an angle on her head, she had a felt hat which looked like a saucepan lid that had slipped to one side.

"Well, where're you from?" she asked. Her voice was surprisingly deep and sounded harsh and unfriendly.

Out of the corner of his eye Adolf saw Max hunch his shoulders. "We already told the other lady," Max explained sullenly.

"Stand up when I'm speaking to you!" said the woman. Max and Peter stood up reluctantly and even Adolf attempted to get up. "Not you!" commanded the woman, and she added sternly: "Take off your caps, we're not in a Jew school here!"

The girls behind her started to giggle. But one girl, near the stove, said: "Those are some boys from the annex! I recognize them." Turning to the old woman she added: "Miss Redwitz has already spoken to them, professor."

The old woman said, "Is that so?" It sounded as though she had an iron file in her mouth. Then she turned around and stalked away.

The girl sat down on the floor in front of them. The others now came closer, too.

"Is it true that you're going along with us now?" she asked. Max started.

"Who said so?" he asked back.

"Our camp commandant," said the girl.

"She has no right to make any decisions about us," said Max. He hastily put his cap back on. He was very distrustful.

Later they got two slices of bread with artificial honey. It was just enough to rouse their appetites. Afterward they were even hungrier than before.

Max cleaned out a space behind the counter which was

full of empty beer crates, and made up a sleeping place. In the aisle between the counter and the wall they were unseen and had some privacy.

Gradually things settled down for the night. Max and Peter sat next to each other, half under the counter. They had the map spread across their knees and had measured that it was no more than five miles to Klattau.

"We could have been there in an hour and a half," said Max, disheartened.

Peter bent over the map, and after a while he calmly said: "We can get out through the bathroom window."

Max's mouth fell open. "Why?" he whispered.

"D'you want to go along with them?" asked Peter.

Max silently shook his head. "But what about Adolf?" he asked.

"They'll take good care of him," said Peter. "He'll have to go to hospital with those feet, anyhow. It shouldn't make any difference to him whether he goes along with us, or with them. They're going in the same direction. The Emperor will fetch him when his feet are okay again." He spoke quickly and without hesitation, as though he had given it a lot of serious thought.

Max wriggled to and fro restlessly. "When d'you want to leave? Right now?" he asked.

"Not at night," said Peter. "Tomorrow morning, as soon as it gets light. Then we'll be in Klattau at six. The others can't possibly have left at that time yet."

"Who'll wake us?"

"If we drink enough, we'll have such pressure on our bladder that we'll wake up."

They both drank from the tap on the counter, until they could not get any more down, packed their knapsacks, and wrapped themselves in their blankets.

Adolf woke from a nightmare; the sounds of shouting and breaking glass still ringing in his ears, but he was awake. He was suddenly wide awake, and lay on his back, listening breathlessly in the black darkness, rigid, like an animal who senses an enemy close by.

A smashing blow made him jump. It had been right above him. Now came the crashing sound. Glass splintered on the ground.

He sat up with a jolt, banging his forehead hard. Stars exploded before his eyes, and he gritted his teeth to stop from crying out. Gradually the throbbing in his head receded, and with painful clarity the shouting from outside assaulted his ears again. A thunderous bass voice, a strident laugh like a hen cackling, sharp, squeaky shouts that ended in a warbling giggle, spluttering men's laughter, and many voices intermingled, squealing, screaming, hysterical voices and bawling singing, and the whimpering sound of a mouth organ, and again and again the crash of splintering glass.

He drew back into his dark compartment, making himself as small as possible, then brought his head close to the edge of the sliding door and tried to open the door a crack so he could see out. Suddenly he heard something there, directly next to him, separated from him only by the thin wood of the sliding door. Something was breathing, coming closer, moving. Voices, whispering as though they were afraid. A high voice, and a deep, droning one, so muted he could not understand them. It was not Max and Peter. These were strange voices. They were right in front of him now, and he could feel something bumping his door, scraping along it outside. He pulled back and flattened himself against the back wall of his hiding place, which suddenly seemed like a trap in which he had been caught. Then he heard the voices again, one growling, the other hurried, with a complaining tone that rose distinctly above the shouting in the background, repeated itself and became louder. Tortured breaths, becoming louder and faster until they finally broke off in a whining moan.

Adolf braced himself in his dark hole, rigid with fear. Where were the others? Where were Max and Peter? And the girls? Where had those people outside come from?

The shouting stopped abruptly. There were hurried steps on the floorboards, clicking heels, chairs scraping, broken glass clinking, terse commands, doors banging. An engine roared to life outside and moved away fast. Then silence. Not a sound.

Adolf waited. He listened, holding his breath. Then he opened the sliding door. There was no one in the aisle behind the counter. He got out of his hiding place and looked over the counter. Not a soul. Emptiness. Clouds of smoke in the light from the bulb, overturned chairs and tables. Suitcases, dresses, coats scattered everywhere. The floor strewn with broken glass. Nothing else. He was alone.

3

Tilli

Max walked along mechanically. Peter was close behind him. They walked in step. Quick march. A four-footed machine. After about an hour they saw Klattau ahead of them. They had not said a word since they had set off. Neither said anything now, either. Max kept up the pace and walked on doggedly without a breather. He was thinking of Adolf.

He was no longer sure that the little boy would really be looked after well by the girls' school. Adolf would not believe that Max and Peter had left him alone. Maybe he would wait. Hide behind his sliding door and wait till they returned. He was obstinate. He would prefer to follow them with sore feet till he collapsed than to stay behind. He just looked small on the outside. He had trusted Max, and that was what troubled Max.

Max walked as though trying to get away from his

thoughts. For four years they had been in the same class, for four years they had been in the same camp and shared the same room. To begin with he had not even noticed the little boy with the large head. The thing that now bound them had only started a year ago.

They had got a new camp team leader at that time. A really tough guy, just five years older than they were, almost delicate with a pale face, but incredibly harsh. During the very first roll call he had said that he would make them into the hardest bunch in the whole region. And he proceeded to do just that. Drill, field sports, relay races, long-distance swimming, carbine shooting, tests of courage, and repeated marches. Marches by day and by night, with and without packs, forced marches, straight marches, obstacle courses, and marches with ambushes. Marches, marches, marches.

It had happened during a night march. Shortly before midnight the whistle had dragged them from their beds and chased them into the yard, carrying their fieldpacks. Competition marching. Room against room. Only the third and fourth classes. The third class had been given a head start, otherwise the rules were the same. Eight miles on a marked course. Without flashlights. At a fast pace. Starting at minute intervals. Arrival at goal timed with a stopwatch. The room with the best total time had been promised a three-day trip to Prague, the losers would have pack drill.

Everyone in the room had been capable of covering eight miles, even Adolf and Heini, the two weakest ones. They should really have won. But Adolf did not cross the finish line.

They had not only lost the competition because of him,

they had had to go out and look for him. And they had found him less than two miles from the goal. He was neither injured nor exhausted nor anything else. He had merely stopped because he had not wanted to leave a boy from 3A, who had collapsed, alone in the dark in the forest. That was his only excuse.

They had cut him dead for weeks after that. No one had spoken a word to him, not even Max. But then suddenly he had taken his side. The little boy had impressed him. In his own way he was stronger than all the others in the room. He had a kind of strength you could rely on. From that time they had been pals.

Max stared at the road which was running past under his boots like a gray ribbon. The first houses of Klattau were just ahead of them.

He asked a man the way to the station. The man pointed straight ahead, and when they started off he called after them, "What d'you expect to find there? — it's all in ruins!" They walked even faster, almost ran. The smell of cold smoke and wet soot hit their noses. Rubble lay in the street — shattered roof tiles, bits of glass, torn twigs. Wide gaps were torn into the rows of houses on the left and right, quite recent; they must have used heavy ammunition there, for not even the stairwells were still standing.

Then they saw the station, the building half blown away. In the middle of the square in front of it was the cab of a steam engine like a twisted memorial. Children were climbing all over it.

They asked a passing woman where the town hall was. When she heard what they wanted she told them it was useless. The Czechs had taken over all the offices. If they wanted to find out anything, they would have to go on to Neuern. Walking through the ruined town they asked other people if they had seen the school group. No one had. They only heard the same advice repeated.

"We'll just have to go to Neuern," said Peter finally; "the man from the fire department said so, too."

"We'll pick up Adolf first," said Max.

Peter looked at him, flabbergasted. "Are you crazy?!"

"He'll wait for us, he won't go with the girls. You can be sure of that," Max explained firmly.

Peter stood still. "You've got a screw loose!" he screamed.

Max calmly said, "You don't have to come along!" He turned into the street along which they had come, and marched off at the same speed as before. Peter had to run to catch up with him.

"Man, don't be an idiot!" he said breathlessly. "If we traipse back now, we'll never catch up with the others. We can wait in Neuern. The girls have to pass through there, too. Then we'll see if Adolf's with them, and if he isn't we can still ..."

Max ignored him and walked on stubbornly. There was no sense in trying to convince him; it would not do any good.

Peter tagged along behind and fell into step with him. "Such nonsense!" he grumbled to himself. "Such rubbish!" But he walked on behind Max keeping pace with him.

Their return journey again took one and a half hours, but when they came to the inn and walked up the stairs, they were so exhausted that their knees buckled. They had to sit down.

Then they heard a bolt being drawn behind them, and saw the door open a crack. Adolf stood behind it. He waved at them hurriedly, motioned them to come in, and bolted the door as soon as they were inside.

"People keep coming and trying to get in," he whispered. "Czechs. They came to the back door, too, and rattled the shutters."

"Where are the others?" asked Max when they went into the restaurant.

"They were gone when I woke up," said Adolf.

"You're alone in the building?" asked Max.

Adolf nodded. "I think so, I haven't heard anyone." He said nothing about what he had experienced during the night, about the fear he had endured alone in the eerie silence of the building, about his uncertainty over Max and Peter's whereabouts.

"The others aren't in Klattau," said Max without looking at him. "We asked. We were there."

Adolf nodded. So that was what had happened. He smiled at Max, a courageous little smile, as though he wanted to tell him that he should not worry, that they would make it. At that moment he did not care where the others were, as long as Max was here again.

"We have to go to Neuern," Max continued, "as quickly as we can. Maybe we can still catch up with them."

"I can walk again," said Adolf. He had bound footcloths made of strips of bedsheets and oilcloth around his feet. "I've found a cart, too," he said and pointed to a recess next to the door. It was a little handcart, half buried under a heap of clothes. They pulled it out.

Peter was busy looking for treasures, poking into everything. "Isn't there anything to eat here?" he asked, annoyed. "All they've left are old clothes."

"There isn't anything," said Adolf. "I've already looked." He was embarrassed, as though it were his fault that there was nothing to eat in the building.

Max emptied the handcart. "Get your things," he told Adolf. They took everything into the lobby and called Peter who was still looking around.

Then suddenly they heard voices outside, a confusion of sounds. Czech voices. Then a thunderous blow against the door. And another. They cowered against the wall and watched rigid with fear as the strong bolt gave way under the blows, as the wood splintered and the door burst open and crashed against the inside wall. Bright light streamed in, making them screw up their eyes. A man was standing in the bright rectangle of the door. He was holding a long sledge-hammer in his hand like a weapon. His eyes were full of suspicion and anger as he looked down at them. He bellowed at them in Czech. It sounded mean, threatening, dangerous.

Others pushed past him, hurried through the lobby, and disappeared into the restaurant. That was lucky for them. The man with the sledge hammer seemed to be afraid that the others would beat him to whatever there was. He bellowed again and pointed to the door with his hammer.

They did not hesitate for a second. Grabbing the cart with their knapsacks, Peter and Max trundled it into the street, put Adolf into it, and took off. The cart rattled over the paving stones. Someone yelled behind them. They did not turn around. They ran on as quickly as they could.

They did not stop until they were almost a mile past the village, where the road led into a wood. They pushed the cart between the trees and dropped onto the ground next to it. Their lungs were working like bellows.

Adolf sat quietly on the cart. He was ashamed because he had not had to exert himself in the least.

Peter took his map out of his knapsack, and they worked out that it was just twenty miles to Neuern. They could not make that by evening with Adolf in the cart. And now hunger was also gnawing at them. They had to get something to eat, or they would not get much farther. They set off.

The forest stretched endlessly, and at some point Peter started to talk about American Indians. He had read not an adventure book, but a true story about real American Indians. It had said how you could live on buds and root tips and the soft inner bark of young trees. Then with his sheath knife he carefully cut squares of bark from beech and larch trunks, scratched out the juicy inner bark, and swallowed the stuff without so much as a frown. He broke off twigs, stripped off the buds, and ate them from his cupped hand. He did not say what they tasted like.

Max tried it distrustfully, and Adolf put a bud in his mouth. They chewed gingerly, and spat it out at the same time. It tasted as bitter as gall, a taste you could not get rid of. Peter calmly went on eating. He scratched resin from fir trunks and chewed on it and talked about his great-grandmother who came from East Prussia and had lived to be 107 years old because as a young girl she had helped her father felling trees, and there had been resin on her hands when they had eaten their sandwiches. And she had become so old because of this resin.

Half an hour later, just as they were coming out of the forest, he suddenly turned quite green, stood behind a tree, and puked his guts out. He could not stop; it seemed to twist his stomach inside out, and what came up was a poisonous green color. They had to stop, and the other two were now desperately hungry.

Max walked over to two farms lying back from the road. Twice he returned empty-handed. The Czech farmers had chased Max away after the first word he had said in German. At the next farm Adolf went to ask.

He limped away on his footcloths, walking with short, stiff steps across the field. The other two stayed on the road. They did not have much hope.

Adolf prayed. Over the whole distance to the farm he prayed that the farmer would give him something, sell him something. Anything. Just so that he did not have to go back empty-handed. He took his money out of his breast pocket, rolled the bills together and held them in his hand. He had forty marks.

When he opened the farm gate a dog started barking, and a woman came out of the house. A large, skinny woman in green overalls and with tall rubber boots on her feet. She looked him up and down so sullenly that he lost his courage.

"*Dobry den,*" he said timidly, "Would you please have a piece of bread, *chleba prosim.*" He held out his hand with the money.

The woman did not answer. She looked at him, her face immobile, appraising him, hostile. Then she beckoned him over and pointed to the open house door.

Adolf hesitated to go past her. Suddenly he was afraid. The woman's face was hard, unfriendly, and taciturn. And she was huge, almost as big as The Emperor. She pushed him through the door into the dark kitchen with its soot-darkened ceiling and small windows. Pushed him behind a table and made him sit down on a bench. There was a chair on the other side of the table with a double-barreled shotgun hanging on the backrest. Adolf clasped his hand around the wad of money.

The woman disappeared through a low door, bending to get through the opening. When she returned she was carrying a loaf of bread under her arm which to Adolf looked as large as a cartwheel. She placed it on the table and cut a broad wedge with a knife, starting in the middle as if it were a cake. She speared it on the point of the knife and held it out to Adolf.

Adolf turned the wedge of bread in his hands until the narrow end pointed toward his mouth, and carefully bit into it. He had to swallow several times; his mouth was suddenly full of saliva.

The woman watched him. Suddenly she said something to him in a deep, hard voice, in Czech. He did not understand what she said, raised his shoulders and smiled in an embarrassed way, a smile that asked for forgiveness.

"You German?" she asked in his language. He nodded uncertainly and watched as she went to the stove and put a log on. When she came back to the table he placed the money in front of her. She shook her head, pushed it back and said something that sounded nasty, and which she accompanied with a sharp gesture.

Adolf pointed out of the window at Max and Peter waiting on the road. "Two friends," he said quickly, lifting two fingers. He pushed the money back to her. Then he pointed out of the window, to the bread, then to the money. He was terribly afraid she would misunderstand him.

She took the knife and cut two more wedges from the bread and carried the loaf back into the storeroom behind the low door, mumbling something to herself loudly and grumpily. She returned with a piece of bacon in her hand and laid it by the wedges of bread on the table. It was light-brown, smoked bacon, a whole piece, as big as a pack of cigarettes.

"*Dekuji, dekuji,*" said Adolf. She interrupted him with a throaty sound, as though she wanted to shoo him away. He stood up holding the bacon in his hand and clutching the wedges of bread to his chest. "*Dekuji, dekuji,*" he said.

He forced himself to walk slowly across the yard and out of the gate, although he felt like running and shouting for joy.

They ate the bread except for the crusty ends, which they carefully stowed away in their knapsacks, and each of them cut off a piece of bacon as big as a nut. They sucked on it while they marched on.

They marched well into the afternoon, past Klattau, and farther down a river valley in the direction of Neuern. When the road ran downhill they all got onto the handcart. Peter steered at the front with the pole between his legs, Adolf sat in the middle holding tightly to the side slats, and Max stood at the back, leaning forward, his legs bent to take the shock of the bumps. Sometimes he jumped off halfway down, ran a few steps, pushed until the cart was moving fast enough, and then jumped back on with a mighty leap. Often they passed horse-drawn carts which had passed them earlier going up the hill, and they yelled and shouted as they rattled by, and made the horses shy.

Around two o'clock they came upon a group of refugees camping by the edge of the road. Five covered wagons stood behind one another along the road. The horses were grazing in the meadow by the river, along with the cows and goats. A large fire was burning behind the covered wagons and the occupants were sitting around it. Just women and children, there were no men there except for an old grandpa and a boy who was at most two years older than they were. The boy invited them to the fire and asked whether they were hungry. They ate potatoes and fish. As much fish as they wanted — trout and other kinds which had red fins. A whole clothes basket full. They must have emptied an entire fishpond. God only knew where they had got so many fish.

They speared them on sticks and held them over the fire, ate with both hands, and threw the bones over their shoulders. They stuffed themselves full to bursting. They could not remember ever having been so full as after this fish meal.

Max handed out a ration of vitamin tablets, and the refugee boy gave them a dab of grease for the wheel bearings of their handcart. It was a great day. And when darkness fell they even found a sand shed to spend the night.

In the morning the fields were white with hoar frost. They froze under their thin blankets and hurried to get back on the road. They wrapped Adolf in blankets and marched off so that they would warm up, and while they were walking ate the bread left from the previous day. It had so much flavor that they chewed it a long time.

The sky was blue, but it was a cold blue, and the sun had no warmth. They could see the mountains in the distance. High, dark mountains, forested to their peaks. That had to be the Bavarian Forest and Mount Arber. That was where they had to go. It was not all that much farther now; maybe they could reach it by evening.

Suddenly Peter stopped, listening with his head to one side. They could hear a hollow, dry explosion, like a muffled drumbeat. And another, and another, one after another at regular intervals. They came from the direction in which they were heading. They came from the mountains.

Six more booms. "That's artillery," said Peter quietly. "That was a salvo. That was a battery!"

"Could have been bombs, too," commented Max hopefully. "Sequence release."

Peter stood his ground. He was well versed in this subject. "That was definitely artillery."

They listened, holding their breath. Six more booms, one after another. If that really was artillery, the enemy was very close. The Front was wherever the artillery was. In that case they could be running straight into the Americans' hands.

But they could not be that close. That was impossible. Maybe it was something else, after all. Target practice? A heavy antiaircraft battery?

They marched on in silence.

A signpost showed them that they were only eight miles from Neuern. Two fighter planes zoomed over their heads, Mustangs or Thunderbolts, they could not be sure. But whatever they were, they were American machines with a white star. Later, far ahead of them, they heard aircraft guns rattling away, long bursts of fire, the roar of engines during the approach, and the dull boom of explosions.

The road fell away in a long-drawn-out curve. When they came out of the curve the smell of burnt paint and scorched rubber rose to their noses. Then, in front of them, they saw the charred remains of a truck in the middle of the road and burned-out skeletons of cars, and an overturned military ambulance lying thirty yards from the road in the field. Among the wreckage of the cars was a boxcart with knock-kneed, buckled rear wheels, and strewn all over the road were steel helmets, gas mask boxes, jagged bits of metal, splintered wood, and torn-off branches. The whole convoy had caught it, maybe those were the shots they had heard. Smoke was still pouring from the truck.

They let the cart roll to a halt. It stopped right behind the smoking truck. There was an eerie silence, not a sound to be heard, not even a bird. But they were not alone. Far ahead, in front of the truck, something was moving. Two figures in dark coats were sitting on the ground like large black birds. A horse was lying there on the road. The carcass of a horse — its bones were exposed. All the meat had been cut off.

The two old people who were hacking at it now had to be content with a few remnants. When they saw the three boys approaching they took off with a handcart, like thieves caught red-handed.

At the edge of the road, under a canvas, covered only in a makeshift way, lay those who had been hit. Lots of soldiers, piled on top of each other like firewood. A few steps farther, in the ditch, was another canvas. Something was under it.

They had left their handcart standing on the road, and walked around among the wreckage, their shoulders hunched, stepping very softly so as not to make any noise. Peter looked over the sides of the boxcart. There was nothing there; everything had been taken already.

"Isn't that the cart we got a lift from?" Adolf said. The overturned cart looked exactly like the one the refugee had had. And the carcass of the horse lying in front of it had once been a sorrel — they could still tell by the head. But there was only one horse there. The refugee with whom they had traveled had had two. Max climbed down into the ditch and picked up a corner of the canvas. There, lying in an oozing mass of blood, bone, and guts, was the refugee. And the woman who had ridden on the cart. And the boy who had walked along behind the cow. And it was the canvas from their cart which covered them. Max dropped it again.

Adolf turned away and ran across the road into the meadow. His stomach turned over, and he was gagging and swallowing hard. He ran farther into the meadow, away from the road. Then stopped suddenly, his arms hanging limply at his sides. He had a horrible, bitter taste in his mouth.

Ten paces away from him something moved in a bush on the other side of a ridge in the field. At first it looked like a piece of material caught in the branches and tugged at by the wind. But then he saw a face hidden under the fabric, eyes which were staring at him intently. And at that moment he knew he had seen these eyes before, at night, half asleep, when the refugee had lifted him from the cart and carried him into the inn.

He walked around the bush slowly, keeping some distance from it. He knew he would have to be careful. The little girl was hiding from him. She was afraid. He must not scare her.

When he was level with her, he stopped. She was sitting on her heels behind the bush, not moving. Like a rabbit in the grass trusting that the hunter will not see it. She had a red scarf around her head. It was that that had caught his attention. She hid her face in her hands, but he saw that she was furtively watching him through her fingers.

He walked toward her a step at a time. Stopped. Waited. Took another step. Squatted down, just like her. Looked away as though he did not want anything from her.

When he looked toward her again, she had taken her hands away from her face and was staring straight at him, still suspicious and fearful. He smiled, a soft smile that started with his eyes. It took a long time before she answered it, uncertainly and carefully at first, then with growing trust.

Adolf kept smiling. He did not say anything. He just waited. He waited for her to make the first move.

"I know you," she said quietly, almost roguishly. She spoke with the same accent as her father, but in her case it did not sound hard, but soft and melodious. She hid her face in her hands again, while she waited for an answer.

"I know you, too," said Adolf.

She clasped her hands around her knees. "I saw you," she said.

"I saw you, too," said Adolf.

"You came along in our cart!"

"That's right, I came along. The day before yesterday."

She nodded. And after a pause she said: "D'you want to see something?" and edged toward Adolf until she was squatting next to him. She pulled out a small leather bag that was hanging on a strap over her shoulder and took out a matchbox.

"D'you want to see what's inside?"

Adolf nodded. He already knew what was inside, he saw the holes in the box. But he pretended not to know. And when she opened the box he pretended to be surprised. "A June bug!"

"I caught it this morning," she said proudly.

Adolf studied the bug. "It's a male," he said.

She looked at him in astonishment. "How d'you know that?" she asked.

Adolf pointed to the antennae. "If the feelers are thin, it's a female. If the feelers are fat, like this one, with little pollen combs on them, then it's a male."

She looked closely, she was not convinced yet. "D'you think so?"

"I know so," said Adolf firmly.

She looked at the bug with renewed interest. It was much

more exciting to have a male June bug, rather than just an ordinary June bug.

She put the box back in the bag and stood up. "I've got a horse, too," she said, her head cocked to one side, and watched from the corner of her eye to see whether Adolf was sufficiently impressed.

"A horse?" asked Adolf, genuinely surprised.

"Over there!" she said and pointed over her shoulder. There really was a horse in the meadow not a hundred yards away. "It's a female," she said. "She's called Herta. Shall I fetch her? She obeys me. She's a good horse."

Adolf made a vague gesture and doubtfully raised his eyebrows. She took it to mean yes.

"Herta, Herta, come here!" she called. The horse lifted its head and looked across at them. The girl waved both arms and ran into the meadow. The leather bag at her side bounced up and down, and her blue coat fluttered as she leaped through the grass. Adolf followed her with his eyes.

He thought about everything she must have seen from her hiding place behind the bush. Her dead parents and her dead brother, carried into the ditch by strangers and covered with a canvas there. The plunderers who had emptied her cart and had fallen upon the dead horse lying on the road, a horse she probably had loved as much as the one she was going to get now.

He heard Max calling and waved and shouted: "Come here! Come over here!"

Max and Peter came hesitantly across the meadow toward him. "What's the matter?" they asked when they were halfway across, and urged, "We've got to move on, man!"

Adolf said: "There's a girl. She belongs to the refugee cart." He waved his arm in her direction. "Over there! She's getting the horse."

They watched as the little girl caught hold of the large animal's halter and patted its neck. The horse was still wearing the harness collar and was dragging the long reins behind it. They saw her grasp the reins and drive the horse on. She seemed to be used to handling horses.

"D'you intend to take her along?" asked Peter.

"We can't leave her here," said Adolf.

The little girl made the horse stop in front of them. She nodded to Max and Peter. She did not seem to be shy anymore. They did not dare go closer. The animal was huge, and it was standing in front of them snorting and tossing its head. "She won't hurt you," said the little girl and stroked the horse's nostrils. "She's good. She's the best in the world."

Adolf suggested they harness their cart to the horse. So they did. They lifted the little girl onto the horse, and the three of them got into the cart, Peter on the shaft again, and Max on the back as brakeman.

They rattled lazily along. They had not traveled so comfortably since they had left the train. When Adolf said something about Ben Hur, they called to the little girl that she should go full speed ahead, and the little girl spurred the horse to a trot. She looked back at them and laughed and shouted. They curled up quite small in the cart, so they would not offer any resistance to the wind, and enthusiastically waved to her until the cart suddenly crashed into a pothole, was thrown upwards, then thudded down on two wheels, so hard that the shaft almost jumped from under Peter's feet. They started to call "Hey! Stop! Hey you!"

The little girl was lying on the horse's neck. She did not seem to hear them. Maybe the cart was making such a fiendish noise that she really did not hear them, or else she thought they were shouting encouragement.

At last the horse slowed down of its own accord. Maybe it was uneasy about the bucking vehicle behind it; maybe it just got tired.

The little girl turned around and beamed. "Again?" she called.

They yelled, "No!" and Max asked softly, "What's her name, anyhow?" Adolf called to her: "Hey! What's your name?" And the little girl called back: "Tilli!" and laughed, and beamed from ear to ear.

Half an hour later they arrived in Neuern. A fighter plane roared above their heads and farther ahead it started to fire. They could not see what it was firing at, they only saw it circling around and heard the repeated rattle of its guns.

Max and Peter got off the cart and continued on foot. Only Adolf remained sitting on it, and the little girl led the horse by its halter.

They asked a man wearing an armband how to get to the station, and went in the direction he pointed. There was an endless line of refugee carts on the street leading to the station.

Eventually they could see the railroad station straight ahead, and a mass of boys in front of the building, sitting on the curb like birds on a telegraph wire. Maybe they were boys from their school—they looked exactly like them. Max and Peter started to run and Adolf craned his neck to see past the back of the horse, which blocked his view. He saw the other two hesitate and stop dead in their tracks. And in that instant he knew.

The boys turned out to be from Berlin. Their camp had been farther to the north and they had traveled the whole distance to Neuern on foot. They looked like it. They said that they had been sitting in front of the station for the last three hours, waiting for their camp commandant who had gone to find accommodations. They had seen a whole mass of CEC go by. But when Max described The Emperor they could not remember.

Max and Peter went into the building. The hall was empty, and they decided to go through to the platform. But before they reached the plank door leading to it, they were cut off by a man who came out of a side door and blocked their way.

"What're you looking for?" he snarled. They could not see whether he was a railroad man because he was wearing an oilskin cape and was not wearing a cap. Max asked him about their school. The man was very short with them. He knew nothing about their group and, no, no one had left any message. While he was herding them toward the exit, he added that they should ask at the church—it was full of CEC from Berlin. He seemed to be in a hurry to get them out of the station hall.

A Red Cross nurse at the church said that they should ask at the school. Berlin schoolchildren had been put up there, and if they did not find anyone there, they were to come back and join another group. All CEC groups were being sent on to Eisenstein-Zwiesel, farther into Bavaria. There was an assembling point in Zwiesel. They would be certain to find the others from their school there.

They had to go through the middle of town to get to the school. Max and Peter walked along next to the cart and the little girl led the horse by the halter.

"What are we going to do with her?" asked Adolf so quietly that she could not hear.

"Red Cross," said Peter. "That's what they're here for, isn't it? They've got orphanages."

Adolf was not happy about this answer — Max saw it in his face. "Maybe she's got some relatives somewhere," he said. It was meant to sound reassuring.

Peter said, "Well, she's got a horse. Maybe she'll find people who need a horse."

"You can't help feeling sorry for a little girl like her!" said Max.

Tilli led the horse across the square. She talked to it in a foreign language they did not understand, and the animal lowered its head as though it were listening attentively.

Max was about to ask two members of the territorial army standing by some stairs how to get to the school, when he realized they were in front of the town hall. He went in with Peter. Since they were here, they might as well ask about the little girl.

Adolf's eyes followed them as they trudged up the steps to the entrance. He heard the little girl draw closer and stop just behind him.

"What're they doing in there?" she asked.

Adolf tried to think of an answer. "They're asking where our school group is," he said.

"Like they did at the church?" she asked.

Adolf nodded.

"And then?"

"If they don't know anything, we'll ask at the school."

"And if they don't know anything either?"

"Then I don't know . . ." He hesitated. "Then we'll have to think again."

"And then?"

"Then we'll go to Bavaria, to Zwiesel. That's a town in Bavaria."

"And then?" asked Tilli.

"What 'then'?" Adolf asked back.

"When you get where you said?"

"Zwiesel? When we're in Zwiesel, we'll find our school again."

"And then?"

"Then we'll go to Berlin with our school."

"And then?"

"Then we'll be home," said Adolf. He was still sitting with his back to her, and heard her breathing behind him. He waited uneasily for her next "And then?" but she did not ask.

4

The Yanks

A man in a leather coat had stopped at the foot of the steps and was talking to a one-armed man with a walrus mustache and a beret on his head. They came closer, and the one-armed man pointed to Tilli's horse. The two walked around the horse and whispered to each other, and the man in the leather coat suddenly asked, "Does the horse belong to you?" He was standing directly in front of them, and Adolf had the impression he was at least six and one half feet tall.

"It belongs to her," said Adolf, nodding his head in Tilli's direction.

"Where's your family?" the man asked.

Adolf grasped the knapsacks lying next to him in the cart and wound the straps around his wrist. He did not say anything.

"Are you alone?" the man asked.

When Adolf still did not answer, the man bent down, hooked two fingers into the lapels of Adolf's jacket, and pulled him up. "Come on, you little shrimp, speak up!"

Adolf stiffened and hunched his shoulders.

The one-armed man pushed the one in the leather coat aside. He did not look so dangerous, and his voice was friendlier. "Where're you heading with your horse?" he asked. "Have you lost your family?"

Adolf shook his head. "We're looking for our school. We're CEC."

"Well, well, so you're looking for your school," said the one-armed man. He spoke the way you talk to a small child. "Well, maybe we can help you. Where d'you think it is? — Your school?"

The man in the leather coat had stepped up to the horse and was examining the collar, reaching for the halter. Tilli, watching him with growing suspicion, suddenly yelled: "Go away!"

The man hesitated for a moment and looked down at her in surprise. "Heyheyhey," he said. "Don't open your trap so wide, little girl!"

"Let go!" Tilli screamed, suddenly beside herself with fury, and when the man laid his hand on the horse's neck, she stepped up to him and kicked his shin so hard that he let out a scream and doubled up, grasping his leg with both hands and hopping around.

"You dirty little beast!" he bellowed and tried to grab her. But she had taken refuge behind the horse and kept close to its front legs so she could duck under the animal's belly at the first sign of danger.

Two men from the territorial army came over from the steps. They were holding the straps of their carbines taut and looked severely from under their helmets. The taller of the two straightened his shoulders so he would not look quite so shriveled up next to the tall man in the leather coat. "What's going on here? What d'you want from the children?" he asked gruffly.

"They want to take my horse away!" shrieked Tilli from under the animal's belly. "They want to take my horse away!"

She yelled so loudly that people stopped and looked around. The taller of the two men from the territorial army took the carbine from his shoulder.

"Now hold on a minute!" said the man in the leather coat, who looked ready to start a fight. The one-armed man pushed his way between them. "It's okay, it's okay — nothing's happened!" He pushed the man in the leather coat aside and pulled him along with him. They walked away across the square.

The man from the territorial army said, "Good God, children! Watch out and don't just hang around! Go on home!" He seemed to be sincerely concerned, like an old grandpa. "There's too much foreign riffraff running around, all of them pickpockets. Nothing's safe from them. They steal like magpies. Just watch out!"

Adolf nodded patiently and said, "Yes, yes, yes."

Then, at last, Max and Peter returned; now they could leave.

The boys had not been able to learn anything.

They set off, crossing the river and walking up a long hill.

They took their time because the one-armed man and his companion, were somewhere in front of them, and the children did not want to get too close.

There was not a soul on the street apart from themselves. It was quiet. Even the artillery firing had stopped. They crossed the street and turned into an alley between dark wooden fences. Behind the fences were long, rambling huts with corrugated iron roofs and no windows. The alley opened into a tree-dotted meadow, which dropped steeply down to the river. Refugees were camping around a fire beneath the trees and two horses were standing in the meadow. Tilli left hers with them so it could graze.

They still had the thick noodle soup in their mess tins which they had been given by some women on the road to the station. They dug into it. It was so cold it made their teeth hurt, and they had to warm every bite in their mouths before they could chew it. It took them half an hour to finish it, and then Tilli fetched the horse.

Just as she came back and they were getting ready to leave, there was an explosion close by. A dry explosion, followed instantly by a whistling hiss above their heads.

On the opposite side of the valley, in the middle of the houses, a fountain of dirt and rubble rose into the air, and two seconds later a thunderous crash burst on their eardrums. Then another blast and the hissing sound above their heads, and another hit across the valley, next to the other. It was like a newsreel in the cinema, and they were sitting in the best balcony seats. A roof rose slowly and fell back again, squashing the walls under it, and white clouds of dust poured out of the sides and enveloped the ruins. Tiny little people were running around among the houses and throwing themselves onto the ground between the spurting fountains of dirt. They did not look like real people; they looked funny, running around aimlessly and falling down.

The explosions continued and jumped to their side of the riverbank. One ripped into a red building that looked like a factory. A chimney stack snapped, pieces of red debris, beams and blocks from the walls flew through the air. The building sprayed apart and black smoke surged upward.

They ducked behind a pile of wood for cover. Only the horse's head stuck out over it, and Tilli desperately tugged at the halter trying to pull it down.

A man on crutches hurriedly lurched in their direction. He jackknifed forward, swinging between the crutches like a gymnast on bars. "Now they're going to bury us, the swine!" he cried. He looked over the top of the wood pile. Tall and gaunt and bald, his eyes bulging, he had a silly grin on his face. "Are they coming yet?" he asked breathlessly. "Did you see them? Where did they come from?" He gasped for air and kept grinning fixedly. "Good Lord, those are tanks! Here they come! How many are there? Good Lord!" A wailing buzz ripped the air, and the face was suddenly gone. One leg buckled at the knee, and the body slipped down between the crutches. Then the crutches fell together with a clatter onto the heap of human being lying on the ground. It did not have a head anymore. There was just a red stump out of which a red froth of blood oozed.

Max moved his lips. He tried to say something. But he could not get a word out. He leaped up. A horse was galloping over by the wood fence. Was that their horse? That *was* their horse! Where was the little girl? She was still standing with her back to the woodpile, staring at the man at her feet.

"Let's get away! Away from here!" screamed Max. He grabbed the girl's shoulders, lifted her onto the cart, helped Adolf up, pulled Peter along with him, and started to run with the cart.

They stopped by the wood fence. Silence had suddenly fallen, no more firing, no more explosions. The horse was nowhere to be seen.

They raced on. A row of houses stood in front of them. Behind them a fire was burning. A dark cloud of smoke rose over the roofs. The wood fence turned to the right; there was a path leading back to the main street and to the school. And there was the horse. It came toward them.

Tilli jumped off the cart and ran to it, shouting, "Herta, come, come here, come to me!" as fearless as a circus rider. "Come Herta, good girl, good girl!" The horse stopped and pranced in place, tossing its head, snorting, showing the whites of its eyes, its ears flat against its head.

They could now clearly hear the crackling of the fire, the booming explosions of dry wood bursting in the scorching heat, the hissing of the flames.

"Be a good girl, Herta, quiet now; Herta, it's me, Tilli. Come to Tilli!" Carefully, taking small steps, she drew closer, talking reassuringly to the animal until she was able to catch hold of the halter. "There, Herta, it's all right, Herta, everything's all right again."

She could not see that the two men from the market place,

the one-armed one and the one in the leather coat, had appeared behind the horse.

"Well, here we are again," said the one-armed man. He had his hand on his hip and looked at Tilli with his head cocked. He smiled and winked at her. "You can count yourselves lucky that we came just in time!" he continued, still smiling. "If we hadn't stopped the animal, it would have been over the hills and gone!"

Then suddenly the smile was gone. His eyes became hard and there was not a trace of friendliness in his voice when he started to speak again. "Now listen closely, you dumb kids. The charming fireworks display we just witnessed was made by the American armored spearhead. The only reason they've withdrawn is because it'll soon be dark. But tomorrow they'll be back again, and then we'll be trapped here. None of us want that, do we?" He paused and took two strides over to the horse, ran his hand down its neck and caught the halter as though by accident. Tilli watched him warily, but she did not move.

"Well, then," the one-armed man continued, "we want to get away from here as quickly as possible, across the border. You want the same thing. We have a car, you have a horse. So we'll go together. Is that clear?" The friendly smile reappeared on his face again. "Unless you want to stay here. In that case, we'll go alone."

They all looked at Max, who was standing in front of the one-armed man, his shoulders hunched.

"We'll come along," he said. And in a helpless attempt at asserting their rights he added, "But we have to go to Zwiesel!"

"That's where we want to go too, lad," said the one-armed man. "What d'you know? we're going in the same direction!" He twisted his mouth into a broad grin and commanded in a harsh tone, "Let's go then!" and pulled the horse along with him.

Tilli released the halter and waited for the other three to come up, then she trotted along behind the cart. She hung her head. She did not want anyone to see that her eyes were brimming with tears.

They followed the men to the main street and through a gate where the huts were. Behind the gate stood a Tempo three-wheeled truck without its windshield and with holes from shrapnel in the roof and in the hood. The bed of the truck was covered with a tarp. On the tarp lay a man in a *Wehrmacht* sheepskin coat with a green collar, and a leather driver's cap. He sat up and swung his legs over the side. "Well, I'll be . . . a nag with harness, what luck!"

The one-armed man maneuvered the horse in front of the three-wheeler. "Stop speechifying!" he said in a harsh, commanding tone. "Harness the old nag!" He was the ringleader; there was no doubt about that.

The man wearing the leather cap put a rope around the window posts of the three-wheeler. The one-armed man climbed into the cab behind the steering wheel and asked for the reins. "You can lift the little girl and the luggage on top, but the three of you'll have to walk," he said. "We have to go easy on the horse. It's quite some distance we've got to cover."

Max pointed to Adolf. "He can't walk!" he said defiantly. The one-armed man threw him a suspicious glance. Then he said, "All right, he can get up too, but make it snappy!" A second later he cracked the reins and moved off.

The man with the leather cap helped them heave the luggage and the cart onto the truck bed, and helped Adolf and Tilli climb up. He seemed to be the most decent of the three. When they were out of the town he took two loaves of sourdough bread from under the tarp and divided them up. He gave each of them a piece of hard red salami to go with it. It was so hot and spicy that it brought tears to their eyes, but they ate it anyway — after all, it was salami. When was the last time they had eaten salami? They could get rid of the hotness by chewing lots of bread.

The horse was tired and slow. When they went uphill even the two men in the cab had to get out, and when it was steep they had to push. The road often went uphill.

Tilli and Adolf went to sleep under the tarp. Max and Peter held onto the sides, concentrating on placing one foot in front of the other. Their legs seemed to be made of rubber. The road was rubber too, soft rubber into which their feet sank deeper and deeper with every step. It was harder and harder to pull them out again.

The men in the cab did not stop to rest. They did not need to: they could rest while they rode.

Darkness fell and Peter and Max could no longer see the road on which they were trudging. The truck was a black shadow in front of them that would drive away if they let go of the sides. They had to stay with it, hold on to it. They hung on. Uphill, downhill, until they could not tell uphill from downhill anymore. It was all the same: one step after another, straighten the knee, right foot forward, left foot forward, right, left, right, left. They let themselves be dragged along, linked their elbows around the side and laid their heads on their elbows, supporting themselves on the truck. Their legs followed along behind, their heads swayed to and fro in time with their steps. Their eyelids drooped. Only their legs still moved. They walked in their sleep.

At some point there was a loud noise that penetrated their sleep, a sudden stop that confused the even rhythm of their steps and startled them. Hands pitilessly grabbed their shoulders and shook them, a slap on their backs, and a loud voice: "Come on boys! Lend a hand!" The luggage pulled heavily on their arms; they heard Tilli's fretful, questioning voice, and smelled the hay, the odor of stables, while watching the shifting beam of a flashlight. Then finally peace, no more walking, a soft place on the ground where they could lie down, could stretch out, curl up, sleep.

Max listened to the others breathing, quietly and regularly. They were still asleep. He lay awake and kept his eyes closed. Suddenly he heard something else — a muffled drone that swelled and receded, then intensified until the air trembled from it. And above the drone, like a shrill musical accompaniment, there was a grating screech that hurt his ears.

Max had heard the noise before. He knew what it was. Tanks. He sat up with a jerk and opened his eyes. Semidarkness around him. A narrow shaft of light came through a window on the left. Max stood up. His whole body was stiff, as though he were frozen through and through. He went to the window and pushed open its broken shutter.

He saw the shadow of someone running past the window

and cautiously poked his head out. To his left, not three yards away, a man was standing against the wall of the building, peering around the corner. A small, bow-legged, fat little man in a black SS uniform, with gleaming top boots and polished visor as though he had just come from a parade. He turned around suddenly, and before Max could pull in his head, he had passed him and was galloping down the street, his stomach sticking out in front of him. He ran toward a railroad embankment where the street ran under it, and disappeared into the tunnel opening.

The drone of tanks had become even louder, so loud that the windowpanes began rattling. Max ran around a wooden partition, past a wooden stepladder that led to the upper floor, and came to a large, windowless room. Against the wall were a grain-binder and other machines, dusty and draped with hay. A strong smell of stables was in the air. Where was the horse? Where were the men?

Max ran to the door which lay to the right and opened it a crack. Three slate-roofed barns stood in front of him. Beyond them he could see a village on the crest of a hill.

Then they came, out from behind the last houses of the village like huge, clumsy beetles. One after another. Five, six, seven, more and more. Between them were small, squat cars such as he had never seen before. They were driving between the tanks and soldiers were marching in long columns on the road in front, their weapons ready. The troops were walking close to the edge of the road, taking cover, keeping their distance. Those were no Germans. Those were Americans with round helmets. Even more vehicles rolled over the crest of the hill, big-wheeled trucks and more tanks, and the small, squat cars that whisked past the convoy. The soldiers in the lead were now only about five hundred paces from the first of the three barns. They took cover behind the trees along the road and in the ditch. Only their round helmets and the barrels of their guns were visible. Three ran along the ditch, leaped across the road toward the barn. Max stared in fascination and could not tear his eyes away. Damn it! If he waited much longer, it would be too late. They would not be able to get away.

He raced back under the partition. "Wake up!" he called to the others, shook them, pulled them up. It was hard to wake them. "The Americans!" he cried. "Come on, get up! We've got to get out of here!" He grabbed his knapsack, threw the blankets over his shoulder, pulled Tilli to her feet and shook her. She went on sleeping on her feet. Peter and Adolf finally got the message. "There's tanks all over the place!" said Max. He ran ahead of them and pointed through the crack in the door. The soldiers were already heading toward them.

"Hide!" he called to the others as he ran back into the farthest corner where the machines were stored and crawled behind them. Adolf and Peter followed him in silent haste. At that very moment Tilli let out a scream, a horrified scream that overrode the drone of the engines and the screech of the tanks' tracks. "Where's Herta? Herta isn't here! Where's she gone?" She was standing behind the door next to a pile of still-steaming horse droppings.

"Tilli, come here!" called Adolf in a hushed voice. "Quickly! Come here!" She stamped her foot and did not move an inch. "I want to know where Herta is!" she screamed.

Something crashed against the door and it flew open; a soldier leaped in and in three bounds was against the wall. He crouched there, poised to jump, submachine gun ready. A small pointed face under a large, fabric-covered, round helmet.

A split second later another one came in. He was two heads taller than the first. A giant. They could not make out his face. The small one called something to him and the giant ran to the ladder and charged up. They heard his steps above, then brusque shouts and splintering wood. When he came back down, the small one pointed to Tilli. They seemed to notice her for the first time.

She was standing in front of them, clutching her little bag tightly and staring at them, her mouth wide open. She was not really afraid; she was much too surprised to be afraid. She stood rooted to the spot.

The giant suddenly bent down to her and said something. In speechless shock she saw that his face was black as coal, as though it had been smeared with shoe polish. She had never seen a black man before, and suddenly she was terrified.

She started to run as quickly as her legs would take her into the corner where the others were hiding. There she cowered behind a stack of boards and hid her face in her hands as though that would make her invisible.

When she looked up again the two soldiers had disappeared. Engines roared outside. The ground trembled under her feet. The whole building shuddered, so that the plaster fell off the walls. Then, slowly, a tank clumsily moved in front of the open door. The stench of gasoline rose to their noses. The tank stopped directly in front of the door, its engine gurgling. The engine noise outside got louder and louder. They heard the earsplitting screeching of the tanks' tracks on the paving stones on the road and short commands barked in a language they did not understand.

None of this impressed Tilli. Nothing compared to the hair-raising sight of that raven-black face which had been so close she could have touched it. She turned to Adolf. "Did you see! A bogeyman!" she said. Her voice shook with excitement, and her eyes were as round as glass marbles.

"That was a Negro!" said Adolf hastily. And Peter hissed at her: "Get over here and shut your trap!" The whole time he had been afraid that the small American would fire a volley into the corner where they were huddled, and the thought of it made him almost sick.

The small American reappeared in the doorway and this time another man was with him, a tall, gaunt, white man with bloused trousers that were much too short for his long legs. He cast a searching glance around and craned his long, thin neck. As he did so, his head wobbled under the huge helmet as if it might fall off his neck at any moment. He did not look very frightening.

He called out something, and after the third time they realized he was speaking to them. "Hello, kids, come on out!" he yelled in German with a flat *r*. They crept farther into their hiding place, but the small man had seen them and waved his machine gun.

They came out slowly and stood in line in front of the soldiers, staring down at the ground like thieves caught red-handed, clutching their luggage.

Two more soldiers came in, one of them with binoculars around his neck, and disappeared behind the wooden partition.

"Have you seen any German soldiers?" the tall man asked. He spoke German with a strange accent, but they now understood him better. They shook their heads. *"Nicht Wehrmacht, nicht SS?"* he asked. *"Nicht soldaten?"* They shook their heads again, silent and suspicious, with the vague fear that their headshaking could have bad consequences.

Max thought of the SS man with the potbelly whom he had seen through the window, but he did not say anything. He was confused. He had imagined war to be quite different. War would have tanks that dashed forward, firing, assault and close combat, flame-throwers, sharp-shooters, paratroopers who fell from the sky, and fearless combat patrols who stealthily sneaked through enemy lines at night. And now? These Americans asked, Where were the enemy lines? Where was the Front? Why were they asking? Surely they knew where the Front was!

"Are you alone?" the American asked. Peter nodded vigorously. "Where is your" — the American searched for the right word — "father, mother, where?" he asked.

"Berlin," said Peter quickly, "in Berlin!" He was afraid that the American might not believe him.

The soldier with the binoculars came back from behind the partition, stopped in front of them, and gave them a penetrating stare. When the tall man said something to him he grimaced, then made a violent gesture with his hand, growled something that sounded nasty, and strode away quickly.

The small man chewed continuously. He sat with half of his backside on a sawhorse and chewed, not taking his eyes off them. As soon as the tall man was outside, he slowly walked up to them and stopped in front of Peter. With outstretched arm he opened the flap on the leather camera case that Peter had hanging on his belt, took out the camera, and put it in the opening of his jacket. He grinned and chewed the whole time. Then he pointed to the door with his machine gun, and when they started walking he followed close behind.

They squeezed past the tank in front of the door. The small man behind them yelled something over their heads, a squawking sound that screeched in their ears. Farther down the road, on a level with the last barn, a man answered and raised his arm.

They trotted off down the road. Max and Peter in front, loaded with their luggage, the two smaller ones behind. Tilli hung on to Adolf's jacket sleeve.

There were soldiers everywhere. Some were sitting, some were lying by the roadside smoking and chewing, and some were sitting in small, angular, open cars from which long antennas towered up like gigantic whips. Beyond the barns were columns of tanks and trucks, standing on the road and in the fields.

On the embankment behind came a sudden bark — two short bursts of gunfire. Soldiers dropped to the ground and one, still standing, threw up his arms. Everything else seemed to have frozen. Only that one soldier on the embankment moved. Silhouetted against the sky, he fell backward with outstretched arms and rolled down the slope. Then a wave of noise broke around them. It was as though they were sitting in the middle of a roaring, howling, engine-droning organ of hell.

They saw flashes from guns on the slope of the forested hill beyond the meadows. They saw the tanks awkwardly start off; saw how they shook when firing their cannons. They saw the building they had just been in collapse in a whirling cloud of rubble; saw the earth spray up; saw trucks, their wheels spinning, race across the fields; saw a soldier who had waved to them lying on the ground, one of his legs twisted grotesquely. They could see that he was screaming, but they could not hear him in the hellish noise.

At last, Max started to run, pulling Tilli along with him. He raced, bent double, across the road, threw himself into the ditch, and pressed against the ground, his face in the grass. There was a droning in his ears, but through the droning he suddenly heard a scream. Someone was screaming close by, screaming and screaming at the top of his lungs. "Take cover! Take cover! Take cover! Take cover!" He kept screaming. It was Peter. And when Max looked up, he saw him standing in the middle of the road, his arms half lifted, as though he were trying to protect his head, a twisted, tearful expression on his face. Screaming over and over: "Take cover! Take cover! Take cover!"

Max ran to him and grabbed his arm. Peter did not move. He stood rigid and stiff. Max kicked him, hit him in the face,

pulled him, pushed him forward across the road and down
into the ditch. Peter finally stopped screaming, dropped
down on his stomach, and scurried along the ditch like a
beetle looking for a dark hole. He turned in a circle, crawled
under the blanket which had fallen from his shoulders, and
hid under it.

Gradually the noise subsided. Only isolated bursts of fire
from the tank cannons could be heard over the droning of
the engines. Far away on the other side of the embankment
they could hear machine gun fire.

An American suddenly appeared on the road, loaded with
ammunition belts, egg-shaped hand grenades on his belt, and
an automatic rifle with bipod on his shoulder. He looked
monstrously fat in his wide, green-brown jacket with its
pockets stuffed full. He called something to them, motioned
over his shoulder, his arm outstretched: "*Mach' schnell!*
Quick!" he called again in his bad German. He became im-
patient when they did not understand right away, and waved
his arm.

Max scrambled up and out of the ditch onto the road.
Adolf and Tilli followed. Silent and frightened, they stared
at the soldier. He pointed to a truck standing next to the last
building on the road, its rear end toward them.

Peter was still lying in the ditch. "Move! Come on, you
asshole!" yelled Max. He was suddenly furious, and furiously he began to run, the two smaller children jogging
along behind.

A red-faced giant with blond hair and hands like shovels
lifted them onto the bed of the truck under the tarp, one

after another as though they were little puppies. Tilli watched him open-mouthed, and when he noticed her astonished stare he started to grin so that his mustache stood on end. He reached into his jacket pocket and quickly popped something into her mouth. She was so frightened that she could not close her mouth quickly enough. When she did, there was something already between her teeth. She drew back her lips, made a face as though she had swallowed an earthworm, and was about to scream, when the truck jerked into motion, throwing her hard against the side.

The blond man stayed behind. He laughed, pointed to his mouth with his forefinger, and chewed with a grinding movement of his lower jaw so that it looked as if he wanted to crush his finger. Tilli did not take her eyes off him until the trees along the roadside hid him from view. Then she carefully pulled out the thing between her teeth. It was flat and rectangular, wrapped in silver paper. She studied it suspiciously. A gray strip, dusted with white and smelling of peppermint, was hidden under the silver paper. She licked it and put it in her mouth. It tasted sweet and became soft between her teeth.

"Maybe it's poison," said Peter.

"Oh shut up!" Max snapped at him.

Ahead of them on the truck bed, a man suddenly began to shout. Both of his hands were thickly bandaged. "Come! Come!" he called. He wanted something. "Come here!" he called again.

Tilli was sitting closest to him. He nodded to her and beckoned with his bandaged hand. "Come! Come!" he urged. She was afraid of him, but she was even more afraid that he could become angry if she did not obey. She hesitantly slid toward him.

"Here!" he shouted and pointed to his jacket pocket. "Here!" He had to shout to be heard over the roar of the motor. Tilli reached into the pocket and pulled out a pack of cigarettes. He nodded to her, pointed to the pack and then to his mouth.

She understood. With nimble fingers she took a cigarette out of the pack. It was difficult, because the truck kept bouncing and she could not hold on. She put the cigarette in his mouth and looked at him, eager for praise. Just then the truck jerked and flung her with full force against the soldier, against his bandaged hand. The soldier screamed and Tilli rolled across the floor, then crawled on all fours to Adolf in the farthest corner, and hid behind his back. The truck skidded around a bend, slowed down, drove through a gate, and stopped.

They could hear music — loud, fast, gay music. The tarp was whipped back, and a man with a dark-brown face lowered the tailgate. A large yard lay before them, enclosed by buildings on three sides: a long house, sheds, barns, stables. The fourth side was closed off by a wall. In the middle rose a mountain of manure.

The man with the brown face shooed them from the truck and pointed to the road outside the gate. They started off, walked to the middle of the yard and past the dung heap. There were stacks of rifles, pistols, machine guns, stick hand grenades, and helmets scattered all over the ground. Then they saw German soldiers. They were standing in the open shed on the other side of the yard, packed close together.

Hundreds of them. Officers in riding breeches, paratroopers and air force men, privates in long coats and in camouflage jackets, and with torn, dirty triangular tarps around their shoulders. Wrinkled jackets, crumpled pants, empty knapsacks, gray, tired, stubbled faces. They had been captured, and now they were prisoners.

The children threw a furtive glance in the direction of the prisoners and shyly walked on through the gate and along a wide, paved lane to the road.

They stopped where the lane joined the road. They had to sort out their things and find out where they were. That was the most important.

Peter fished the map from his knapsack and handed it to Max. He was quiet and embarrassed, and slipped quickly away.

Alone, Peter ran to a stream that flowed through the fields beyond the road. He struggled out of his pants in a flying hurry. Luckily it had all been caught in his underpants. He washed them, then stepped into the water and washed between his legs. He put the wet underpants in the leather camera case, which he still had on his belt, and put on his pants. He did not button them up until he came out from behind the bushes. Let the others think that he had just peed!

Tilli sat on the edge of the road, her face hidden behind her hands. "Where have they taken Herta?" she wailed.

Adolf, small and helpless, stood near her. "We couldn't have done anything, Tilli," he said. "There were three of them — we couldn't have done anything against them anyway." He felt like crying himself.

Max was folding the map again; there was no sense in

studying it. The large mountain behind them had to be Mount Arber, but they did not know where they were in relationship to it. To the south? Or to the north? The sky was gray, no sign of the sun.

Peter thought they were to the north. But that was impossible. The men with the three-wheeler had said they wanted to go to Zwiesel. And Zwiesel was to the south of the Arber. They set off marching along the side of the road in single file, Tilli bringing up the rear.

There was a sign at the next crossroads pointing in the direction from which they had come: KONIGSHUTT 5MI. They had memorized the map. They were to the north.

"I told you so!" said Peter. "Told you so!" Max threw him a venomous glance.

They sat down on the embankment above the road and took out the map again. It was at least twenty miles to Zwiesel. The men with the three-wheeler, those swine, had turned north from Eisenstein. They could follow the route clearly on the map. Now they were here, Zwiesel was to the south, and the Arber was in between; there was fighting still going on around the Arber.

"We'll go south first," said Max hesitantly. "There's a railroad track. It leads to Zwiesel." He stood up and buckled on his knapsack. Then he turned into the side road that branched off past the signpost. It led into the forested hills winding upward in sharp bends.

Adolf's feet had begun to hurt again. He could only take small steps. It took them almost three hours to reach the top and another two before they came out of the forest. A small village lay ahead of them with dark, slated-roofed houses.

The church clock showed twelve and from the window above the clock hung a long, white cloth, billowing in the wind.

The village was as quiet as a graveyard, not a soul in sight. Nor had they met anyone on the road during their five-hour march. They had not realized that until now.

Slowly they went farther into the village. Two small girls were standing behind a picket fence watching them curiously. They ran away when Max and the others came closer. Then, above them, a window opened and an old lady leaned out and asked something in a high, piping voice. They only understood the word *Americans*. She probably wanted to know whether they had seen the Americans. Max pointed in the direction from which they had come and at that moment they heard the soft hum of engines, and the woman looked up, crossed herself, and slammed the window. A white cloth hanging down over the windowsill swayed in the wind.

5

Destination Berlin

The roar of motors approached quickly. It had to be a whole convoy. Then they saw it racing up the village street. Right in front was one of those small, squat cars with a mounted machine gun. Behind it came a column of trucks, all the same kind. In them were German soldiers, crowded shoulder-to-shoulder like sardines, as though they had been stuffed in from above. A few waved, and the children waved back as the trucks thundered by, one after another.

On the second to last truck a man leaned far over the side, waved his arm, threw them something, and shouted, "To Berlin! To Berlin!"

They waited till the convoy had passed, then Peter picked the thing up from the ditch. It was a tightly folded note with an address written in indelible pencil on it: "To Mrs. Annette Schatzman, Berlin-Reinickendorf, Schaferstrasse 12."

Max took the note from his hand and carefully stowed it away in the breast pocket of his jacket.

"What are you going to do with it?" asked Peter. Max said nothing. He started off again and Peter hurried to catch up with him. "D'you know where Schaferstrasse is?" he asked.

Max shook his head.

"I thought you knew your way around Reinckendorf."

Max shrugged his shoulders, "But I don't know Schaferstrasse," he said.

In the village square stood an army truck with its hood up, loaded with steel helmets. Behind it was a house with pink-colored plaster and across the whole facade in thick black letters was written: ONWARD TO VICTORY WITH THE FÜHRER!! Next to the entrance hung a sign with the inscription COMMUNAL ADMINISTRATIVE OFFICE.

Adolf was the first to notice it and hoped that Max would overlook it. But Max turned into the square and walked past the truck straight toward the building. "Wait here. I'll be back soon," he told them.

Max went in. It smelled like a school, and when the door closed behind him, it was so dark he could barely see a thing. He was about to turn back when a door opened next to him, and a thin old lady stared at him with undisguised suspicion. "What d'you want?" she asked. She had a voice like a man.

"I just wanted to ask . . ." he stammered. She did not let him finish. "Where've you come from?" she asked. Max told her, but she remained suspicious until he told her about the Americans. At that point she suddenly pricked up her ears.

"Where'd you say that was?" she asked. Max described it to her. She called upstairs: "Mrs. Scheurer, Mrs. Scheurer! You wanna hear the latest? The Americans are in Eisenstein!" Turning to Max she said, suddenly quite anxious: "You hungry son?" And then in a trumpeting voice: "Mrs. Scheurer, C'mon down! Bring some bread!"

"I just wanted to ask," Max started again, "I just wanted to ask whether the Red Cross is here, or something like it. It's just that we've got a little girl with us. She lost her parents. We can't drag her around with us forever. We have to hand her over to someone."

A heavyset, massive woman with a thin crown of hair and watery eyes came down the stairs, clutching some bread to her breast. It was half a loaf, but it almost disappeared under her fat, red hands.

The small woman with the man's voice turned to her: "Y'ever heard such a thing, Mrs. Scheurer?" She was almost in tears. "Isn't that dreadful? Yes, merciful Lord in Heaven, these children are roamin' round the countryside, utterly alone. How could somethin' like that happen?" She went on and on. Max was not listening anymore; there was no point to it. They would never get rid of the little girl here. He just stared at the bread and waited for them finally to give it to him. The fat woman was still clutching it to her bosom. And the thin woman kept talking at him: where he should go because of the little girl, first here, then there, and if he did not have any success there, he should go to the priest. And he should give the priest her regards. She wrote something on a scrap of paper and stuffed the note into his jacket pocket. Max kept nodding and waiting for her to give him the bread. At last she took it from the fat woman, grasped his hand, laid the bread in it, and then grasped his other hand and pressed it against the bread, as though he were incapable of holding it himself.

The fat woman did not say a word. She just kept staring at him with her watery eyes and pressing her folded hands against her mouth. The small woman went on talking. He could still hear her wailing after he had gone out of the door. At least he had got the bread.

As he walked he took his knife out of his pocket, and when he reached the others he cut off four slices and handed them out. It was not until he had eaten half of his own slice that he said casually, "Nothing doing."

The two women were still standing in the doorway of the communal administrative office, watching them. A man with a pickle barrel was in the process of painting over the words on the pink wall with black paint. The only part still legible was WITH THE FUH. The rest was a wide, black stripe.

"Why's he doing that?" asked Tilli. "Why's he getting rid of it?"

"So you can't read it anymore," said Adolf.

"Read what?" asked Tilli.

"The writing up there!"

"What's it say?"

"Read it yourself," said Adolf curtly. He wanted to seem hard because Max and Peter were there, but when he saw how Tilli hung her head, he was sorry.

"*Can* you read?" he asked.

She did not say anything, and turned away until she had her back to him.

"How old are you, anyhow?" asked Adolf. "Come on, how old are you?"

"Seven," she said almost inaudibly.

"In that case you must be in school," said Max. "You must be able to read."

Adolf quickly swallowed the piece of bread he had in his mouth. "They've been traveling since Christmas," he whispered in Max's ear, so quietly that she would not hear.

Max looked at the little girl and really saw her for the first time: her short, flaxen hair straggly and matted to the nape of her neck; her blue, woollen coat that was too small for her; her thin legs in the long brown stockings; the little bag she clasped tightly. He looked at her, raised his shoulders, and would have liked to say something friendly. But instead he hooked his thumbs into the knapsack straps and pulled them taut. "Come on, let's go!" He turned and walked off.

They walked until Adolf could go no farther. He did not say anything, but he walked slower and slower, and they could see the pain in his face. They stopped and Max again handed out some bread. He had hoped they would reach a larger town by evening, but they would never make it now. They would be lucky to find somewhere to spend the night.

He thought of Tilli's horse and the three men who had taken it, and imagined what he would do to them if he met them again in five years' time. He would remember their faces. He would never forget them.

He unwound Adolf's footcloths. They were soaked through at the back and the heels were raw again. The scabs had rubbed off. He wrapped a new bandage around them. He had to tear it in half since it was the last one they had.

Adolf endured it all without a word. He did not move a muscle even though tears came to his eyes.

"Maybe it would be better if I put the shoes on again," he said. "If I lace them up tight, they can't rub. Maybe I'll be able to walk on again." He smiled uncertainly and looked to Max for help.

"Wouldn't be able to get the shoes on," Max said gruffly. He jumped up, screwed the footcloths into a ball and violently flung them across the field. "Those rotten swine!" he said. He rummaged in his knapsack and took out something from the bottom that had been carefully wrapped in packing paper.

It was a pair of shoes, brown half-boots made of sturdy skiver leather. They were double-stitched, laced with leather thongs over hooks, and had strong soles with metal at the front and back. The shoes gleamed as though they had just been polished. Max had never worn them. He would rather have gone barefoot than put them on. His father had made them for his qualifying exam for journeyman cobbler.

For as long as he could remember they had stood in a glass cabinet in the living room with the framed master craftsman's certificate. Four years ago, when he had left home, they had still been standing there. Then last Christmas they had suddenly arrived in the package his mother had sent him. "Look after them well, son," she had written. "You know how attached father is to them, and your brothers should be able to wear them after you." In the same letter she had told him that his father had been reported missing in action on the Eastern Front.

He had never been very close to his father. The man had

been too strict for that, had always been too ready to grasp for the leather belt. And Max, as the eldest, had been on the receiving end the most. Nevertheless, he had taken care of the boots as though they were a treasure.

He loosened the thongs so that Adolf could slip them on more easily. The leather was soft and pliable, for Max had oiled them regularly. He knew how to care for shoes. With two pairs of socks on his feet, they fit Adolf perfectly. If he took short steps, bent his knees slightly, and walked flat-footed, they would not rub and he would hardly feel his heels anymore.

They started off again and towards evening they came to a river. The bridge had been blown up, so they followed tire tracks that led away from the road across the meadow, upstream to a ford. Max and Peter took off their shoes and socks and rolled up their pantlegs. First they carried the luggage to the other bank, then they made a seat with their hands and got Adolf. They wanted to carry Tilli across the same way, but Peter said he could do it alone. He lifted the little girl onto his shoulders and waded through the water with her. When he had almost reached the other bank he slipped, and Tilli fell off his shoulders and splashed headfirst into the water. It happened so quickly that she did not have time to scream, and after she had recovered from the shock she was shivering so hard that she could not make a sound. Max and Peter caught her by her hands and pulled her toward a barn that stood a few hundred yards upstream.

The barn door was locked but they found a loose board on one side that they could crawl through. Inside there were stacks of hayprops, roof tiles, and boards. Overhead was a loft made of loose-laid boards with hay hanging between.

They carried Tilli inside, and Max tried to take her coat off. He swore because the sleeves were so tight that they might as well have been glued to her arms. They panted with exertion as Peter pulled at her shoes, Max at her coat, and Adolf rummaged in the knapsacks for dry clothes.

They were so busy that they did not hear a movement above them in the hayloft. Only Tilli saw the head above her. Someone was looking down from the loft. The surprise made her teeth stop chattering and before she could warn the others, the man above called, "You'd better not hurt the little girl, you punks!"

They jumped with surprise.

"We just wanted to . . . well . . . because . . . she fell in the water," Max finally stuttered.

The man above let down a ladder. "Then leave her clothes on," he said and sat on the edge of the opening to the loft with his legs hanging down. "Bring her on up!"

Tilli hesitantly climbed up the ladder.

"Come here, little girl," said the man. He stretched out his arms and lifted her up. "Boy, you really got wet; you're still dripping!" he drawled in an agreeable Saxon dialect. He seemed so friendly, so nice that Tilli trusted him immediately.

He carried her to a corner where the hay was piled shoulder-high and began to dig a hole into it. "We'll have you warm as toast in a jiffy. You'll see."

With growing curiosity she watched him take one handful after another out of the hole. It was already so deep that his head disappeared into it, and when he straightened up he wheezed and sneezed and laughed at her. "I'll have it deep enough in a minute. You'll see how nice it is, warm as an oven!" Then he lifted her up and put her into the hole, after which he stuffed hay firmly around her until only her head peeked out.

"Bring me a towel and a blanket," he called. He spread the blanket around Tilli, so she looked like a severed head on a blanket on the hay. Then he rubbed her hair dry. "Well, can you feel the warmth? Are you getting warm?"

Tilli nodded absently. All her senses were turned inward as she started to sense the warmth slowly rising up in her. A blissful, tingling warmth that made her feel heavy, made her tired, her legs, her arms, her eyelids. The towel stroked over her hair. "Feet warm, head cold, you'll live to be a hundred years old!" she heard the man say. She opened her eyes again and saw Adolf in the brown boots that were too big for him. She smiled at him, and a second later was fast asleep.

"See, she's asleep already," said the man. He led the three boys to the other end of the loft. There was another pile of hay there and a wooden ventilating shaft. Behind it sat another man, taller and thinner than the first one, and much younger. Maybe twenty years old. He did not look so young around the eyes. The boys could see that both the men were privates: their uniforms were lying behind the pile of hay, along with blankets, and belts, helmets, canteens and carbines. A carbide stove was standing on two roof tiles, and hot water was steaming in a mess tin.

"Where've you come from?" the younger man asked. He

was from Berlin, he told them. They suddenly felt at home.

"We come from Berlin, too," said Peter happily.

"Well, then, make yourselves at home," said the Berliner. He gave Peter one end of a leather strop and proceeded to sharpen a razor blade on it. It scraped as he worked the blade to and fro. "D'you have a cigarette on you by any chance?" he asked. "Nothing? No smoke?"

They shook their heads, both astonished and flattered by his question. They would have given a lot to be able casually to pull a pack of cigarettes out of their pockets.

"I guess you're heading for home now?" the Berliner asked.

Adolf held his breath and stared at Max. Peter also waited in suspense.

"Hmm," said Max, shrugging his shoulders. It could have been taken as a yes.

Berlin! Why shouldn't they head for Berlin? Why should they look for their school first? They could just as easily go home alone. The two privates seemed to think the war was over. The man from Saxony had already stripped all the military insignia from his uniform jacket: decorations, epaulets, cuffs and collar patches. And he had sewn on artificial staghorn buttons in place of the metal ones. It looked like the jacket from a peasant's costume. The Berliner was not wearing any part of his uniform, not even the army boots. He was wearing elegant, low summer shoes, wide brown trousers, a shirt that looked like a lady's blouse, and a white linen jacket over it.

"And you?" asked Max. "Where're you going?"

"Mmm," said the Berliner. "We'll see how far we'll get."
He lathered his chin and the small mustache he had on his
upper lip. Max watched him shave.

"Listen Egon," the man from Saxony said suddenly.
"What would you say if I played father?"

"I've thought of that, too," said the Berliner, his mouth
twisted. He was shaving his right cheek, puffing it out. "Let's
sleep on it," he said. He had shaved his whole chin, and on
his upper lip only the Hitler mustache was left. He rubbed in
a small dot of lather under his nose.

Suddenly he sat up straight, combed a lock of hair onto
his forehead with his fingers, puffed himself up, and
frowned. Then, in a voice they all knew from school when
they had stood in front of the radio in formation with the
whole Hitler Youth team, from the camp commandant on
down to the smallest squirt, he growled and roared: "Na-
tional Comrades! It is not my fault that Providence failed!"
Then he pulled his nose up with two fingers, lifted the razor
blade, and shaved off the mustache.

Tilli woke up. Through the chinks in the barn wall broad
shafts of dazzling white light streamed in. Outside, the sun
was shining, a cold sun. The blanket under her chin felt ice-
cold; and when she breathed out, a thick cloud of steam
rose. But she was not cold. Her whole body was filled with
warmth. The warmth rose up in her, and she had to blow the
steam out through her mouth so she would not become too
hot. She thought of what the man had told her before she
had fallen asleep, and she thought how beautiful it would be
to stay in this warm hole until she was a hundred years old.

She remained quite still. Not a sound to be heard except the quiet, squeaky twittering of birds. The birds are freezing outside, she thought, and stretched in her little hollow.

Where were the others? She carefully turned her head. No one was lying on the pile of hay opposite. Maybe they were lying behind her?

She listened, holding her breath. Not a sound. A slight unease welled up in her.

"Adolf!" she called. And again: "Adolf!" Her voice was as squeaky as the twittering of birds outside. No answer.

All at once the fear was there. A fear which made her deaf and blind; which screamed inside her and squeezed her throat shut. In wild panic she kicked her way out of the hay, ran around the hayloft looking in all the corners, calling "Adolf! Adolf!"

Nothing. No one. No knapsacks, no blankets. She slid down the ladder, climbed over the woodpile. Her coat got caught; she tore it loose, pushed the board in the barn wall aside, and crawled out. Shimmering, glittering, sparkling brightness dazzled her, blinded her. Everything was white, glaring white, glistening white. She ran off into this white brightness, ran, tripped, fell. There was something cold on her hands, on her face. She scrabbled up, ran on. "Adolf! Adolf!" She stopped, looked around. The field was covered with frost. Beyond it was the forest, like a black wall. Everything blurred before her eyes. "Adolf! Adolf!" she screamed.

Then she suddenly heard shouts. Someone was calling her, calling her name. "Tilli! Hey, Tilli!" It was Adolf's voice. Adolf was calling her. She saw him coming from the forest, running toward her across the white field and carrying something in his arms. Huge, dry branches. He had not gone. He had not left her alone. He had only gone to gather wood.

She was suddenly ashamed. And before he reached her, she quickly turned away, lowered her head, and furtively wiped the tears from her face.

"Did you dry out?" asked Adolf.

Tilli felt her coat. It was dry. Terribly dusty and full of hay, but dry. She nodded and picked the hay off her coat and brushed the dust off.

"I can't believe it!" said Adolf. "Weren't you cold at all?"

She shook her head. She was afraid that he would hear that she had been crying if she spoke.

"Come on, we've got to make a fire," he said. "The others'll be here soon."

They stacked the wood into a pyramid in front of the barn, stuffed hay under it, and lit it. They needed only one match to light it. Adolf dragged a hayprop out, placed it over the fire like a tripod, took their mess tins from under the hay, and hung them on it.

By the time the others arrived the water was boiling. Peter and Max came back first. Peter emptied a knapsack of potatoes onto the ground and started to jabber: what terrific guys the two privates were; they were really with it; they knew their stuff. Tilli and Adolf should have seen the Berliner crawling on his stomach to a potato pit and taking the potatoes as quick as a flash, even though the farmer was only fifty yards away in the field. They were in the village now trying to swipe a chicken.

The two privates did not bring a chicken. But they did

procure five eggs. Max cut up the rest of the bacon that the Czech farmer's wife had sold him into the eggs; the privates contributed a can of sausage; and they ate scrambled eggs, bacon, potatoes and sausage. They ate till they were full.

"Guess it's time to pack up," said the Berliner.

Max watched him from the corner of his eye.

He knew the two privates wanted to go home: the Saxon to a place near Wittenberg where he had a farm, the Berliner to Spandau. They had talked about it the evening before, and had planned out the route they wanted to take, using Peter's map. But they had not said anything about taking them along. Not yesterday evening, and not this morning. And Max had not dared ask them because he was afraid they would say no.

They stood in front of the barn, ready to go. The Berliner was the last to come out. He looked up at the sun and said casually, "What's the name of the next hole? Cham or what? That's what the map said, wasn't it?" Turning to Max he went on: "That's fifteen miles. D'you think we can make it by evening?"

Max thought about it for a second. "Of course," he said. He said it as casually as he could. "Of course we can make it."

They set off toward the north, walking through the woods on small paths off the road and taking their bearings by the sun.

The Saxon carved a little whistle from a hazel twig for Tilli and she played it in time with their steps. Then the Berliner lifted her onto his shoulders and they played the game "I spy with my little eyes," and once Tilli saw something blue in the middle of the forest. It was not the sky, not a flower, but an air force uniform, including pilot's cap, hanging neatly folded over a feedbox for the deer. Some men who looked like local farmers came toward them. But when they asked them the way, they did not know.

"It looks as if we're not the only ones on the road," said the Berliner. "That worries me a bit."

From the next hazel bush he cut himself a long, supple stick, carved a groove in the thin end, then pulled his belt from his trousers. It was not a regular belt, but a sturdy, double-thick, leather strap. He tied it tightly to the stick and snapped it in the air a couple of times.

The Saxon watched him uneasily. He looked worried and said, "Don't do anything stupid!" But the Berliner just laughed and said, "Nothing's happened yet! It's just for safety's sake!" He carefully gathered the strap into loops and used the stick as a walking stick.

The village consisted of just a few farmhouses on the right and left of the street. After they had passed the first house the Berliner suddenly said to Tilli: "I hear with my little ear something that smells good!" He looked mysterious and when she opened her mouth to ask, he laid a finger on his lips and whispered, "Wait and see!"

The gate to the second farmhouse was locked. They knocked and a young woman looked out of the window and called down that she had nothing to sell, and certainly had nothing to give away.

A gaggle of geese ran past them cackling, and the gander charged at them, hissing. Tilli hid behind the Berliner and suddenly saw him take two swift steps toward the gander and swing the whip he had made. She saw how the tip of it curled around the gander's neck as quick as a flash; how the strap pulled tight with one tug so that the neck snapped; how the animal was lifted off the ground with a second tug and made to disappear into the Berliner's open jacket; how he turned and at the same time slipped off his knapsack and stuffed the goose inside, and threw it over his shoulder again.

It all happened so fast that Tilli thought she must have been dreaming. But when the Berliner winked at her and showed her the bulging rucksack with a slight turn of his shoulder, she believed it. She began to grin.

When the gate closed behind them, she burst out laughing. She could not hold back anymore. She bent double with laughter. Then she caught the Berliner's hand and kept in step with him and sang: "I spy with my little eye, something that's white!"

About midday they took a rest. The Berliner suddenly became very serious and said: "Okay, listen kids. The thing is that we don't have any discharge papers from the army. That means that if we fall into the hands of the Americans they will probably nab us despite our beautiful disguises." He looked at them one by one, grinned at them, and then went on. "But if we travel together, we might be able to get through. Because a guy with kids doesn't look like a soldier."

"We'll pretend that we belong together, that we're a family," said the Saxon, chewing. "Got it?"

They set to work making up a story. The Saxon had been
a train engineer and the Berliner had been his stoker. The
children were from Berlin, but had been evacuated to
Zwiesel in 1942. They had lived there until it had been
bombed three days ago. The house had been buried, their
mother buried, all papers destroyed. They had been able to
save only what they had been wearing.

As they marched on they elaborated on the story. The
Berliner set Adolf on his shoulders, the Saxon took the little
girl, and Max and Peter walked along next to them, and they
all practiced as in school.

"Who am I?"

"You're Uncle Egon."

"What's your father's name?"

"Alex Heinze, forty-eight years old."

"Where did we live in Zwiesel?"

"In the Bahnhofstrasse, number fifteen, first floor."

"Where is your mother?"

"She died during the air raid. We were already in the air
raid shelter at the station, she was still at home when the
planes came, and she was buried."

"When was that?"

"Three days ago at two o'clock in the afternoon."

The Saxon said doubtfully, "Don't you think they may
check? Wouldn't it be better to say two months ago?"

"What the hell!" said the Berliner. "Let's leave it at three
days ago. Then it's still quite recent, and if they can't answer
something, we can say it's the shock."

On the gravel road between two villages they came upon
a wood-fueled truck standing at the side of the road. The

driver was working on the carburetor. When the Berliner asked him whether he would take them along if he got the old crate going again, the man agreed.

Ten minutes later they were riding among milk cans in the back of the truck. It was cold and drafty and except for the downhill stretches the truck moved at a snail's pace. But at least they were not walking.

The Berliner began to pluck the goose and Tilli helped, throwing the feathers off the back so they whirled around like snowflakes.

Peter, who was standing behind the driver's cab, suddenly started to shout, and excitedly pointed ahead. There were five boys — Peter and Max recognized them immediately. A few days ago the same group had passed them, as though in a military march. They had sneered in passing — "Slow-pokes! Kids! No discipline!" — and the leader had called out: "Hamburg! Straight ahead!" Now, the group was not marching so arrogantly.

Max and Peter leaned over the side and as they passed, yelled at them: "Straight ahead! Keep walking straight ahead and you'll get there!" and jerked their thumbs in that direction and laughed.

But when the truck came to the next hill the engine began to stutter and even though they jumped off and pushed, it was no use. They could not get the truck up the hill. The Berliner set to work again. After he had checked the carburetor he said that it was a bigger job this time, and they might as well make themselves comfortable in the ditch.

They all sat down farther up the hill by the edge of the forest, except for Peter who walked all the way to the crest.

From there he had a wide view of the countryside, but there was not a town in sight. He pulled out the map, spread it on the ground, and aligned it to the north. He hoped he could work out how far they were from Cham by using the mountains drawn on the map as a guide. He was so engrossed that he did not notice the five boys they passed earlier coming up the hill.

Suddenly they were standing next to him. He felt uneasy. He had laughed at them, and now it was one against five. But the one in front, who seemed to be their ringleader, merely asked whether he could look at the map to see what route they should take. His upper lip curled back when he spoke and exposed long, protruding teeth.

Four of them bent over the map, but one who held a long stick seemed uninterested. He sat down next to Peter at the side of the road.

"You're heading for Berlin?" he asked.

Peter shrugged his shoulders. "So what?" he asked casually.

The boy with teeth like a horse briefly raised his head. "Don't be such a smartmouth," he said. "We know you're a little baby going home with your daddy!" And he motioned down the hill to where the soldiers tinkered with the truck.

"What d'you know?" Peter snapped back. "That's just an arrangement we made, you idiot!" If they had not outnumbered him, he would have taken the map away.

"What d'you mean — arrangement?" the boy with the stick asked.

"So they won't be nabbed," said Peter. "They're privates, we only met them last night."

The four boys bending over the map apparently ignored him and discussed the route they would take, and one of them wrote down the names of the towns and villages along the way on a slip of paper.

"Where've you come from?" Peter asked.

The boys were heading to Hamburg from their CEC. They had been on the road for five days. "You kids have had it easy," said the leader. "We've been in the thick of it."

"We've been through some hard times too," said Peter loudly. "There was a man standing next to us and a piece of shrapnel tore his head off. You should've seen it. Sliced clean away. He was standing barely a yard away from us!"

The boy with the horse's teeth stood up and threw Peter a scornful glance. "Show off!" he said. And to the others: "C'mon, let's go!"

They walked off without saying goodbye. Only the one with the stick turned and briefly nodded to Peter before he started to amble on.

It took the Berliner a good hour before he had the wood-fueled truck running again. Afterward he swore like a mule-skinner when he found out that he would have been spared the trouble if the truck had made the last fifty yards up the hill. Because from that point on, it was downhill all the way. When they arrived in the valley, a town lay before them. The driver stopped and asked whether they wanted to go on with him, because a Yank guard would be at the entrance to the town, inspecting everything and everyone entering it.

The Berliner said, "We'll risk it," but the Saxon disagreed. He did not want to end up behind barbed wire when they

were so close, after having come so far. He would take no
more risks. Certainly not now that the work in the fields was
beginning and his wife was home alone on the farm and
urgently needed him.

The truck drove on without them.

They walked halfway around the town, keeping close to
the edge of the woods. The Saxon went ahead, the Berliner
following some distance behind. He was furious and swore
under his breath.

"Why don't we just keep away from the town altogether?"
Adolf asked after a while. "Why do we have to go in?"

The Berliner patted his shoulder. "We need papers, lad,"
he said affably. "We can't struggle through the bushes for
three hundred odd miles." He smiled at Adolf encourag-
ingly. "And apart from that, we have to find some place for
the little girl somewhere."

Adolf wished he had not asked.

They found a dirt road that offered them enough cover to
reach the outskirts of town unseen. They came to a soccer
field and then a housing development and a paved road leading into the town.

There was no one in sight. All was dead silence, as if they
were in a ghost town. Their heels clicked loudly on the paving stones, and the Berliner stopped and said, "Damn it!
There's something wrong here, I can feel it in my guts!"

At that moment a man shouted from a window: "Curfew,
you idiots! They're in the jeep up ahead! Can't you see
them?"

Just then an engine roared to life and not fifty paces in
front of them one of those squat, agile cars shot out from

behind a house, turned into the street on squealing tires, and came straight at them.

It was too late to run. "Just keep your mouths shut, let me handle it!" the Berliner hissed at them.

A fat black man was sitting behind the wheel of the car, and next to him sat a baby-faced white man. They were wearing fabric-covered helmets and thick, puffed-up jackets. The white man was holding a huge revolver loosely in his hand when he got out.

"I.D., — *Ausweis* — please," he said, grinning amicably.

The Berliner began to wave his arms about, tore the hat from his head, tapped his breast, showed his empty hands, and said, *"Nicht Ausweis,* all destroyed! Bombs! You understand? Bombs!" He made a movement with his hands meant to convey the idea of bombs falling. *"Ausweis kaputt. Mutter kaputt!"* He pointed to Tilli. "All is gone, destroyed!"

The American did not seem to be particularly impressed. *"Nicht Ausweis?"* he said, still grinning. He came closer and asked: "What's the time — *wieviel Uhr* — please?" It sounded as though he were particularly proud of his knowledge of German.

The Saxon hastily looked at his watch. "Quarter past seven," he said, and to make sure the American understood, he held the watch under his nose. The latter grinned at him and undid the watch strap, as quick as a magician, and put the watch in his breast pocket. *"Danke,"* he said. Then he appraised the others from head to foot, one after another. Still grinning, he stopped in front of Peter, opened the camera case on Peter's belt with nimble fingers, and reached inside. Suddenly his grin froze as he saw the brown-stained underpants in his hand. He swore, spat a few words of English in their faces, and waved the revolver.

They moved off, staying close together, and walked down the road. The jeep with the two Americans drove along behind them.

"It's all your fault, you asshole!" the Berliner hissed at the Saxon. "Curfew! If we'd gone in the truck we would have made it easily. But you and your goddamn caution! You hang your ass out of the window, and still shit into the room. And I have to clean up the mess!" The Saxon did not say a word.

They came to a small square with a slender tree in the middle. There were cars everywhere, American ones and German ones, all with an American star painted on them. An American flag was hanging from one of the houses. Two sentries stood in front of the entrance below it. The man with the revolver herded them over there.

Inside it was stiflingly hot. A large iron stove stood glowing behind the door.

There were three doors on the left and right, with benches standing between them, and at the back was a double staircase. Music floated down the stairs. The same lively, joyful music they had heard before, and which somehow seemed to be a part of the Americans.

The man with the revolver motioned to a bench and they sat down close to each other.

"We'll stick to our story," said the Berliner. "We haven't lost yet. Just don't hang your heads."

They looked up at him hopefully. You could trust the Berliner, he was certainly not saying that just to cheer them up. He was a crafty, old Front line soldier, who would get them out of this.

Half an hour later one of the young, neatly pressed American soldiers came and stood at attention in front of them. He stared at the two adults and asked in fluent German: "Are you members of the army, the SS service, or the police?"

Both indignantly shook their heads, as though he had accused them of something indecent, and the Berliner immediately began to tell the story of the air raid. But the American merely moved his hand to silence him, and ordered them to go with him.

They disappeared into one of the rooms opposite. Five minutes later they came out and the Berliner winked his eye at them from the doorway. When he sat down he said softly, "Just fine!"

They went on waiting. Darkness fell outside and from time to time American soldiers came in, lighthearted, loud, and noisy, and warmed themselves at the stove. They laughed till it echoed from the walls, smoked and chewed and talked to each other, still chewing. It appeared as though they had to chew every word before they could say it.

Then a sentry came from outside and led in the five boys from Hamburg. The boys seemed to have lost all their self-assurance, glanced around timidly, and sat down on the bench next to the stove. The boy with the stick nodded to Peter and began to poke around under the stove, as though he were looking for something. He seemed to be obsessed with poking around with his stick.

Half an hour later another man with sharply creased trousers came, motioned the boys from Hamburg into his room, and closed the door behind them.

"It could still take some time," whispered the Berliner. The heat was beginning to make them drowsy. Tilli slumped over to one side and fell asleep against Adolf's shoulder. The clatter of a typewriter came through the door, and music droned incessantly from above.

Then the American appeared again in the doorway. The boy with the horse's teeth was with him. He pointed to the two privates, and they heard the American ask, "These two?" They saw the boy nod without looking up, and the American pull him back into the room again and close the door behind him.

The Berliner stiffened, stared at the door, and said through his teeth: "That little swine! What does he know?" Turning to Max he asked with a dangerous undertone in his voice, "Did one of you open his trap, godamnit?!"

Peter had held his breath. Now he let it out slowly. He was trembling.

The man in the sharply creased uniform stepped out of the room. "Come here!" he snarled at the two men. His voice was sharp and cutting now. "Bring your luggage with you!"

The Berliner pulled his knapsack from under the bench and while he was bending down he whispered, "It's not going to work, boys, I'm sorry!" They watched him until the door closed behind him.

The boys from the road were led out of the room, showed

the sentry at the door a note, and walked out in single file. Not even the one with the stick turned around.

Max's group waited in silence until the American poked his head round the door once more and called something to the sentry. They could see the Berliner through the crack in the door. He was stripped to the waist and he was holding his left arm. It was the last they saw of him.

The sentry beckoned them to him, and when he noticed that Tilli was asleep he picked her up and they quietly followed him out of the building and across the square to an inn. They heard him talking to another sentry and waited until a huge black man came who took Tilli from the first sentry. Then, moving as though sleepwalking, they followed the black man to a car with its top up and crawled into the back seat as the black man told them to.

The engine roared, the headlights flashed on, and suddenly the whole square was flooded with dazzling white light. They were startled, and Peter almost yelled, "Lights out!" He had been trained to fear any light at night which could attract bombers. They all still had to get used to the idea that there was no need to be afraid of the bombers anymore. There were lights in the windows of all the houses they passed as they were driving down the street.

6

Boxing for Candy

They drove out of town and through the countryside. The trees along the road whooshed by, and then they drove through a forest and up a long hill. When they were over the top, the car turned into a side road which went uphill in two steep curves and ended in front of a large, yellow house.

The black got out and walked to the door framed by the headlights. An old woman opened it. She seemed to know him and let him in.

Above them a bell rang out, deep and droning, and echoing for a long time. Just one single stroke. The black and the woman came out again. The woman was carrying a lantern and had put a coat around her shoulders. She was small and walked quickly, and from the waist up she swayed sharply to and fro. Her right leg was stiff.

The black lifted Tilli out of the car. The woman stood next to him, craning her neck, and when she saw them get out of the car, one after another, she said "Ecch, how many are there?" and she held the lantern so that it shone into the car.

She went ahead with the light along a gravel path and up a long row of wide, worn stone steps, then along another gravel path with tombstones and crosses on both sides to a tall church door. She unlocked it and waited till they had all gone past her. Then she pulled it closed again.

In the pale glow from her lamp they could make out the high, wide church aisle. There were rows of pews to the right and left, and ahead, at the front end, a large candle was burning. It shed a golden glimmer behind it. The limping steps of the woman echoed as she walked forward between the rows of pews. She put down the lantern, stretched her stiff leg to one side, and made a crooked genuflection. The black who was carrying Tilli also touched his knee to the ground and crossed himself with his free hand. Then he wrapped Tilli in a blanket and as though she were breakable, carefully laid her on the first row of pews.

"D'you have blankets?" asked the woman in Bavarian dialect, and when they nodded she said, "Then lie down in there for now," and pointed to the pew behind Tilli. "Tomorrow mornin' we'll see what to do next." They obeyed in silence.

The woman waited until they had spread out their blankets and had lain down in the narrow pew. "Wrap yourselves up well; it gets real cold," she said before she left.

The flickering light withdrew, and they heard the door slam shut and the key turn. Then there was silence. They lay on their backs, their arms by their sides, as if in coffins.

Above, they could make out the dome of the church ceiling, indistinct and blurred.

Max suddenly sat up, listened, his head on one side. Something was moving. Wood creaked. Peter and Adolf sat up, too. They heard whispering, someone was there.

Then, quite clearly, they heard a voice talking in a loud whisper, "Hey, you up there! Who are you? Where d'you come from?"

They got up. Five rows behind them a head rose above the pews. A girl. "Where d'you come from?" she asked again.

"Are you from Berlin?" Max asked back.

She nodded. "You too?"

"CEC," said Max, "we were in Kusice."

"We were in Bad Lettin," said the girl. Another head popped up, and yet another. All over the place between the pews they popped up, all girls; the whole church seemed to be full. It looked eerie — only the heads floating above the pews, moving to and fro.

"How many of you are there?" asked Max.

"Twenty," said the girl. "Our teacher is in the hospital."

But there were others there, too. Refugee children from Silesia and Moravia and Hungary. They had lost their parents, some had been in the church for weeks. They told their stories. Then one by one they disappeared behind the pews again.

Adolf awoke. He was freezing. His legs were like icicles and he had the feeling that they would break off if he moved. He heard muffled echoing noises, a lot of confused voices. It took him some time to remember where he was. When he opened his eyes there was a face above him, the face of a small boy who was looking down at him with serious eyes. Adolf sat up. Max and Peter were gone, but their knapsacks and blankets were still lying on the pew behind him. Then he saw them come in through the church door. They were walking behind the woman with the lame leg, carrying a large, steaming pot with handles. And behind them came a girl carrying two round loaves of bread.

"Come, children, breakfast's ready," said the woman.

The smell of hot malt coffee filled the church. They sat in the front two rows of pews as though for a mass. Each of them had a slice of bread in one hand and a mess tin full of hot, milky-brown malt coffee in the other. How long had it been since they had last drunk hot coffee?

Adolf took little, careful sips and felt its warmth running down his throat and spreading through his body. His legs tingled as they thawed out. Tilli sat next to him, dunking her bread in the coffee, munching away, both cheeks full. Adolf watched her as she dunked and munched. He suddenly felt they had known each other for ages. He was happy that she was sitting next to him.

They were still eating breakfast when the door opened and a man wearing a long black coat entered. He was short and stocky and so wide that he could only get through the door sideways. A square head with bristly red-brown hair sat on his shoulders. At first he seemed to be fat, but he was not; he was just wide, heavy and stocky. He was pushing one boy ahead of him and carrying a second in his arms who was clinging tightly to his coat front. They were followed by a stooped, old man carrying a third boy.

The woman with the lame leg dropped the ladle into the coffeepot and fluttered toward them like a lame bird, calling in her shrill voice: "Oh Lord, Father, how many more're you gonna bring me!"

"Bring some blankets!" said the priest in a deep voice that filled the whole church. Turning to the woman he said in broad Bavarian: "They need something to eat, but something light!" When she did not move he added gruffly, "Quick!"

The girls in the front pew stood up and made some room.

Something terrible had happened to those boys. They resembled figures from a gruesome puppet show with their large, wobbling shaved heads, and the limp, grey overalls in which there seemed to be no body; with their matchstick-thin arms and legs, and the unnaturally plump, swollen hands and feet at the ends. Frightened animals, dragged from their cave into broad daylight.

"I wouldna've found 'em," said the old man while he bedded down the smallest of the three on a pew. "The dawg sniffed 'em out in the hayloft."

"Where're they from?" asked the priest. "Didn't they say where they're from?"

"Na, they don' talk," said the old man.

The priest wrapped the three in blankets and talked to them reassuringly.

"They'll probably turn out to be Jews," said the old man. "Or Poles. They drove masses of 'em past durin' the last days!"

The priest stood with his arms crossed in front of the pew,

murmured something to himself, then turned to the girls standing shyly around him.

"Any of you speak Polish?" he asked. When one of the girls came forward he said, "Ask 'em in Polish!"

The girl asked a question, and the oldest of the three answered. But even though it sounded as if they ought to understand each other, the girl shook her head.

"At any rate, they're foreigners," said the priest.

"They're Czech," said a girl in the second pew. She pushed her way forward.

"They're Czech," she said again. Then, in a quiet voice she talked to the eldest of the three, and when he answered, she listened attentively.

"He says they're from a camp somewhere near here," she translated. "He says that they'd been walking for five days — just women and children." She listened again to what the boy was saying and bent down closer to him. He spoke so softly that his words were almost inaudible.

"They had been afraid that the SS would shoot everyone. Many were shot because they could not walk anymore. The women hid him and the two others. At night. Under some grass." She asked the boy something again. It sounded as though she wanted to be sure she was translating it right. "Hidden under bits of grass in a field."

"So they're Czechs," said the priest and loudly cleared his throat. "If they're Czechs, the Americans are responsible for 'em. I'll have to report it to the Americans." He looked at the old man as though he expected an answer.

The old man grabbed his hat and hastily pulled it off.

"Well, then . . . ," he began, embarrassed, "then I'll be off." The priest did not seem to hear him.

The old man slowly withdrew and walked down the middle aisle to the door. His hand was already on the door handle when the priest's voice stopped him in his tracks.

"Lederer!" called the priest so that the whole church echoed. "Lederer, listen, you've got room to take two or three of 'em, haven't you?" The old man raised both arms in a defensive gesture, but the priest did not give him a chance to say anything. "So I'll be around in a couple of days; you be prepared now!"

The old man took two steps back into the church, then he let his arms drop, turned, and went out, shutting the door with a bang.

Above them the church bell began to ring. Ten droning booms. The priest waited until the echo of the bell had died away. Then he straightened up, laid a hand on Max's shoulder since he was standing next to him, and said, "There's a bicycle behind the altar, bring it here!" He bent down to the girl from Iglau and said, "You look after those three till the lady gets back. And make sure no one slips 'em somethin' extra to eat. They're so starved, they'll die if they get too much at once."

Straightening up again, he called, "Well, where's the boy with the bike gone to?" He caught sight of Peter and said to him, "You come along, too!" And when he saw Max pushing the bicycle across the altar carpet he shouted, "Hey! Can't you carry it? You don't ride a bicycle in front of the altar!" and walked off with short, quick steps, pushing Peter along in front of him.

Max followed him. He had got such a fright that he carried the bicycle all the way to the church door and did not dare put it down until he was outside.

The priest took it from him, pushed it to the steps, then carried it down in outstretched arms. He seemed to have the strength of a crane.

He vigorously pumped up the tires and clipped clothes pegs on his trouser legs. He let Peter sit on the crossbar, and Max on the luggage rack behind, and peddled off. They raced around the sharp curves down the hill from the church. The tails of the priest's black coat flapped in Max's face as he desperately clung to the saddle support and drew up his legs. At each curve he was afraid the brakes would give out.

They turned onto the highway and rode down the hill. It stretched on endlessly. At night, in the car, the distance had seemed much shorter.

At last they reached the town. Max tried to keep his hands under his backside as they rattled over the cobblestones, but he still felt every single bump.

They did not go to the square they had been to before, but turned off sooner and stopped in front of a bakery. In front of it was a line two houses long with at least sixty people waiting there.

The priest handed them four bread ration cards and a slip of paper on which he scribbled a few words. They were to give it to the baker he said. Afterward they were to be sure to wait for him. He might be late returning, he warned them, but they had better be there when he came back.

Max and Peter took their place at the end of the line.

Peter tried to push past a lady but gave up when she snapped at him nastily and threatened to box his ears.

Max and Peter decided that they did not both have to stand in line. Max picked up a pebble and put his hands behind his back, holding the stone in his right hand. Peter picked the left, so Max said he'd be right back. He'd just go and see what was going on.

Peter could see the church clock from where he was standing. He waited five minutes, and then another five minutes. When Max still had not reappeared, he asked a boy standing behind him to keep his place, and ran off.

American trucks were standing bumper to bumper in the entrance to the courtyard next to the inn. Peter ran between the house wall and the trucks to the back. He stopped at the corner of the building. A large, paved yard lay before him, surrounded by dark brown wooden sheds and stone garages with their doors wide open. Jeeps were parked in all the garages and in front of them were trucks and scout cars. Only the back wall of the inn was kept clear. A crowd of children were standing there, at least thirty of them, from very small ones to fourteen-year-olds. They were standing with their backs to him, blocking his view.

He walked along the building. American soldiers were sitting opposite — on the truckbeds, in the jeeps, on mattresses on the ground, and on chairs and armchairs that had been brought out. The soldiers had stretched out their legs and were drinking coffee out of large mugs and eating white bread. Each one had a pile of small cans in front of him and little packets in silver foil and cellophane. They kept opening cans and when they were empty, they threw them aside, so they fell clattering to the ground. They threw them down from above, too; some men were standing on a balcony over the main door, and others were hanging out of the windows next to it.

The children were continually on the move. Each time a can clattered to the ground, they ran to it, scuffled for it, licked it clean using their fingers, and waited greedily for the next can. They were always on their toes.

Max was standing against the house wall, his hands in his pockets, shoulders hunched, bent slightly forward. He did not take part in the pursuit of the cans. He stood there quietly, as if he were watching something that needed his total attention. Now Peter, too, saw what had caught his eye.

Directly opposite on the other side of the yard, in front of a truck, in the middle of the crowd of Americans, stood the boy from Hamburg with the horse's teeth. He was wearing black gym shorts and a white T-shirt, with a blanket around his shoulders. On his hands were large, heavy sparring gloves that an American soldier was tying for him. The four other boys were sitting behind him, including the one with the stick. They did not seem to have noticed Max yet.

The boy with the horse's teeth hit the gloves together, making a slapping sound, and bounced around and threw a few jabs in the air.

"What's he doing here?" Peter whispered.

"Boxing," said Max without turning. He did not seem surprised that Peter had suddenly appeared behind him.

"Where'd he get the gloves?" asked Peter.

Max motioned toward the Americans with his head. "It's all from them," he said, "gloves and all." He took a hand out of his pocket and pointed to a jeep opposite. A lanky black man was sitting on the backrest of the driver's seat; he had a gleaming, black top hat on his head and was clapping in time to the music coming from the windows of the inn. Next to him sat a red-faced white, chewing with his mouth open, calling loudly to another soldier on the balcony. Then he showed him a bill and folded it lengthwise and pushed it in the peak of his cap, so it stuck up like a feather. In front of the two, on the hood of the jeep, lay a pile of cans and packages, all of them the same olive drab color. And on top lay a pack of cigarettes. "Whoever wins, gets that," said Max.

Peter had not taken his eyes off the boy with the gloves on. He stared steadily at him over Max's shoulder as though he wanted to hypnotize him. Until now, he had not noticed that a second boy was standing just a few steps from the first, also wearing sparring gloves. An American was with him, too. He helped him put on the gloves and then put a blanket around his shoulders.

"He hasn't got a chance," said Peter.

"No, he hasn't," Max agreed. The boy was almost as big as the one with the horse's teeth, but he was much more lightly built. It looked as though he were having trouble just holding up the heavy gloves.

An American who was sitting in an armchair near the main door suddenly stood up and looked at his watch, and the others started to whoop as though on command. They laughed and whistled, and threw their caps in the air. The black man with the top hat danced on the driver's seat of the jeep and the red-faced man waved his cap and bellowed like an ox.

The man with the watch seemed to be acting as referee. He inspected the gloves and brought the two boys together in the middle of the yard.

"He's already knocked down one weakling like that," said Max. "They don't care about losing. All they want is the consolation prize."

The referee looked at his watch again, raised his hand and waited until one of the soldiers pounded on the hood of a truck with his fist. Then he let the boys go at each other.

It was an unequal fight. The boy with the horse's teeth went at his opponent like a steam-hammer, hitting at him wildly with both fists, pushing him along in front of him, landing mighty blows and swinging punches that hit from below. The other boy tried to hide behind the huge gloves as much as possible, but it did not help. His opponent could take as wide a swing as he wanted without fear of being hit back. As a result his blows had so much force that he once landed a punch just by hitting the other boy's glove — he simply hit the glove into his face.

After a while the Americans fell silent. The fight was too one-sided. Only the red-faced man in the jeep was still having fun. He had jumped up and was leaning far across the windshield and was boxing along with them. He was on the winner's side, and the more he hit the other boy, the louder the soldier shouted. He pulled the cash from his cap and waved it toward the balcony and shouted so much that his face got even redder.

"You can't win against him, he's much too strong," said Peter quietly. "He'd just knock you over. How can you defend yourself when he pounds away like a crazy man?!"

"So what?" said Max. He did not take his eyes off the boy from Hamburg. "He's just flailing his arms like a windmill."

Peter caught his breath. "You want to fight him?" he asked incredulously.

"Why not?" said Max.

"You're crazy, you'll never win," said Peter. He felt a pang of fear. "What d'you think you can do, man? You can't do anything technical. You can't get through with those gigantic gloves, man!"

"If he goes on waving his arms around like that, he won't be able to hold them up much longer," said Max calmly. For the first time he turned and looked Peter in the face. "Not him," he said. "After two rounds he'll tire. He won't be able to raise his arms after two rounds. You can be sure of that."

"And how are you going to last two rounds?" asked Peter. Max shrugged his shoulders and turned back again.

The loser was now so weak that he was just staggering around, and his knees sagged after every blow.

The referee raised his arm to stop the fight but he was a second too late. The boy fell before he could get his hand up. The winner had not even landed a good punch. He did not seem satisfied with his easy win.

"He won't get away from me, the skunk!" said Max. It sounded as if he were trying to screw up his courage.

The winner basked in the applause. His four friends

danced for joy and tossed the cans he had won into the air. One of them instantly brought him the blanket and put it over his shoulders. The red-faced American ran over to him, slapped him on the back, lifted him high above his head and carried him on his shoulders to the balcony, and did not put him down until he had made a victory round with him.

Max stared across at him. Finally the boy recognized him. He took two steps toward him.

"He-e-ey!" he called derisively and showed his teeth. "D'you want somethin', kid?"

"Bastard!" said Max just loud enough for him to hear.

The other boy turned to his pals. "He's tryin' to be smart, the jerk!" he said and took another step toward Max. "You tryin' to be smart, you chicken?"

Max did not answer but calmly took off his jacket, threw it to Peter, and slowly walked toward the boy from Hamburg, rolling up his sleeves as he walked along.

The black man in the top hat jumped from the jeep and came closer with mincing steps. With every step he bobbed up and down, swaying his hips and pulling faces. He waved up to the balcony with his long arms. Max hesitated when he saw him, and stopped dead in the middle of the yard. He became even more uncertain when the whooping and whistling started up around him. He stuck his hands in his pockets and looked around, his shoulders hunched.

"You've got cold feet, haven't ya?" shouted the boy with the horse teeth. "You're scared shitless! Just shove off!"

Max heard the Americans shouting and laughing. For a second he thought they were laughing at him, and he was seized with such fury that he would have flung himself at the other boy if the black man in the top hat had not blocked his way. The black man grinned at him and said something that Max did not understand. But it sounded friendly, and the black man looked friendly, too.

"Can I have proper gloves?" asked Max and tried to explain what he meant with gestures. "Proper gloves with bandages, not sparring gloves!" The black man at first did not understand him, but when he saw Max's wrapping gesture, an enormous smile suddenly spread over his face. He turned and called something up to the balcony, waved his arms, and threw the large sparring gloves across the square onto the bed of a truck. Suddenly they were surrounded by soldiers who brought boxing gloves of all sizes, and bandages, too. They wound the bandages around both of Max's hands at the same time, and pulled the gloves over the fists. They talked at him, slapping his shoulder and jabbing him in the side in a friendly way, and pushed him forward until he was standing next to the winner of the last match.

The latter looked at him with open hatred. "Hope you've put numbers on your bones!" he hissed at him. "I'll knock you around till you think you can hear the air raid siren!"

"Bastard!" said Max calmly.

"I'll push your teeth down your throat so far that you'll be able to play piano on them in your ass!" said the boy from Hamburg.

"Bastard!" said Max again.

Suddenly they were standing alone in the yard; the only person with them was the referee. He looked at his watch. Why doesn't he start? thought Max. Why the whole ceremony of inspecting the gloves and shaking fists and the gong? What they had in mind was not a boxing match, it was going to be a free-for-all, and free-for-alls did not have any rules.

The referee caught hold of Max's glove and pulled him closer until his glove touched the Hamburg boy's glove.

"Prick! Asshole!" said the boy from Hamburg.

"Bastard!" repeated Max.

Then the boom from the hood of the jeep rang out amid the whoops of the soldiers, and the boy with the horse teeth attacked. He set to like a bull on the rampage, his head thrust forward and both arms whirling.

Max was prepared for the assault. He had fought opponents like this one before. He knew there was no point in playing the hero now. To begin with he would have to pretend to be a mouse, to duck away, evade the punches, dart aside, until the other was out of breath. And then, just as the other was wondering why his attack had failed, he would give two sharp punches in order to get him mad again, to tempt him into another windmill attack which would sap his strength. Max knew precisely what he would have to do. But now the other boy was hitting damned hard. And despite the gloves the Americans had given them, Max felt the blows even when only his guard was hit. He also felt the effects of not having trained during the last few weeks in camp. A wild concert of boos and whistles broke out. The Americans were booing him.

Then he attacked, hitting out without thinking, thrashing at the other boy, not getting through. The other had longer arms and pushed him away again and again. Max paused.

He could not risk such an outburst again; it cost too much strength. He had to stick to his plan, had to wait until the other had exhausted himself.

He thought of Bernd, the first camp team leader he had had in the CEC. Bernd Koniger, who had got him interested in boxing. Everything he knew, he had learned from him. Train your left jab, Bernd had said, it is the wasp, the poisonous wasp, which stings again and again. One sting is not particularly painful, but repeated stings, five stings, ten stings, twenty — then the opponent's face will swell up, he'll crack. That's when you start punching, that's when you use the right. He had to stick to that. His opponent was half a head taller than him, and quite a bit stronger. He could only win against him by using strategy.

He stepped back, blocked, weaved to and fro, ducked away from the hammerblows that were showering on him. Those wide swings were easy to calculate and dangerous only if he let the boy come too close. He had to stay out of range, always keep his distance. Let the Americans whistle and boo.

A few times though he brought his left through and connected. But the gong came much too quickly — just as the bigger boy was beginning to weaken.

The black man came up with a blanket and put it around Max's shoulders. He fanned his face with his top hat, and gave him something to drink from a can, some sweet, sticky juice. Max spat it out again.

He watched the boy from Hamburg, who was sitting opposite. Max knew he had to hit him in the body. He was so tall that it was difficult to get at his head. But he could wear him down with body blows. He felt in top form when the second round began.

"Now I'm really gonna give it to ya!" said the bigger boy. "I'll smash your nose to a pulp!"

Again he let fly, howling with sheer fury because Max would not stand up to him, kept backing away from him, covering his head with both fists. Suddenly Max was in a corner. His opponent hit at him with both fists, right-left, right-left, so hard that Max fell where he was standing. The big boy wanted to throw himself upon Max, to finish him off. The referee had to hold him back by force.

Max got up dazed; he heard the referee counting. Was this it? Was he finished? Were they counting him out? Good Lord, the boy had not even hit him properly, he had only pushed him over. He shook his head, and put up his fists. On no account could he let this bastard win.

He faced him. He must not let himself be forced into a corner again. He shot out a left jab and then another two, one after the other, right between the other boy's fists. A hellish noise suddenly broke out, shouts and cheers of encouragement from all sides. Again he came through with his left and then for the first time he hit with his right. Hit just above the belt. It was not a hard blow, but the other boy was not expecting it. He gaped like a frog and doubled up, and before he had his fists up again, Max landed two blows to the head. Now Max had the advantage; now he had him in his power; now it was a textbook case. Left jab to the head, feint, and then the right with a hook to the liver.

The bigger boy defended himself desperately, but his punches just whistled through the air. Max no longer needed to fear them, there was no force behind them anymore. Max was quite calm now, boxing with a cold fury. He wanted to hurt the other boy, to give him a good beating. The swine, he was going to be flat on the ground. Left jab and right hook, and two more jabs to the head. The blood was pouring from the boy's nose.

And then he brought through a hook that almost lifted the Hamburg boy off his feet. He had almost made it. Max did not let up for a second, he wanted to lay him on the ground in this round.

Then something hit Max on the ear. A terrible blow, like a sledgehammer. A harsh light zigzagged before his eyes, and there was a terribly high-pitched sound in his ears which almost split his head. He desperately tried to straighten his knees, held his fists in front of his face. Where had the blow come from? He had not seen it coming. Where had the guy got the strength to land such a punch? He had not even seen him start to swing. He staggered and stumbled sideways toward the house wall, his knees buckling. He must not fall, he must not fall down now. The gong would sound at any moment.

Someone was pulling at his gloves, trying to tear them off. Was that the referee? Had he been counted out? He tried to twist his hand out of the grasp, but could not get free. His hand was stuck as in a vise. Then, suddenly, a thunderous voice drowned out the strident buzzing in his ears. "Hold still! You miserable wretch!"

The priest! Where had the priest come from? The shock cleared his head.

There he was, in his black coat, his face bright red. He

threw the gloves at the feet of the Americans who were standing around him laughing and shouting. He was so furious that Max was scared, but the priest took no notice of his reaction. He rushed from the yard, his coat flapping, pulling Max along behind him like an unmanageable puppy.

Peter was waiting on the street outside. He kept out of reach and flinched at every movement the priest made. His cheek was glowing red. He had gotten it, too.

The priest stopped in front of the bakery, took his bicycle which was leaning there, and while he was clipping the clothes pegs onto his trouser legs he growled furiously: "You'll come back on foot. And if you aren't back by one, I'll give you such a beating you won't forget it!"

They nodded in silence, took their place at the end of the line again, and watched as he rode away.

Tilli was in the garden behind the rectory when the bell rang twelve. She was raking one of the neatly heaped up beds, silently moving her lips as she wielded the rake. Adolf was watching her.

He was sitting on a wooden bench along the wall of the rectory, and had put up his feet. The girls from Berlin had given him new bandages, and he had changed the dressing and taken off Max's shoes. The swelling in his feet had gone down and he could put on his own boots again.

A rooster began to crow, loudly and persistently, as though it were trying to drown out the midday bell. Adolf could see it in the back part of the garden behind a chicken-wire fence. It was a small rust-brown rooster.

"That's Joseph," said Tilli. "The priest's wife told me he crows loudest."

"That's not the priest's wife," said Adolf. He had already told her that several times.

"D'you see the fat white one?" called Tilli. "He's called Hermann. He's going to be killed tomorrow because he's so fat, she said."

Adolf looked at Hermann so as not to disappoint her, but he took no notice of the rooster. His thoughts were elsewhere.

The girls from Berlin had told him that they would all be put up at various places in the neighboring villages until the trains to Berlin were running again. Adolf had had to enter their names on a list in the rectory. "Max Milk, Berlin," he had written, "Peter Reuther, Berlin," and "Adolf Zeesen, Berlin." And on the line below, just the first name "Tilli" followed by two dots as if he had not known her surname. But he had put the two dots directly under the name "Zeesen" so they looked like ditto marks: "Tilli Zeesen."

Now he had to explain to Tilli what he had done to keep them together, so she would not give him away. But he did not know how to tell her.

A rooster crowed again. This time it was a black one sitting on the roof of the hen coop.

"D'you see him?" called Tilli. "Y'know his name? It's the same as yours. The lady said she can't kill that one. The hens like him best."

Suddenly they heard the hum of an engine coming up the hill to the church. They ran around the rectory and just as they came to the corner the priest pedaled out of the street and across the courtyard on his bicycle. He was snorting like an old carthorse, and sweat was running down his forehead despite the cold. Each time he breathed out his head disappeared behind a cloud of steam. He mopped his forehead with a white handkerchief which was as large as a bedsheet, and then stuffed it back into his coat pocket again.

The car they had heard turned into the square and came to a scrunching halt on the gravel. It was a kind of delivery van with a massive nose and the rough-ribbed radiator that all American cars had. At the rear it had a box-shaped construction which displayed the Red Cross on all sides.

A pale young soldier got out and opened the back door. Max and Peter jumped out. Each of them was carrying two loaves of bread under his arms.

The priest stood as though rooted to the spot when he saw them. He sucked in his breath loudly, puffed himself up like a turkey, and got even redder in the face. Everyone saw that he was about to explode. The only person who seemed not to notice was the pale young soldier. He put his arm round Max's shoulder.

"I didn't know this was one of your children," he said guiltily. "My friends were having fun with him. I'm sorry."

Quite slowly the priest deflated again to his normal size. "Take the bread into the building!" he snapped at the two boys. They ran off, making a wide detour around him.

The young soldier took his helmet off with an awkward movement and went toward the door with the priest. He looked like an apprehensive sinner on his way to confession. He did not look at all like an American. "I'm sorry," they heard him say again, "it all happened too quickly." Even the way in which he spoke, his head nodding and his hands folded under his chin, distinguished him from all the Americans they had met so far. And he wasn't chewing. Maybe he was not an American at all; maybe he was just wearing an American uniform.

After lunch in the church the priest announced that the children would be lodged with farmers. They were to stay there until conditions improved. He would look after them, and if they had any troubles they could always come to him.

Half an hour later a truck drew up. The pale young soldier was in it, but this time he was wearing an elegant uniform and the priest addressed him as "Lieutenant" and was very friendly to him.

They all stood in line in front of the rectory and the priest took the list of names from his pocket and began to call out the names. First of all the girls from Berlin, then the refugee children. As each name was called, the child stepped forward and was lifted onto the bed of the truck.

Adolf felt his heart begin to race.

"Max Milk!" called the priest.

"Yessir!" said Max and went to the truck. "Peter Reuther!"

Adolf held his breath. He and Tilli were the only ones left. But it all turned out to be very simple. The priest glanced at his list, nodded to them, and said: "And finally we have you two little ones, that'll be all." And lifted them into the back of the truck.

The young lieutenant raised up the tailgate behind them

and closed the tarp, leaving only a narrow slit open. Then the truck moved off.

For at least a quarter of an hour they drove through forests and along roads full of potholes, and once they crossed a river over a wooden bridge that lay on huge inflatable rafts. Their first stop was in a small village by the river.

They watched as the priest went from farm to farm, came out with a farmer or farmer's wife, lifted two or three Berlin girls from the truck, and the girls disappeared into the houses.

He found accommodations for the whole Berlin class in the village. Then they drove on southward through the woods. They stopped at six farms in succession which lay secluded between the river and the forest. At the first one the truck drove into the courtyard and the girl from Iglau got out with her two sisters. They could hear the farmer's wife asking the priest whether he did not have stronger children, and pointing to Max, saying she could better use one like that. Then, at the second farm, they saw the American lieutenant take a swing at the farmer, so as to persuade him. They became quieter and quieter.

Finally just the four of them remained. The truck rumbled along a dirt road leaving deep tracks, drove through a farm gate, and stopped right behind it. They waited till the priest came around to the rear. He lifted all four of them down.

The farmyard lay before them: a two-storied building to the left, the ground floor with stone walls, the upper floor wooden; the living quarters in front, the stables behind.

Along the back was an open shed in which were cars and tools, and on the other side a barn, so that the buildings formed a horseshoe enclosing the yard.

In the middle of the horseshoe was the dung heap, over which towered a dovecote. The ground was one big mire, and the priest rolled up his trousers before he went any farther. He called "Lederer!" and when nothing happened, he called again in a loud voice "Lederer!" They stopped in the corner between the wall with the gate and the house wall, and waited.

A large, shaggy sheepdog stood barking in front of its kennel next to the stable door, its head stretched as far forward as its chain would allow, its teeth bared.

At last the stable door opened, and a tall, lean man came out, pushing a wheelbarrow toward the dungheap.

"Lederer!" called the priest and took a few steps toward him. "Lederer, I've come with the children I spoke about last Sunday."

The farmer set the wheelbarrow by the dung heap and looked in their direction. "What'm I meant t' do with 'em?" he asked after a long pause. "They'll collapse just under the weight o' a hayfork! If ya' don' have any bigger uns, then there's nothin' doin'!" He picked up the wheelbarrow again, tipped it over energetically, and cleaned it out with a pitchfork.

They could hear the priest puff himself up and hold his breath so long they thought he would suffocate.

"Good Lord, Lederer!" he finally said, and you could see that he was making a tremendous effort to stay calm. "Not everyone can choose exactly what he wants. The refugee doesn't want it, the evacuees don't want it, the children don't want it. But there's no other way! If you don't take the children, they'll lodge someone else here!"

The farmer pushed the wheelbarrow back to the stable. He did not seem to be listening. Just before he reached the stable door he stopped. "If ya have some bigger uns, I'll take 'em," he growled and disappeared into the stable.

"Then fatten 'em up!" bellowed the priest so loudly that the startled doves fluttered up from the dovecote and the dog began to bark. "Fatten 'em up, then they'll be stronger!"

The farmer came out of the stable door again and shouted at the dog. "Shut up you lousy critter!" Then he turned, took his hat off, put it back on again, and growled: "Ya can leave the boys here, but not the girl!"

The priest sighed. "Good Lord, Lederer, they're brothers and sister. You can't tear 'em apart!"

"I won't take the girl!" repeated the farmer.

The priest took two steps toward him, then gave up and turned back, shaking his head. He seemed exhausted.

Tilli looked up at him. She was clutching her little bag tightly, and her eyes were full of distrust.

"Listen, little one," said the priest. He leaned down to her and tried to stroke her hair, but she ducked away from his hand. "What would you say if I took you over to the sawmill — it's just over there, you see?" He pointed to a large property which lay a quarter of a mile away at the edge of the wood. "There're other children there. It's a nice place."

Tilli silently shook her head.

"You can visit each other every day; it's not far," the priest went on in a pleading tone. He jerked his head in

Adolf's direction. "You can visit him, and he can visit you as often as you want."

Tilli shook her head.

"But there's no other way!" the priest shouted suddenly. The dog, which had crawled into its kennel after the farmer had yelled at it, now rushed out again, its chain rattling, and started to bark twice as hard as before.

Adolf was trembling with anxiety. He looked at Tilli and saw that her eyes were filling with tears. He was next to her in three steps, put his arm round her shoulders, and whispered something into her ear.

He talked to her for a long time, and she whispered back, and Adolf nodded. Then he looked at the priest, his face pale, peaked, his eyes serious. He nodded to the priest.

The priest sighed again, took Tilli's hand, and went back to the truck with her.

"What did you tell her?" asked Peter.

Adolf watched the truck drive through the gate and jolt away over the dirt road toward the sawmill. He watched it until it disappeared behind the boards stacked in front of the mill.

Then he turned around and said softly, "I told her she can come home with me to Berlin when we get away from here."

7

Escape

Max was sitting on Ladek's laundry basket by the window. He stuck his head out of the window. It was so narrow that he could only just get his head through.

In the west, above the roof of the toolshed, the sky was still light. Narrow bands of black clouds hung over the horizon. A quarter of an hour earlier these same clouds had glowed deep red. Tomorrow it would be just as hot as today. Maybe there would even be a thunderstorm again.

The evening wind carried the soft chime of bells across from the village. Max did not need to count the chimes. He knew it was eight o'clock even without the bells. They had been living at the farm for five months and by now had acquired an accurate sense of time.

At twelve they had lunch. At seven dinner. If anyone came too late to say grace, he was lucky if the farmer's wife sneaked some leftovers to him later. In a case like that, you automatically got a good sense of time.

Directly under the window was the dog's kennel. The dog lay in front of it. The damned dog. If it had not been for the dog, they would have left long ago. That blasted animal.

The entrance to their room, the only way in, was up a kind of ladder that ran up the outside of the stable wall. The kennel was less than five yards from the foot of the ladder. And since Ladek had gone, the farmer had come out every evening after he had put out the light in the kitchen, and had unleashed the dog. So they were imprisoned more securely than behind any lock. No one could get past that dog.

The dog allowed only three people to go near it. The farmer, because he was its master, the farmer's wife, because she brought its food. And Ladek. It had been afraid of Ladek. Ladek could have strangled it with his bare hands. And the dog apparently sensed it.

Once Max and Ladek had driven to the sawmill with fir logs — fifteen-foot logs. Ladek had thrown them down from the cart like toothpicks, and then lifted them onto the scales. And the scales had shown three hundred pounds, four hundred pounds, four hundred and fifty pounds. Even the farmer had been afraid of Ladek, and — as long as Ladek had been there — things had been fine.

Ladek came from the Ukraine, from a village by Lvov. In 1941 he had been taken prisoner and since then had worked on the farm. Had it not been for him, they would not have been able to stick it out here. The farmer was quick to hit them if they did something wrong. He hit them with his hand, with the horse whip, and if they were standing too far away, he threw clods of earth at them. Ladek, however, had been patient.

He had shown them how to use the plow, how to kill chickens, how to blow up stumps using powder from the ammunition that they had found in the stream. He had taught them how to catch rabbits with a noose, and how to use a scythe. He had explained that they did not have to be afraid of the horses and oxen. When they had had diarrhea he had come with herb tea, and when they were exhausted he had done their work.

Ladek had also wanted to help them run away. But one day the Americans had arrived in a jeep with a Russian interpreter and had picked him up in order to send him home. That had been at the end of May. It seemed as though three years had gone by since then, not just three months.

The kitchen window went dark. Max withdrew his head. He heard the farmer coming, heard the dog whine and the chain rattle, and steps retreating again. Then the farmer threw a switch and light went out in the boys' room.

Max listened to Peter's and Adolf's regular breathing. That was another thing Ladek had taught them: use every break to sleep.

Gradually his eyes got used to the dark. It was a starry night. Around eleven o'clock the moon would rise. If they left around two o'clock, they would have enough light to find their way.

He stuck his head out of the window again and waited till the light in the farmer's room went out. Half past nine. At ten he would wake Peter, who would keep watch until twelve. For the last two hours it would be Adolf's turn. He was tormented by the thought that Peter would fall asleep. He would have to make sure he was wide awake. He did not have to worry about Adolf. You could rely on him.

For a while he had intended to take off with just Peter. He and Peter could cover twenty or twenty-five miles a day; they wouldn't tire. And Max would have taken off just with him, during the day, but the farmer had prevented it. It was as though he suspected. He had always kept Peter or Max close to him, never Adolf.

The dog lifted its head. Maybe it had caught Max's scent. It growled quietly. Max held his breath and very slowly withdrew his head. How in the world had Adolf succeeded in making friends with this murderous beast?

A week ago Max had seen it for the first time. Adolf had come down the ladder, had sat on his heels in front of the kennel and the dog had crawled out, whining and wagging its tail, and had rolled onto its back. That huge dog had lain on its back for the kid to scratch its chest, and had licked his hands like a puppy.

Next morning in the stable while they were cleaning out the dung, Adolf had said quite casually that he might be able to arrange things so that all three could get past the dog.

Now Max stared into the room. He could not see Adolf in the darkness, but he knew how he was lying — the blanket kicked off, and hugging the pillow, as though he had to cling to something. Adolf was okay. The only trouble was that Adolf was so small, and he was so devoted to Tilli. Now Tilli had made a new friend at the sawmill where she had been placed. This new one, what was her name again? Billie? Billie and Tilli. It sounded like a clown act, ridiculous. But

Billie also wanted to run away according to Adolf. What did they want with another girl? She'd just get in the way. Yet Adolf wouldn't go without Tilli and Tilli wouldn't go without Billie. How much easier to leave them all behind.

Max quietly got off the laundry basket, did two quick kneebends, and shook his legs, which had gone to sleep. Maybe it was quite unnecessary to worry about Tilli. Maybe the new girl, Billie, would not come along. And if she did not go along, they could leave the little girl with her. She would be well cared for, and maybe Adolf would then stay here as well. But then again maybe it would be better if Adolf came along. It was always good to have someone like Adolf along. You could count on Adolf.

The bell chimed ten. Max waited till the tenth chime had died away, then he woke Peter. He had to shake him for a long time before he was awake, and after Max had lain down on his straw mattress he desperately kept his eyes open for fear that Peter would sleep through the change of watch. But soon Max was asleep.

When Adolf woke him, he sat up with a start. His eyes flew open and he looked toward the window. Everything was okay. It was still pitch-black outside.

They took their knapsacks out of the laundry basket. Everything was well tied and tightly lashed so that nothing would rattle or dangle.

Adolf opened the door and called softly: "Rolf! Rolf!" waited quietly and called again. The dog moved in its kennel, slowly came out, raised its head, stretched, and wagged its tail. Adolf talked to it smoothly and softly. Then he climbed down the ladder, went over to the dog and squatted near it. He waited till the dog crawled up to him and laid its head in his lap. He scratched its ears and chest.

Max and Peter watched out of the window and, holding their breath, waited for Adolf's sign. At last he waved to them.

They ran down the ladder, Peter first, ears straining, ready to make a dash for it. Adolf had told them not to turn toward the dog while they were going down; they should not look at it. They heard Adolf talking to it. When Max reached the foot of the ladder, he and Peter ran on, close to the stable toward the back wall, and climbed out through a window of the open shed built into the wall.

The moon hung above the woods lighting their way. But they could have found it even in the dark, they were familiar with every stone. About a hundred paces past the farmhouse they stopped behind some bushes.

A few minutes later they saw Adolf come out of the shadow of the farmhouse. He ran toward them. He was not as short-winded as he used to be. The work he had been forced to do on the farm had actually done him a lot of good. He had grown stronger; all three of them had grown stronger. There had always been plenty to eat.

They walked in single file to the woods, along the edge of the woods to the sawmill, and sat down behind a stack of boards. They saw the house in front of them, and the stables behind it.

They waited. "D'you think she's going to come?" asked Peter after a while. He had turned over the question in his mind for a long time.

Max drew down the corners of his mouth. "Shouldn't think so," he said.

Adolf was uneasy. He liked Billie. He liked her because she had looked after Tilli. And because the little girl had got used to her. He stared at the house until he saw black spots before his eyes.

Tilli came first. She was running so fast, her legs could hardly keep up with her. A few minutes later Billie followed.

"Pretty late," said Max without looking at her. She looked up in surprise, raising her eyebrows. "A couple of minutes can't matter, can they?" she said. Max turned round and walked off.

Just before they reached the forest a fat cloud pushed its way across the moon, and by the time they turned onto the dirt road that led to the embankment, they could not see their hands in front of their faces. They stumbled along blindly behind Max, who hardly slowed his pace. He walked along, his head bent back, watching the slightly lighter night sky along the gap in the black ceiling of the forest that indicated the course the path took. He had been on so many night marches at the camp that he knew how to find his way even in the deepest darkness.

A quarter of an hour later they came to the embankment, clambered up the slope, and walked along the cross ties between the tracks, in step with each other, single file, two cross ties apart.

The tracks led in a wide curve around a hilltop, then ran halfway up a hillside, and finally took a sharp bend over the valley bottom. Max stopped at the beginning of the bend. This was where he wanted to wait for the train.

He had nursed this plan for a long time, had checked everything in detail. Every Monday morning between three and eight two trains passed by going north. The first one usually came exactly at three, the second one came irregularly. He had only been able to hear the first one. The second one he had sometimes watched, and whenever he had seen it, it had always been a freight train. If they did not succeed in jumping onto the first, they were certain to get onto the second; it had always had open cars. But maybe they could ride on the first, which should be coming any minute now. Maybe it was a freight train as well. Max held his ear to the track. He could not hear anything yet. They sat down under the trees at the edge of the woods by the embankment and waited.

The first train appeared shortly after three. It was made up of an express engine and two long passenger cars; brand-new, clean cars with lights in the compartments and glass in the windows. A Yankee train. Nothing doing.

They drew farther back among the trees and lay down on the ground, their heads on their knapsacks. They were not worried that they would miss the next train if they fell asleep. The pounding of the engine was sure to wake them.

Max awoke on the dot of six. He just caught the last chimes of the church clock. He saw Peter and Billie sitting ahead at the edge of the woods, and went over to them. The sun was already warm. The bees were buzzing among the trees, and butterflies fluttered above the embankment.

"Hey, come over here!" called Peter. "You've got to see

this!" He was lying on his stomach, watching something on the ground. "Come quickly, or you'll miss it!" he called urgently. Max sat down next to him.

"You missed it," said Peter, but added reassuringly: "Wait, I'll do it again." There were small craters in the fine dry sand of the forest floor, one next to the other. Peter loosened a few grains of sand with a twig and let them roll into one of the craters. At the bottom of the crater something moved, two dark claws poked up through the sand, tiny pincers, ready to snap shut.

"He keeps on throwing ants in there, on purpose!" said Billie reproachfully. "I think it's so mean, I can't even say how mean I think it is!" She trembled with suppressed fury.

"So what!" said Peter. He let a small red ant crawl onto the twig he was holding in his hand and flicked it into one of the craters. "Now watch," he whispered. "Wait till you see what it does now!"

The ant tried to climb up the side of the crater. It scrabbled desperately with its legs, but kept sliding back as the sand gave way beneath it. But it went on paddling, wallowing, and fighting its way forward, as though it sensed the danger lurking at the bottom of the crater. It had almost reached the safety of the edge of the crater when a small fountain of sand shot up from below, hit it, and dragged it back. The ant made another attempt, and again a load of sand hit it. The thing with the claws, the thing hiding somewhere down there, was aiming at it, was shooting sand at it, pulling it back again until it slid down, exhausted. Instantly the pincers snapped shut around the ant and a moment later pulled it into the sand. Only the ant's head with the trembling feelers was still visible; then it was gone. The sand still moved a little where the ant had disappeared.

They watched, holding their breath, a tingling feeling at the nape of their necks, a gooseflesh tingling feeling.

"What kind of creature is it?" asked Max with slight awe in his voice.

"Don't know, either," said Peter.

"It's an ant lion!" said Billie indignantly. "Everyone knows that!" She eyed Peter with hostility, stood up, and went over to the embankment.

Two men came toward them along the tracks, lightly hopping and trotting across the ties. They were foragers with bulging knapsacks and briefcases in their hands. They looked satisfied, as though they had been successful, nodded to the children amicably, and sat down next to them at the edge of the wood. One of them lit a partly smoked cigarette. They handed it to and fro a couple of times, and then, the first one carefully stowed the butt away in the tin box from which he had taken it. "You wouldn't by any chance have a whole one?" he asked without much hope.

Billie went to her knapsack without a word, took two cigarettes from a pack she had hidden, and brought them to him.

"Good Lord, girl!" he said. And the other one immediately reached for his briefcase and asked, "D'you want something to eat? I can give you a piece of bread and molasses." Billie shook her head. "We've got some ourselves," she said. She watched the two men stretch out on their backs and draw on the cigarettes with their eyes closed. They drew in so deep that there was no cloud of smoke when they breathed out.

The train announced its arrival from afar. It came closer, pounding laboriously. They hid behind the trees and let the engine pass. A greasy brown-black cloud billowed and laid itself heavily over the cars behind. The first cars were laden with lumps of coal, then came several tank cars and high, closed freight cars with sliding doors. This was the time to jump on — right now! But the train was going too fast and the cars were too big for Tilli and Adolf to get onto easily. It was too dangerous. They would have to get between the cars, and the engine was picking up speed again.

"What's the matter?" shouted one of the scavengers, who was already on the car.

"We can't!" Billie called back. The man jumped off, lifted Max on his shoulders, and ran with him next to a car. Luckily just then the train jolted to a short stop.

"Move it, kid, open the bolt!" It was a heavy drop bolt with a handle and a pin at the end which fit into a ring. Max hit the handle with his fist. The bolt flew open and sprang back with a crash. "That's right, boy!" said the man. "We'll make it yet!" He braced himself against the sliding door, which rolled open with a screech. "Quickly now!" He lifted one after another into the car, then pulled himself up, too. "Well, we made it." And the train slowly started up again.

The car was full of straw and cow dung. "It stinks too much for me, kids," said the man. "I can't stand it." He waited till the train slowed for a bridge, then jumped out, ran forward, and swung himself onto the buffer.

They cleaned a space for themselves behind the door, scraping the dung together with their feet, then pushing it through a hole. They did not mind the stench. They were traveling. They were riding in a train. No one could stop them now. They were on their way home.

The train slowly moved in a northwesterly direction, rumbling along hour after hour. Sometimes it stopped on an open stretch, but they could not make out why. Then it started off again laboriously, traveled through forests, along steep hills, past signalmen's huts and past small, abandoned railroad stations.

The countryside flattened out, the woods receded. The two foragers jumped off and waved to them. The train had turned more and more to the west, now it turned north again, in their direction.

They traveled through open fields where people were digging. The field-workers straightened up as the train passed, and stretched their bent backs. There were many children with them who waved. Max and the others waved back. They had succeeded in avoiding the potato harvest. Never again would they work in the fields, never, not ever again for the rest of their lives.

Peter got out his map and tried to find how far they had gone. The railroad tracks had not been plotted on the map he had and they had been unable to see a sign with a name on it since they boarded the train. They had no reference point, but they calculated the train's route by the direction and speed, and figured they would have to be close to

Weiden. Despite the detour the train had made, they should be at least thirty-five miles closer to Berlin than when they had set off that morning. They were in high spirits.

Around midday the heat in the car became more and more unbearable. Swarms of flies buzzed around the dung. The only place where it was tolerable was in the breeze by the open door. They sat right on the edge and let their feet hang down.

A large town came into view, and Peter and Max pulled the door closed before the train entered the station. The train rumbled over several switches, slowed down and stopped. Looking through a crack in the door, they could not see anything — a freight train on the next tracks blocked their view.

"Let's get out," said Max. He shouldered his knapsack and carefully pushed the door open a few inches. Abruptly he stopped and listened and motioned to the others to keep quiet. They could hear footsteps coming closer. A moment later the door rolled forward and crashed shut. The bolt locked with a hard snap.

For seconds they stood there paralyzed, staring at the closed door. The door could not be opened from the inside now, and there was no other way out.

"We've got to call someone," said Billie, sounding panicky. She was about to start kicking the door but Max held her back. "Are you nuts?" he hissed at her. "There's time enough for that if we don't come up with any better ideas."

"What ideas?" asked Billie agitatedly.

Max pointed upward. There was a jagged hole in the roof

above the door, as though a bomb fragment had torn it open. "Perhaps we can get out through that if we make it a bit bigger," said Max.

Billie did not think much of that idea, it was plain to see, but she did not say anything.

So Peter stood with his back against the door and acted as a ladder, and Billie helped Max up. He could just reach the hole with his arm outstretched.

The roof was made of narrow boards laid lengthwise and covered with tar paper. Max was able to break out two boards. The tar paper was also easy to tear away. But the opening was still too narrow. Another board had to come out.

Max asked for his knife. He would have to cut through hardwood, and he had a wobbly foothold on Peter's shoulders. His arms quickly became tired because he had to hold them high above his head.

Outside, trains and single engines traveled by, and they could hear steam whistles and loud shouts. They must have landed in a shunting station.

Max carved a notch into the board. The board was cut halfway through when the car was jolted so sharply that Peter lost his footing. Max tumbled off, and fell with his full weight on top of Tilli, who was sitting on the ground. He pulled her up. She looked as though she wanted to scream, but could not. Her head was covered with muck and flies. Her eyes were as big as saucers, her mouth was wide open. She could not breathe.

Helplessly they stood in front of her, watched as she gasped for air, groaned and tried to relax the spasm which was squeezing her lungs, and finally, panting, started to breathe again.

Another sudden jolt went through the whole train, a steam whistle started to wail, and the train began to move. They were off again.

8

Minefield

The train picked up speed and the station noises were left behind. But suddenly Max realized something: the train was traveling back in the direction from which it had come! The ray of sunlight coming in through the hole in the roof showed it as clearly as a compass. They were traveling south.

They set to work again to free themselves. This time Peter got up on Max's shoulders, then Billie took her turn. When they changed places for the third time, they finally succeeded in breaking out the board. The others supported Max's legs so he could pull himself up. He squeezed halfway through the hole and leaned out.

The bolt on the door was right below him. He thought that if he could get a hook into the ring, he would be able to pull it open. They knotted three ropes from their knapsacks together and, using Billie's nail file, fashioned a belt buckle into a hook.

Max climbed up again and leaned out of the hole and lowered the hook. It was not easy to get it into the handle of the bolt, what with the car swaying and the wind pushing the rope back, but finally he succeeded. He pulled on the rope.

The bolt was stuck. It did not give way until the others rattled the sliding door from inside. Then it flew up. The door was open.

Max dropped back into the car and they opened the door wide. Now they realized that the train had changed direction again: it was now traveling west. And it was moving fast for a freight train, at least thirty miles an hour.

For about an hour they continued to travel at the same speed. Much too fast to jump off. They went through two towns which they could not find on Peter's map. Maybe they were off the map.

Suddenly the brakes went on. It was so unexpected that they had no time to brace themselves. They skidded across the floor and landed in the dung at the front end of the car as the train stopped. Outside they could hear steps on the gravel; someone was running toward the front.

They waited till he had passed. Then Max jumped out. The others threw their knapsacks to him, he helped Tilli out, and the others followed.

They lay on their backs in the dry grass, which had been warmed by the sun all day. They heard the engine steam away and the drone of motors receding quickly into the distance, and a short shrill whistle from the steam whistle, which was thrown back by the dark wall of the tall forest. Then there was silence. Just the buzzing of the bees and the chirping of the birds above them in the trees. The whole forest was full of birds. They had never heard so many birds twittering.

Thirst drove them on. They started off, through the woods in the direction from which they had come on the train. The railroad embankment was their only guide. They had to stay close to it.

After a short march they reached a long, open field that cut through the woods. The embankment rose to their left; to their right, a quarter of a mile away, they could see a river bordered with trees and thick bushes. A row of dark alder bushes ran through the field all the way from the embankment to the river. There was probably a stream there.

They waded through the field. The shoulder-high grass should have been mowed long ago — the stalks were dried out already and wide stretches had been flattened by the wind.

Tilli ran on ahead and when she reached the stream she slipped off her bag and dropped to her knees.

"Are you crazy! You can't drink that!" yelled Peter.

Tilli stopped and stared at him, wide-eyed.

"Why?" asked Billie.

Peter put on a supercilious expression. "Because you have to boil river water. Because of ptomaine poisoning!" He paused and then added, bragging: "Ask any soldier!"

Billie looked him up and down, her head to one side, then turned away and strode energetically to the stream, unbuckled her mess tin, and filled it with water. Before she raised it to her lips she said with a scornful sideways glance: "Ptomaine poisoning! In such a small stream! There's no room for a corpse!" She took long swallows, knelt down, washed her hands and her face, and Tilli crouched next to her and drank greedily. When they had satisfied their thirst, Billie turned to Peter and said caustically, "At most a baby's corpse!"

Peter felt the blood rush to his face. Billie's scorn had hit a sore spot. And when he saw Max and Adolf drinking from the stream, too, it hit even deeper. He stood in the field, rigid, his head held high, and stared past the others.

"Come on, come over here," Max called.

Peter waited till they had disappeared behind the alder bushes. Then he trotted along in their tracks.

On the other side of the stream, halfway between the embankment and the river, was a barn. They decided to spend the night there, although it was not late yet. The journey in the cattle car had exhausted them, and they had to wash their clothes.

The barn was only a broken-down shed, open toward the river, but the roof was still watertight. If a thunderstorm came along, they would at least stay dry. They made themselves comfortable.

Billie took the two smaller children with her to look for something to eat. They had seen raspberries and mushrooms in the woods. Maybe they would find enough for a meal before it got dark. They had to try to save their own supplies.

Peter hung around behind the shed and did not come in until the three had gone.

"Give me some matches," said Max. He had broken up some rotten boards and had stacked the pieces of wood.

"Why me? I haven't got any," Peter said angrily.

Max looked in Adolf's knapsack . . . nothing. "Damned shit!" he said. Peter nodded gloomily. He was thirsty.

Max went to the stream with his mess tin and got some water. "Come on, drink it! It's just a lot of nonsense!" he said.

Peter hesitated, but finally drank it. "She's a show-off," he said.

Max shrugged his shoulders.

"I think she's a show-off, the stupid cow!"

Max pointed to Billie's knapsack. "Look whether she's got any," he said. Peter rummaged in the outside pocket of the knapsack and pulled out a tin box. There was a lipstick in it, and a silvery earring, and a rolled-up leather belt, a mechanical pencil, and a blue notebook. "What d'you know!" he said. "She keeps a diary!" He held up the book, grinning.

"Has she got any matches or not?" Max asked roughly.

"Nope," said Peter in a subdued tone.

They kept a lookout for the others. Two men suddenly appeared on the embankment. They walked along the tracks, stopped, and stared in their direction. One of them raised his binoculars. Peter and Max threw themselves on the ground. The two men continued on their way, searching the field again with their binoculars before they disappeared behind the trees.

"D'you think that's because of us?" asked Peter.

Max shook his head. "Why should they be looking for us?" he asked.

The other three came out of the woods with a field bag full of mushrooms.

"Haven't you made a fire yet?" asked Billie reproach-fully.

"D'you have any matches?" Max snapped back.

"Oh good grief!" said Billie.

Adolf watched the two of them uneasily. He sensed they were on the verge of going for each other's throats and he did not want them to quarrel. Jumping up, he ran back to the woods and returned a moment later with a few cartridges. He broke the shot out of the case, shook the powder over the pile of wood, cut a forked branch from a bush, and wedged a shell-casing in the fork. He pressed the ends of the fork to-gether so that it clamped the shell-casing as in a pair of pliers. He held the mouth of the casing to the little pile of powder and hit the cap with the point of his penknife. A small flame shot out, setting the powder alight.

"Where d'you get the cartridges?" asked Max.

"There're more in the woods," said Adolf. "Masses of them."

"So there you are," said Billie.

They fried the mushrooms with a bit of bacon and ate potatoes with them, and sat around the fire watching it as it slowly died down. Then they curled up in their blankets. Only Billie stayed by the fire and took the blue notebook and mechanical pencil out of her knapsack and began to write, lying on her stomach.

Peter watched her through half-closed eyes. He imagined

she was writing the story about the ptomaine poison. He thought he saw her grin while she was writing. At that moment he hated her with all his heart.

Adolf was sleeping against the barn wall toward the stream. A blackbird woke him. The wall boards had rotted away at the bottom so he could see out. The blackbird was sitting on a bush less than two yards away, chattering away, with drooping wings and twitching tail. Then it flew up and continued to scold from the roof of the shed. Something must have frightened it. Adolf strained his ears. Something was scratching around on the outside of the back wall of the shed, snuffling. It sounded like a dog. He sat up.

It was a dog. A medium-sized, shaggy mongrel with floppy ears and thin legs. Suddenly it was standing in front of him, eyeing him, just as astonished as Adolf was. It stood ready to run, the hairs on its neck raised.

Adolf did not move, just said softly, "Okay, okay now," and "Here, here, here," and clicked his tongue. The dog wagged its tail timidly, and lost some of its fear. It lowered its head and crawled under the boards. It crawled along on its stomach until it was close enough for Adolf to stroke it, then pressed close to Adolf and licked him. Suddenly it looked past him and stepped over his legs, and when Adolf turned around he saw that Billie was also awake and sitting up. The dog was next to her, letting her stroke it.

"My goodness, he's so skinny," she said softly.

They crawled from under their blankets and sat down behind the shed by the stream so they would not wake the others. The dog followed them. It was still early in the morning. Mist hung over the field, and the grass was wet with dew. But they did not freeze; it was not cold.

"I've got a dog at home, too," said Billie, "a dachshund." And after a pause she asked, "Do you have one, too?"

"My father has," said Adolf hesitantly.

"What kind?" asked Billie.

"Shepherd," said Adolf.

"Oh," said Billie.

The dog looked up at them with sad, pleading eyes, snuffled around and trotted restlessly to and fro, then sat down and raised its paw.

"Maybe he won't recognize me anymore when I get back," said Billie. "Last time I went home, at Christmas, he kept barking at me. Didn't want to sleep in my room anymore. Before, he'd always had his basket at the foot of my bed."

"Ours isn't allowed into the house," said Adolf.

"Why?" asked Billie.

Adolf felt the disapproval in her question. "He's trained," he said quickly, "he's a watchdog, he's always outside, he's got his kennel." He gave her a shy sideways glance and hastily continued. "Only my father's allowed to feed him, he's trained so well that he only eats what my father feeds him."

Billie threw him a questioning glance, a deep wrinkle between her brows.

"That's so that if burglars came and threw him some poisoned meat, he wouldn't eat it," Adolf explained, stammering. "That's the way he's been trained. He only eats what my father gives him."

"I thought your father was an officer!" said Billie. Adolf nodded uncertainly.

"Well, who fed him when he was at the Front, then?" asked Billie.

"My father wasn't at the Front," said Adolf. "He was in Berlin the whole time."

"What if your father gets sick?" asked Billie. "If he'd have to go to hospital, who'd feed him then?"

Adolf thought about it. "I don't know," he said hesitantly.

They fell silent. The dog lay down between them and they both stroked it, and when their hands touched, Adolf quickly withdrew his.

"Doesn't he take anything from you, either?" asked Billie skeptically. Adolf did not say anything. "Go on, admit that he takes things from you," she said.

The fog had lifted. Just a thin veil of mist hung above the river, evaporating almost imperceptibly. The trees along the bank began to emerge, and then suddenly the sun broke through. At first there was only a glaring, bright glow behind the mist, then a round, dazzling white disk, and finally the rays penetrated through the veil. They felt them warm on their skin.

"How did you handle Lederer's dog?" asked Billie.

Adolf shrugged his shoulders. He did not know what to answer. He did not know how he had done it. He said: "You just mustn't try to force them to like you." And after a pause he added: "You have to wait till they like you."

Billie stood up. "I'm going to the river to wash my things," she said. "If you want me to wash something for you, bring it along."

Adolf waited till the others were awake. Tilli was the last to wake up. She saw the dog and forgot everything else — threw sticks into the field which it retrieved with breathtaking speed, took it in her arms and stroked it, called endearments in the same language in which she had talked to her horse.

They followed Billie's tracks through the tall grass down to the river. Billie was kneeling on the bank, scrubbing her clothes, rubbing the material against itself, then rinsed them, wrung them out, and hung the things on the bushes to dry. Adolf watched her for a while, and when she told him he should give her his shirt to wash, he felt terribly self-conscious. But he finally gave it to her, and when he was standing in front of her in his undershirt, he was even more self-conscious. His arms seemed even thinner, and his shoulders even more bony. He quickly slipped away and ran upstream. The others were there.

He saw Max and Peter, who were standing on the bank in their gym shorts, jump into the water. The little girl shouted when they dived in, and the dog raced up and down the bank yapping. The water was so deep that Max and Peter could barely stand. They were gasping for breath and spluttering and wildly thrashing around with their arms. Suddenly Peter dived under and when he came back up, he had something in his hand which he threw onto the bank and shouted, "Man, there's a mass of things down there!" He dove again, and this time Max dove, too. He brought a gun up with him and held it over his head. Peter brought up a second gun. "It's as good as new!" he shouted. They waded across to the bank, scrambled out, and Peter called to Adolf:

"You've never seen anything like it! Look at that!" He gave him the gun and dove headfirst into the water again, threw out a pineapple grenade, a bayonet, a cartridge magazine, and a belt of machine gun ammunition. "Boy-oh-boy, the whole river's full!" he shouted.

Suddenly Billie appeared next to them. She lunged toward Tilli who was holding a grenade in her hand, took it away from her, and threw it back into the river. "Don't touch that!" she said threateningly.

Peter came out of the water and planted himself in front of her. "There's no danger," he said casually. "You can't even pull the pin; the cap's still on."

"I don't care!" said Billie venomously. "The little girl, at least, is not going to touch them!"

"Oh!" drawled Peter. He suddenly started to grin. The grin spread from ear to ear. Still grinning, he bent down, grasped a hand grenade, unscrewed the cap, put his finger into the ring of the pin, shouted "take cover!", pulled the pin, and casually threw the shiny black thing into the field.

All of them were already flat on the ground when they noticed the dog leaping after it, yapping wildly. For a moment they were paralyzed with fear. How long did it take for a hand grenade to explode? How far had Peter thrown it? How quick was the dog?

Billie was the first on her feet. "Into the water!" she shouted. She grabbed Tilli and raced to the river, dove under, clutching the little girl who was flailing wildly with arms and legs. Tilli hit out and scratched; Billie could not hold her under any longer. She surfaced.

There stood the dog right in front of them on the bank,

wagging its tail and whining, the hand grenade in its mouth. She thought her heart would stop, thought she saw the black thing fly apart. And then she heard Peter's voice behind her, calm and without a trace of fear. "It's a dud," said Peter. "It won't go off." It was not until then that she felt how cold the water was.

Peter took the grenade out of the dog's mouth and weighed it in his hand. "A dud," he said disdainfully. "Perhaps some water got into it."

Billie yelled at him: "Just throw the thing away, or I'll really give it to you!" She was absolutely furious, and if she had not been afraid of the hand grenade, she would have slapped him.

"There's nothing can happen anymore," said Peter. "Once it hasn't gone off, it can't ever go off. It's ruined. Not the least bit dangerous." He threw it into the air and caught it again. Then he drew his arm far back and threw the grenade upstream in a high arc, so that it flew almost to the edge of the woods. The grenade landed between the bushes along the bank. Suddenly they saw something tear through the branches, saw the explosion before they heard the bang, and the howling whir of the shrapnel. They threw themselves onto the ground.

Peter remained standing. Paralyzed, stunned, dumbfounded. He whispered hoarsely, tonelessly: "That's impossible!" Again and again: "That's impossible! That's impossible! That's impossible!" Then to Max, pleadingly, "Surely that's not possible?! That can't happen! It just can't explode!"

Billie leaped up, furious. "Maybe it didn't explode!" she cried scathingly. "Maybe we just imagined the explosion!"

And as she stalked away they could hear her saying: "Such imbecility! The things one has to listen to! What an idiot!"

It took Peter a long time to calm down. He explained to them in absolute detail how the firing mechanism of the hand grenade works, staked his life on it, and if they didn't believe it, they could ask any soldier and he would confirm it. They let him talk.

They watched Billie walk back to the shed with her washing. She was still furious. They had to give her time.

Billie was sitting in the shed, waiting. She had carefully folded the freshly washed things, wrapped them in a dry towel and tied them to the outside of the knapsack. She waited impatiently. She was still furious, and the longer she waited, the angrier she became. There was no sign of the others. She wondered whether she should get them. She stood up, started off, then turned back again. Why should she chase after them?

She tore an empty page from her notebook, wrote in large block capitals "I'LL WAIT ON THE EMBANK-MENT," pinned the note to Adolf's knapsack and started off. She walked with quick, stiff steps, hitting the grass aside with her hand. She was barefoot, carrying her shoes in her hand. The ground was soft under her feet, damp and cool.

There was a wire fence along the base of the embankment. She crawled through and climbed up the slope. The gravel stones at the top were pointed and sharp. She sat down to put her shoes on. From where she sat she could see across the whole field down to the river. She shaded her eyes with her hand and searched the riverbank, but could not find the others. She sat down on the signal wires at the edge of the embankment and swung on them impatiently.

Below, on one of the fence posts, was a sign, two posts farther another, and yet another three posts farther on. Red-and-white flags were hanging on the topmost wire of the fence. She had noticed them yesterday when they had jumped off the train and slid down the slope. There had been the same kind of fence there, too.

Something was written on the signs. She could not read it from here. But under the writing was a drawing — it looked like a skull and crossbones.

She stopped swinging and felt herself go cold. A moment later she was on her feet. She slithered down the slope, stared at the sign, did not want to believe what she saw. "Minefield" she read. And "Keep out, danger," and the thing that had looked like a skull and crossbones *was* a skull and crossbones. Two posts farther on, the same sign. One sign after another. And the fence ran the whole length of the embankment in both directions, as far as she could see.

Suddenly it all made sense: the unmowed field, the ammunition in the woods and in the river. And now she remembered that when she had been washing, she had seen a fence on the opposite bank, the same fence, hung with red-and-white rags. Minefield! And the others were still in the middle of it!

She yelled, "Adolf!" cupped her hands to her mouth and yelled at the top of her lungs: "Adolf! Max!" She raced up the slope. Yelled from above. Listened, craning her neck.

Nothing. No answer. They could not hear her. The river was too far, they were sitting between the bushes and the water was gurgling. They could not hear her.

She saw the tracks she had made through the grass, and a shiver ran down her back at the thought that with every step she could have been blown sky high.

Should she wait till the others appeared? Perhaps that would be too late. Perhaps Peter had been right about the hand grenade; perhaps it had not been the hand grenade that had exploded, but something it landed on. She could not wait — she had to do something right away. The others were still sitting by the river. If she got to them in time, they would only have to wade through the water. She had to get to the other side of the river, along the fence around the minefield. She had to try it, no matter how far it was.

She let her knapsack tumble down the slope and took off, running alongside the tracks. Below her was the fence with the signs. It ran on endlessly, one sign after another, and red-and-white flags on the wires.

She was panting. Her fear almost choked her. But then she reached a side valley, and the fence turned and ran along a stream toward the river. She ran on with renewed strength. Now her goal was before her; she could see she was getting closer to the river. And she had a freshly mowed field under her feet, hard ground on which it was easy to run.

The row of posts ended at the riverbank. A long wire with a sign in the middle was hanging across the water. On the other side the fence continued again. Billie waded through the water. It reached to her breast and she paddled with her arms to get across quicker. Then she ran on next to the fence which stretched along the bank.

Suddenly she heard the little girl shout and shriek, and heard the dog join in barking. Now she could see her, too, see her head bobbing up and down over the top of a bush.

"Tilli!" she called. She did not have enough breath to shout. She gasped for air. The two smaller children were standing over there. Adolf with the rod held high above his head, his eyes staring at a fish wriggling at the end of the string, Tilli next to him, hopping up and down and shrieking for joy: "He's caught one! He's caught one!" And the dog running around in circles, yapping. Where were the other two?

"Tilli!" called Billie. The little girl heard her at last. "We've got one!" she shouted. "Billie, we've got one!" Adolf was fighting to get the fish, which dangled, wriggling, in front of him. He could not grasp it, because he had to hold on to the rod with both hands.

"Tilli, stand still!" called Billie. "Adolf, tell her to stand still! There are mines where you are! That's a minefield!" Adolf stared across at her. He did not seem to understand what she was saying. "It's all mined where you are! That's a minefield!" called Billie, desperately serious. Now Tilli hesitated, too. "You've got to hold on to the dog!" called Billie.

The fish was hanging directly in front of Adolf's face; it was twitching very little now, swinging limply on the string. It was a long, heavy fish, as long as a big cucumber.

"Where are the others?" asked Billie.

Adolf indicated over his shoulder with his head. Billie saw Max's head appear above the grass a few paces behind Tilli. Peter was next to him.

"How d'you know that?" she heard Max ask in a weak voice.

"There's a fence," said Billie. "It's all fenced in, and it's written on the fence!" She saw Max draw up his shoulders as though he wanted to make himself lighter — as light as he could. She saw him looking at the ground around his feet and, carefully feeling his way, take a first step toward the bank. She held her breath.

Step by step he came closer. Peter kept right behind him, stepping in his footprints and trying to keep his balance by stretching out his arms.

Adolf was still holding the rod, his arms high above his head, not daring to move. His arms were shaking from the strain.

"Throw away the rod!" Billie called to him.

He swung the fish to and fro and threw the rod away. The dog leaped up, yapping, as it splashed into the water. Tilli could not hold it anymore. But Max was there and caught it by the scruff of its neck. They had to bring it across the river with them. It could not be allowed to run loose on the bank.

Suddenly Peter took two bounds past Max and dived into the water in a wide arc.

"Jump in after him!" Max called to Adolf. And Adolf leaped in, went under, came up kicking, then swam with hurried strokes.

Max waited till he had reached the other bank. He was

holding the dog, and Tilli was standing behind him, holding tightly to his belt. He could feel her trembling.

"You don't have to be afraid," he said without turning his head. "I'll carry you across."

He threw the dog into the water, slid down behind it, and pulled Tilli onto his shoulders. He heard the others shout, saw them throw themselves onto the ground, saw the dog paddling wildly back to the bank and clamber up between the roots of the trees along the bank.

He threw himself forward, fought through the current. The little girl got heavier and heavier on his shoulders. "Take cover!" he shouted. "Take cover!" He heard the dog yapping behind him, pushed the little girl to the bank, crawled up behind her calling: "Get away from here! Get away!" He ran, crouching, along behind the others, between the hayprops across the field.

They did not stop until they reached a gravel path at the foot of the hillside. They watched the dog, which was still yapping behind them and searching the bank, its head down. Then it stretched its muzzle and started to howl plaintively.

A black mountain of clouds had built up over the woods and pushed in front of the sun. A thunderstorm was brewing. Billie urged them to hurry.

They ran along the road to the end of the minefield, waded through the river, and ran on along the stream at a safe distance. As they reached the embankment the first gust of wind swept down the valley. They climbed up the slope and trotted back along the ties to the field where the shed stood.

The black watersack in the sky above them suddenly burst

open with thunder and lightning, and a torrent of water poured down on them. The trees bordering the river blurred in gray veils of rain. They could just make out the shed as a black dot in the field. That's where their luggage was.

Billie slid down the slope. The others saw her collect her knapsack from the grass and slowly climb up again. At least Billie still had her luggage.

Tilli had only her little bag. Peter had the camera case holding his money on his belt. Adolf, too, had saved his money. Max had nothing any more.

"Let's go," said Max. He walked ahead across the ties. The rain pelted down on them unrelentingly. Max took off his shirt. He felt the rain drumming on his skin, the water dripping from his hair and running down his back between his shoulder blades. He kept his eyes half closed and breathed deeply. He thought of the boots his father had made. When they had been in the church, after Adolf had returned them, he had polished them thoroughly again, greased the leather, waxed the soles and scoured the metal with flint until it gleamed. Now they were lying in his knapsack, well packed, under the floorboards of the shed. They would stay there till they rotted away.

What should he tell his father when he got home? When his mother had written him that his father was missing in action, he had thought he would never see him again. Whoever was missing in action on the Eastern Front was as good as dead.

But now, unexplainably, Max was convinced that his father would come home; that he would be sitting at home, waiting only for his boots. This thought sent hot and cold shivers down Max's back.

The rain stopped and they trudged on. The route led through endless, thick forest, then turned northward. It was time to find out where they were.

They asked three women who came toward them on the other tracks. According to what they said they were roughly fifteen miles north of Regensburg. The cattle train had taken them far from their route.

They trotted on for at least an hour until they emerged from the forest. Ahead of them was a railroad crossing and a road that led across the tracks. To their right a church steeple towered over a hill, and the road led toward it.

Max wanted to stay on the railroad tracks, but Billie talked him out of it. They could not stay on the tracks where the foragers had already cleaned out everything. They had to go cross-country, through villages. They turned onto the road, toward the church steeple.

There was a small village with a dozen large farmhouses and a few smaller properties in between. They did not leave out a single house. They begged their way from the first to the last farm, knocked on every door, said, "Hello!" in chorus, and pushed Tilli forward so she could recite the request: "Please would you have something for us to eat?" Mostly they did not get as far as Tilli's little speech. The door was instantly slammed in their faces. Sometimes a small child would come to the door and shout back into the house: "Mommy, there're some more here who want food," and from the interior would come the answer: "We don't have nothin'!" Or a suspicious old woman would scold from the window: "Go beggin' somewhere else!"

They moved on. Hunger began to torment them. They had not eaten anything all day. They did not reach the next village until about five o'clock.

They thought up a story for the two little ones to tell: They were from Silesia and had spent six months in a camp. Their mother had died, and the camp commandant had taken all their belongings, and now they were trying to get to their grandparents in Berlin. It was a story two girls had once told the sawmill owner's wife and Billie could remember that the two had at least got a quarter of a loaf of bread and a mess tin full of milk. Apparently it was a good story.

They split up before they came to the first farms, only Adolf and Tilli staying together. They divided up the farms which each of them was to check out, and agreed to meet afterward at the church.

Billie was the first to arrive at the meeting place. She brought back only a piece of bread. A small end bit, as hard as stone — but farm bread, which you could suck. Peter had two potatoes. Max had nothing. He was in low spirits. He was no good at scrounging. Each time he had to force himself just to knock at the door.

You had to be able to talk like a salesman if you wanted to beg. You had to know how to tell stories, be able to start a conversation straight off, not let yourself be chased away. And at the same time you always had to be friendly, polite, bow, let yourself be spoken to in a stupid way without changing your expression; be patient, always have a joke on the tip of your tongue, be thick-skinned; never give up, even if you've been thrown out for the tenth, for the thirtieth time. Max knew all this; he had watched it often enough. But he could not do it himself, he just could not go through with it. His requests sounded like apologies, and all the farmers' wives had to do was throw him a sharp look, and he turned away of his own accord. All of them saw right away that he was easy to get rid of.

The three of them sat on the church steps and waited for the two small ones. The sun went down, but the stones were still warm, radiating the heat from the sun which they had stored up during the day. The clock struck eight, it began to get dark, and there was still no sign of the two of them. They waited in silence.

At last Adolf came running, hot and out of breath. They had found a place to spend the night, and they had eaten three dinners — it had almost made him sick. Each time they had got potatoes with greasy, boiled pork, and Tilli had crammed her bag full so that they would get enough, too.

He led them to a low farm at the end of the village. Only two tiny windows on the ground floor were lit. Adolf knocked, and a little later an old lady came out leading Tilli by the hand, and lighting the way with a lantern. They followed her through the yard. In the back wall she opened a padlock and pushed up the beam, pulled open the door, and let them in. She held up the light so they could look around, and shouted after them that they should sleep on the straw; they'd better not crawl into the hay, or there'd be hell to pay. Then she closed the door.

They sat down beneath a window and set to work on Tilli's bag. It was stuffed to the rim with lumps of meat and squashed potatoes. Billie took out the mush with a spoon, divided it into three portions, and cleaned Tilli's odds and ends from the meat — hair pins and coins, rubber seals from bottles, glass beads, and a shriveled horse chestnut were all sticking to it.

It really wasn't enough. But they did not have to go to sleep with empty stomachs. They had a roof over their heads, and something soft and warm to sleep on. They could not complain.

9

The Summerhouse

*A*t six o'clock the door creaked open and the old lady said that they could earn some breakfast if they helped clean out the stables. Later, in the kitchen, she promised them some lunch and half a loaf of bread in exchange for bringing in three loads of hay. They made a tremendous effort and had the hay in the barn by midday, just in time to beat a thunderstorm. They ate and waited until the storm had blown by and then continued to march along the road northward. They walked for three hours without a break. Then dug for two hours in a potato field, but it had been harvested so thoroughly that they found only tiny tubers, not enough to fill one mess tin. Finally they gave up and walked on and begged their way through a village where even the two small children came out empty-handed. They continued on their way, tired and depressed and dirty from digging potatoes.

There was little traffic on the road. They waved to every truck that passed them, and each time Billie held up her pack of cigarettes, but no one stopped.

The sky had not cleared after the storm. The black wall of clouds had drawn white veils behind it, which had become denser and denser until they covered the whole sky. And a wind had arisen from the west. A steady, sharp, cold wind that gradually chilled them to the bone.

Billie shared all the warm clothes she had left: a sweater for Adolf, a quilted jacket for Tilli. She wore her cardigan, and Max and Peter put her blanket around their shoulders.

They had to find a place to spend the night, because it looked as though it would rain, again. Shortly before darkness fell they came to an inn standing alone at the crossroads beneath tall chestnut trees. Next to it was a garden enclosed by two sheds. Two horses, a goat, and a cow were standing in front of it, and women and children were sitting at the tables in the inn garden. They asked a woman whether they could spend the night there. The woman said they would have to talk to the innkeeper, and asked whether they had any money, because the innkeeper would not let them stay unless they paid.

Billie went into the inn alone. The restaurant was empty except for an old couple sitting next to the counter with a plate of soup in front of each of them. The man surveyed her suspiciously, and asked sullenly between spoonfuls what she wanted. It was the innkeeper.

It would cost them two marks each to spend the night, and the innkeeper demanded that Billie pay in advance. The woman sat bent over her plate, slurping the soup from the spoon, and when Billie put the money on the table, she lifted her head just high enough to see the bills. The innkeeper pointed to the longer of the two sheds. They were to look for some room there.

There was a bowling lane in the shed. The women sitting in the inn garden had already made themselves at home there. The long, narrow room was subdivided by blankets and tarps that hung down from the low plank ceiling. It stank of sweat and boiled cabbage and of mildewed straw and old rags. And a baby was squalling.

The five of them stood uncertainly in the doorway, not daring to go farther until the woman to whom they had spoken came along. She led them to the space behind the door, showed them how to put the tables together so as to have their own sleeping compartment, and told them where they could find potato sacks and straw.

When darkness fell they sat down with the others around the fire in front of the shed. They were refugees from Wallachia who had been living here for a month. They worked for the farmers, foraged through the harvested fields again and again, gleaned corn, and collected raspberries and mushrooms and herbs which they sold as far away as Regensburg. The woman lent them a pot and Billie fried a piece of bacon, sliced potatoes into it, and gave each of them a piece of bread. The refugees gave them a serving of potato and nettle soup.

After the meal they withdrew to their compartment. Tilli had already fallen asleep by the fire. They wrapped her in Billie's blanket and laid her on a straw mattress.

They crept under their potato sacks, curled up, and

wrapped the sacks around them. They lay awake for a long time before they finally fell asleep.

Thundering steps, which shook the floorboards, woke them up.

It was damp and cold, and they were freezing under the thin sacks. When they saw the refugees leaving the bowling lane one after another, they got up, too. The woman said they could come along to dig potatoes. There were still two fields close by which had been harvested just the day before, and they would probably be able to find something.

They left Tilli, who was still asleep, in the care of a ten-year-old girl who promised to look after her.

A cold drizzle spattered in their faces as they turned onto the road. They draped the potato sacks round their shoulders, but it did not help much. They were soaked to the skin before they reached the field. A dozen people who had gotten up earlier were already digging there. And a field guard with a shepherd dog was standing next to them because the neighboring field had not yet been harvested.

They grubbed with their hands through the torn-up furrows. The earth was cold under their feet, and wet and heavy and sticky. It was difficult to find the tubers in the gluey dirt. The farmers had not left much. And the field guard did not take his eyes off them.

At midday they ate their bread, which had become wet and slimy and slithered between their teeth. Then they set to work again with tough stubbornness. They dug their fingers into the soil and crumbled up the clods. In the worst days of the harvest they had not worked half as hard at the farmer's.

Despite that, they had not even succeeded in filling half a sack by the time it got dark and the field guard chased them from the field. The refugees had given up hours earlier.

They were drained and exhausted when they got back. They washed at the pump. Billie paid another ten marks for the night, and cooked potato soup with the refugee women in the inn kitchen.

They ate silently in the dark in their compartment behind the door to the shed, passing around Billie's mess tin.

They crept under their potato sacks again. They had frozen all day long. They were still freezing. They lay awake. The only one to fall asleep quickly was Tilli. She was warm in Billie's blanket.

Max sat up. "This is senseless," he said. "We're not getting anywhere like this." His voice sounded strangely deep, as though it had broken, unnoticed. "We might just as well go back to the farmer. There, at least, we did not have to pay for staying the night."

No one said a word. There was no argument to be made.

"I've got relatives in Weissenbach," said Adolf abruptly. He spoke so quietly that they could hardly understand him. "That's near Hof; perhaps we could go there." They could hear him swallow.

"Where is it?" Peter asked incredulously.

"Near Hof," repeated Adolf.

They all knew where Hof was. They had to cross the border by Hof. It was right on their route.

"Man, you're crazy!" said Peter. "Why didn't you tell us before?"

"I was only there once," said Adolf. "Before the war." It sounded like an apology. He had never said anything about these relatives. Not when they had traveled with the two soldiers, nor in the church with the priest. Not even on the farm. He had wanted to stay with the others, go with them to Berlin. He was afraid they would dump him if he said anything.

Now he had said it. His relatives would not let him go on once he was there. He knew that. He swallowed hard. He felt like crying.

They were sitting at a table in the inn garden, in front of the bowling lane shed, and had spread out the map. Peter ran his finger down the line along the left edge of the map. The towns along the line were circled with wet indelible pencil: Weiden, Marktredwitz, Selb, Hof. Peter now drew another circle on the map right underneath Hof. That was where Weissenbach lay.

Hof was a good hundred miles away. A few miles less to Weissenbach. If they only covered fifteen miles a day, they could make it within a week. They had to make it.

They left about nine and walked without stopping until midday. That was where they found the first signpost: WEIDEN 26 MILES. They stopped and cooked some potatoes in a Yank can that Billie had picked up on the side of the road. Almost a quarter of their stock of potatoes went for this one meal; they would have to start begging again.

As they continued on their way, they made the rounds of all the farms to the right and to the left of the road, taking turns to beg. One would run to the farmhouse while the others waited on the road.

Tilli brought two eggs back from the first farm and their hopes were raised, but they got nothing after that. The two eggs were the only booty right through till evening.

Then Billie traded her cardigan for five eggs and half a loaf of bread. When it was getting dark, and they were about to give up and look for a place to spend the night, Max went off one more time.

The farm he wanted to try lay above the road at the edge of a wood at least two hundred yards away. A narrow dirt road edged with hawthorn led up to it. There was not a soul in sight at the farm or in the fields around.

They sat down in the ditch and watched Max. They saw him knock on the door and wait. No one seemed to answer. He stood irresolutely for a moment and then ran along the outside of the courtyard wall toward a small garden surrounded by a picket fence. He sidled along the fence, looked over his shoulder, and suddenly climbed over.

"He's gone crazy!" said Billie, horrified. "In broad daylight!" They stared at the fence behind which Max had disappeared, saw the farmer come out of the farmhouse door and, stooping low, run toward the garden. He moved fast and had almost reached the fence. He was much too close for them to warn Max.

At last Max started to climb over the fence. It took a torturingly long time before he was over it, before he started to run. He headed for the stubble field and raced across it. The farmer was right behind him. He raised his whip and lashed out. They could not see whether he had hit Max, but the effort had put the farmer off stride and he stumbled. The distance between them increased. Max did not slow down — he ran like a hare.

The farmer slowed down, stopped, and raised his whip threateningly. Then he bent down for something which he threw at Max before turning back.

Max toppled over like a stiff-legged doll, fell on his face in midstep without using his hands to break his fall, slid on his stomach along the ground until he came to a stop. The farmer trudged back to the farm without turning round. Max lay motionless in the field.

Billie was the first to jump up and run across the field. Her knapsack bounced against her back. Max still did not move. He lay on his stomach, his face in the mud. She sat down next to him and called: "Max, Max! What's wrong?"

He did not move. There was blood on the back of his head. It oozed out between the hair in thick drops.

The other three came across the field and sat down next to Max. He groaned suddenly, pulled his arms under his body and tried to lift his head.

"Max!" Billie whispered, "Max!" He slowly turned his head one way, then the other, pushed himself up on his arms and tried to get up. Blood was running down his forehead and from his nose. His nose was hurt, too; it looked as though it had been squashed in. Blood was running down his chin and dripping onto his shirt.

Billie rummaged through her knapsack with trembling hands. She pulled out an undershirt, tore it into strips, and wiped the blood from Max's forehead and chin. He resisted weakly, groaning, and sat there leaning on his arms. He shut his eyes tightly, holding his head at a strange angle as if he could bear the pain only in this rigid, twisted position.

"Max, can you hear me?" asked Billie. She felt terribly helpless. What could she do? How could she help him? All she could do was dab away some blood. He needed a doctor. He desperately had to get to a doctor. They had to get him down to the road and stop a car.

Max moved his lips. His eyelids twitched, and he blinked and swallowed and ran his tongue across his lips. The taste of blood seemed to surprise him. His eyes suddenly cleared, and he brought his hand up to his head, his nose. He grimaced with pain. "What happened?" he asked unsteadily.

"The farmer hit you with a stone," said Billie. Max closed his eyes. The effort it took him to think was mirrored in his face. It looked as though he had laboriously to feel his way back to his memories, as though what had happened had just left very blurred traces in his memory.

"You've got to get to a doctor," said Billie. Max shook his head. He tried to get up and swayed to his feet. Billie held his arm. "Sit down again; we can carry you," she said, almost imploring. He shook her hand off, placed one foot unsteadily forward, and dragged the other one up to it. His knees buckled, but he made a desperate effort to hold himself erect, and shuffled along, step by step. "Let me help you," said Billie.

They walked back to the road across the fields. Max in the middle, his legs stiff, his arms around Billie's and Peter's shoulders. The two little ones followed with Billie's luggage and the potato sack in which they had their food.

At the edge of the road they propped Max up against a tree. He kept his eyes closed. The cut on the back of his head was still bleeding and his nose was swelling.

They waited for a car. Slowly it got darker, and the forest threw dark shadows that spread across the meadows and fields. No car came, no cyclist, nothing. The road was deserted.

A light went on in the farmhouse at the edge of the wood, two shining yellow squares of windows in the black wall of the house. Billie wanted to walk over there and threaten to report the farmer if he did not help her. Peter and Adolf held her back. It was no use, they knew. At night all farms were locked and bolted; no one would open the door. If a child knocked, the farmers were twice as careful. There had been gangs that had sent children ahead, gangs that had concentrated on isolated farms.

At last a car appeared and came down the hill behind them. Short, dim, flickering cones of light, a quietly gurgling engine that spluttered into a roar again when the car left the downhill stretch behind. It was a German.

Billie and Peter stood next to each other on the road, waving, their arms spread wide, directly in the light from the headlamps. The car came straight at them. Its horn blared, but it did not slow down. Peter jumped to one side, the car rattled past, and a man shouted something out of the window. They watched the red lights disappear quickly into the darkness.

They continued to wait. It became so dark that not even the contours of the trees along the road were silhouetted against the black of the sky. Then three cars came along.

Judging by the noise of the engines, they had to be American trucks. They came racing down the hill at such hellish speed that none of them dared stand on the road. They waved at them from the side, shut their eyes against the dazzling brightness of the headlamps, and waved timidly. In the twinkling of an eye the trucks were next to them. The current of air almost snatched their feet from under them. They thundered by, leaving only darkness behind, which seemed even blacker than before.

"It's no use at night," said Max. "No one ever stops." His voice sounded as if he had a cold. They heard him stand up.

"But you can't walk!" said Billie. "It's senseless!"

"We can't stay here, either," said Max. "That's just as senseless."

They started off. Billie and Peter again took Max into the middle, pulling him along with them, holding him upright. Max's feet dragged along behind, his weight rested on their shoulders. He could hardly move his legs anymore. It was useless. They could not carry him; he was simply too heavy. They could not drag him for miles down the road.

Adolf stopped suddenly. "Something's coming!" he said. They listened into the darkness. They heard the clop of hooves ahead, a single horse, trotting toward them on the road. There was no accompanying noise of cartwheels; it had to be a rider on a horse.

They stood in the middle of the road and waited till the horse reached them. There was a cart, after all, one with rubber tires.

Billie called, "Hello, please can you help us?"

They could not see anything, but they heard the horse stop. "What's the matter?" asked a man's voice.

"One of us has cracked his head open," said Billie. "Someone threw a stone at him." And for fear that the man would drive on, she hastily added: "You can see for yourself if you don't believe me!" She struck a match, holding the flame so it revealed Max's head. The wet blood in the hair at the back of his head and on the nape of his neck glistened. The glow from the match flame made it look worse than it had in daylight.

"He's got to get to a doctor!" said the man. "But there's no doctor around here."

"Maybe he's got a fractured skull!" said Billie.

"The nearest doctor is in Schwandorf," said the man. "You must be crazy; that's almost an hour away!"

"His nose is broken, too," said Billie. "He was unconscious for two hours. We thought he was dead!"

The man was silent. They could hear only the horse snorting softly and pawing the asphalt on the road with its hoof.

"Why didn't you stop a car, you idiots!" growled the man. They thought he would drive on, but then they heard him jump down from the driver's box. "I need some light," he said. When Billie struck a match he grasped Max under his shoulders and lifted him onto the cart. Then he helped the others up, too, and said, "Make sure he doesn't hit his head!" He turned on the road and drove the horse to a fast trot.

A short while later they turned off the asphalt road onto a gravel path so bumpy that it shook them around on the floor of the cart. They could not sit anymore, but had to squat on their heels. Billie and Peter held tightly to the side with one hand, and tried to keep Max balanced with the other.

They could see nothing of the road. Impenetrable darkness. Only the horse seemed to see where it was going.

Half an eternity later lights appeared ahead of them, and the outlines of houses became visible. It had turned just a shade lighter. The cloud cover had broken open, and they could see the stars above them. The town they were traveling toward seemed to be a large one. The slim silhouette of a factory chimney was etched against the dark sky.

The cart stopped suddenly and the man said, "I can't go any farther. There's a curfew and that's too risky for me."

He lifted Max from the cart and Billie held out five cigarettes to him. At first he did not want to accept them, but then he took them anyway. Now, for the first time they saw that it was not a man, but a boy, and that he was lame in one leg. They watched him as he drove away.

Max could hardly stand. Peter and Billie dragged him along for a while, then Peter took him on his back and Billie ran ahead to get help.

The first houses were dark, but there was a light on in the fourth. When Billie knocked on the door a window opened above and a woman looked down and asked what the matter was.

"One of us is hurt!" Billie called to her. The woman came down and helped them bring Max into the house.

His nose was very swollen and was turning blue-red, and his whole face was smeared with blood, with thick crusts of blood on his throat and the nape of his neck. It was still oozing bright red from the cut on the back of his head, and dripping from the hair onto his shirt. The whole back of his shirt was soaked in blood.

In the hallway two old men were lying on camp beds, and they looked at Max's head wound. A woman came down the stairs, followed by three girls. All agreed that Max should go straight to the hospital, and the woman who had helped them got a bicycle from the cellar and said she would try to get the Yanks.

A quarter of an hour later they heard a jeep pull up in front of the house and two MPs followed the woman inside, picked Max up, and drove off with him. The woman said they would take him to the hospital and bring them news the following day.

In the meantime the hall had filled with people. Some were looking out of adjacent rooms, some were sitting on the stairs — men, women and children, and old grannies with long, thin, yellow-white hair, wrapped in black shawls, and wearing threadbare dressing gowns.

The woman took a bunch of keys from a hook behind the door, pushed Billie and the other three outside, and walked along the street with them into the town. The moon had come out and lit their way. They could now clearly make out the town lying before them, and the houses on both sides of the street that were dark as though they were uninhabited. They passed a factory that was like an immense black box without a roof. It was burned out, caved in at one corner, and had high, narrow, empty windows. A high picket fence adjoined the trellis fence that closed off the factory grounds. Behind the picket fence were gardens with little houses. They looked like summerhouses.

The woman stopped in front of a gate in the picket fence, unlocked it, and led them along a narrow gravel path. It, too, was bordered by high picket fences with barbed wire on top and wooden doors, barred and bolted with heavy locks. She stopped by the third door, unlocked it, and pushed back the bolt. The door squeaked as she pulled it open, and a dog began to bark nearby, deep and hoarse. A man's voice called, "Who's there?" And the woman called back: "It's me, Mr. Knief! I have to put up a couple of children here, just so you know!"

The woman lit a candle and showed them the inside of the wooden shed. It was stacked full of gardening tools and large boxes and baskets and rolls of wire. Opposite the door was a tall white kitchen cupboard with a lot of shelves with chicken wire nailed across them. Rabbits were sitting on the shelves, their eyes gleaming red in the light from the candle. The back part of the shed was separated from the front by a waist-high wooden partition, and was stuffed full of hay. The woman said they should sleep there. She gave Billie the keys and insisted that she must always keep the gate and the garden door locked. She said she would not come until the following evening, and if they wanted to, they could make themselves useful in the garden during the day by turning over the two rear beds, and picking sorrel and dandelions for the rabbits.

She waited outside on the path and did not leave until Billie had locked the door. She seemed to be very anxious about her little garden.

They sat down in front of the shed and put the candle on the threshold. Peter gave each of them a slice of bread and they chewed on it solemnly. It was the last of the bread.

Nothing moved in the other gardens. Not a sound could be heard except from time to time the plaintive howl of a dog in the distance, answered by another, even farther away.

They were still ravenously hungry after just one slice of bread, but they did not dare make a fire to cook the potatoes. They would simply have to sleep away their hunger.

Peter and Adolf crawled into the hay and Billie dug a hole for Tilli next to them, covered the little girl and was just about to close the door when she heard a cry from the street, so quiet and piteous that at first she thought it must be a kitten mewing. But it was a woman calling; she could hear it clearly now.

She still had the burning candle in her hand and quietly pulled the door closed.

"There's someone on the street, a woman," she whispered to the others. Adolf and Peter sat up and listened, holding their breath. Again the piteous cry, despairing and without hope.

"What does she want?" Adolf asked in a whisper.

Billie shrugged her shoulders. "I don't know."

Adolf slid over the wooden partition and stood next to Billie, listening. Everything was now quiet. Maybe the woman had moved on. They waited. Abruptly Billie came to a decision and opened the door. She held the candle high and turned toward the street. "Yes?" she called quietly.

The woman was still there. "Please can you help me?" they heard her call. They could hardly understand her.

Billie looked for the key in her pocket. "We have to unlock the door first," she called back. Her hands trembled as she put the key in the lock and pushed back the bolt. She was afraid that the big dog could be running loose on the garden paths. She was afraid the woman could have seen that they were alone and was just putting on an act. She was afraid that the woman who had helped them would be angry if they let someone in. She blew out the candle, and crept toward the gate keeping close to the fence.

The woman was standing outside, leaning against the picket fence, clutching the crosspiece with both hands. She did not look as if she were putting on an act: she really seemed to be feeling terrible.

"Just a minute," said Billie. "I have to unlock this, too." She carefully opened the door. The woman was still holding on tight. "My name is Sophie; I'm sorry but I don't feel very well," she said. Billie took her arm. "My legs suddenly gave way. Then I saw your light. All the houses were dark already." Her hand felt hot. Billie led her along the gravel path.

"You've got a fever," said Billie.

The woman shrugged her shoulders slightly. "I don't know. For three days I haven't been able to keep anything down."

Billie said: "I know all about that. It's dysentery. I had it, too."

When they reached the shed, the woman suddenly collapsed and started to shiver so badly that her teeth chattered.

Billie lit the candle, pulled the knapsack from the woman's shoulders, put the blanket around her, and gave Peter the key so he could lock up again. Then she got her canteen and a small tin box in which she still had a couple of Yank cookies. She poured some water down Sophie's throat and gave her the cookies, insisting that she eat them. Then she washed her face with a wet handkerchief.

In the candlelight Sophie was ghostly pale, shivering under the blanket. A narrow face with feverish, glinting eyes, and cheeks so sunken that the cheekbones stood out sharply. The scarf around her head made her look old at first, but she was still young, maybe around twenty-five.

Adolf and Billie half carried her into the shed.

They had to make her a bed. She had to lie down, to stay warm, and she needed a bucket if she had dysentery. Oh, good heavens! She could not be in here with the boys if she had to use the bucket.

Billie pulled Peter and Adolf outside. "There's not enough room for all of us in here," she said. "But I noticed there's a wagon at the other end of the garden." She led the boys to it. There was a door in the front of the wagon, with three steps. But the door was locked.

"The key is sure to be around somewhere," said Peter eagerly. "We've got a summerhouse at home, too. We always have a key there for safety's sake." He felt the tires, the bars of the frame, the piles of wood on which the wagon was resting. He lifted Adolf onto his shoulders so he could get at the channel between the roof and the walls. Billie held the candle for them.

They found the key in a space on the underside of the first step. "Bad hiding place," said Peter disdainfully and unlocked and opened the door. He sniffed the air and said, "There's a goat in here!" And at that very moment the goat began to bleat.

Billie brought the light into the wagon. The goat was standing just behind the door at the front, tied with a rope. It was a young animal, brown and shaggy. It did not really fit into the clean neatness of the wagon. Everything seemed to have its own place: tools, garden implements, bee hives, work clothes. Each object had its own hook, its own shelf in the plywood racks on the walls. A folding bed was built into the back wall, and a folding table and folding chairs stood under a hanging lamp. They could put the woman in here.

They took the goat out and tied it to a tree in front of the wagon. Then they brought Sophie over and laid her down on the bed. The three of them had to carry her; she had no strength left to walk. Billie stayed with her until she fell asleep. It was after midnight when she herself lay down to sleep in the shed.

When Billie awoke, Tilli's place was empty but the two boys were still asleep in the other corner. Billie climbed quietly over the wooden partition, and combed the hay out of her hair and from her clothes with her fingers. She felt tired and drained, and her throat was so dry and scratchy she was forced to cough. It hurt when she coughed.

Outside the sun was shining brightly and the bushes and beanstalks glowed a rich green, the trees stretched out shimmering green twigs, and along the fences the greenery twined and ran rampant. At night they had just seen black fences everywhere and locked doors and barbed wire. Now the garden looked like a large, friendly, green room.

Tilli was sitting next to the wagon at the other end of the garden, feeding carrots to the goat. Billie was suddenly wide awake. She ran to her, and snatched the carrots from her hand. "Have you gone crazy!" she shouted. "You can't just pull things out of the ground here!"

Tilli hung her head and watched out of the corner of her eye as Billie stuffed the carrots back into the bed from which she had just pulled them.

Peter and Adolf went into town in the afternoon. They took money and cigarettes with them. They had to get something to eat, and the woman in the wagon obviously needed medicine. Their supply of potatoes would not last for more than another two days, and the way Max had looked, it would be some time before they could go on.

They soon found the market place. The houses were still standing there. Not a single one had been destroyed, and most of them had beautifully curved and stepped gables. A church towered opposite. They passed an inn occupied by Yanks. A sentry wearing white leather straps and belts was standing in front of it. There was a pharmacy two houses farther on. They went inside and asked about medicine for dysentery. The saleslady said she only had charcoal tablets for diarrhea, but they would not help much. They would have to go to the doctor anyway, if the person had dysentery. They bought the charcoal tablets and asked about a doctor. The saleslady pointed to a large gabled house at the other end of the market place, and said that it was the hospital. They should be able to get more information there.

They went over to the house. It looked like a department store, but the shop windows were boarded over, and a Red Cross flag was hanging from the top floor. The word

HOSPITAL was written above the door, and under it was an OFF LIMITS sign.

The door opened into a kind of waiting room — a long, narrow hallway with temporary walls of plywood boards held together by a wooden frame. In the back wall was a swinging door and next to it a small window over which was written ADMISSION.

They joined the line in front of the small window. A young Red Cross nurse in a blue-and-white-striped uniform was sitting behind it. When they finally reached her they told her their story. But the nurse did not let them finish. She said they were in a hospital and if the woman really had dysentery, they would have to go to a general practitioner. He could send her to the hospital if necessary. Unfortunately she could not give them more information. She seemed to be genuinely sorry. She looked as if she had dysentery herself.

They stood irresolutely outside the front door, then turned into a narrow cobbled alley, wedged between tall, gloomy, gray-plastered houses. A revolting smell of urine and wet, charred wood crept into their noses. A group of men wearing long coats stood in a doorway, passing around a cigarette.

Adolf and Peter went farther down the alley. It became lighter. Suddenly they had a clear view across the valley and town which spread out for several hundred yards toward a river. Not a single house blocked their view. Everything had been leveled, razed to the ground. Just ruins of houses and beyond them ruins of a railroad station, ruins of trains, ruins of steam engines. Crushed flat, as though a booted giant had trampled it.

They followed one of the narrow paths and climbed down into another trench. People were standing around in small groups with suitcases and knapsacks. They were talking in murmurs, glancing around furtively; they disappeared in twos and threes behind waist-high stumps of walls, communicated with each other with sparing gestures, a shake of the head, a whispered question; moved around continually, wandered from group to group, peering round watchfully like crows on a rubbish dump. Among them were Yanks, their heads held high, strutting around with measured tread, followed by children and teenagers. Wherever the Yanks went, the people crowded around, the murmuring grew louder, the suitcases were opened, the briefcases, the baskets. Curious people gathered, craning their necks. Peter and Adolf also pushed their way among them, quickly lost their shyness, listened to the offers. Silverware, Meissen porcelain, gold Party badges, Zeiss 7×50 binoculars. Prewar goods, first-class quality. How much? What's the price? Dollar, whiskey, Chesterfield! Two packs? Two cartons! Chewing, nose-wrinkling, headshaking. Too much!

A path immediately opened up to make way for the Yanks, the curious people made themselves scarce, and those left behind hunched their shoulders, moved close together again, wandered on, whispered to each other, exhibited their goods which they were carrying hidden under their coats. Razor blades, light bulbs, crosscut saws, knives from Solingen, salami, pure coffee, half a pound of butter, hundred marks, kilo flour, eighty marks. Who'll exchange leather for lighter flints? Tobacco cutter for a bicycle tube?

Outrageous prices! Peter's mouth was permanently open.

He ran around excitedly, snuffling like a hunting dog. They could not do much with the little money they had. But he had the cigarettes in his pocket, thirteen Chesterfields. They could get something for that — cigarettes were as good as cash. He could bargain with them; he was not there empty-handed like many others who were merely roaming around, gaping. One man offered him a small can of meat for ten Yank cigarettes. For eight, a three-pound loaf of black bread. Adolf wanted to take the bread, but Peter wanted to check around some more. Maybe there would be better offers. Chocolate, sugar, dried milk. He first had to have an idea of the prices before he bought anything, compare the offers, bargain, haggle. There were more dealers farther down toward the ruins of the railroad station.

They came out onto a wide asphalt street that led along the railroad premises. The sidewalk was buried under piles of rubble. Black, charred tree trunks towered among them, the dead branches reaching for the sky. The fires of hell must have burned here.

Adolf again urged that they should set off for home. They had promised Billie that they would not stay away too long. But Peter was not ready to turn back yet. The rubble field between the station and the market place stretched far on both sides, no-man's-land, which seemed to promise adventure.

Close to them by the side of the road someone was sitting on a bicycle, leaning against one of the black tree trunks. He had both his feet up on the handlebars, his arms on his knees. He was watching them through half-closed eyes, and asked superciliously: "You lookin' for somethin'?"

Peter glanced up at him. The boy was not much bigger than he was, also not much older. Two, three years at most. Knickerbockers, suit jacket, glasses on his nose, straggly white-blond hair brushed straight back. He did not look like anything special.

"D'you have anything to sell?" he asked back.

"Depends," answered the boy. He took his feet off the handlebars, pulled a pack of cigarettes out of his jacket pocket, and offered one to Peter.

"I've got some myself," said Peter.

The boy shrugged his shoulders and lit a cigarette, inhaling deeply. Slowly he blew the smoke out. "You live here?" he asked.

Peter considered whether he should answer. The boy did not seem to be as bad as he had looked to begin with. He shook his head.

"Where d'you come from then?" asked the boy.

"Berlin," said Peter. And casually he added, "We're just passing through."

"Alone?" asked the boy, and when Peter nodded, he got off the bike and slowly walked toward him, shook another cigarette out of the pack, and held it out. "You can take one now," he said, "or don't you smoke?" Peter put the cigarette in his mouth and let the boy light it for him. He drew the smoke in carefully, held it in his mouth, breathed through his nose, and blew the smoke out again.

Adolf watched him uneasily and when the boy offered him one, too, he vigorously shook his head. He knew for sure that Peter had never smoked in his life before, and he did not like the way he was standing there now, holding the cigarette clamped casually between his fingers.

"My name's Karl," said the boy and offered his hand, a soft hand.

The cigarette smoke got into Peter's nose and he cleared his throat loudly in order to suppress a cough. "What're you selling?" he asked with studied casualness.

The boy slapped the saddle of his bicycle with his open hand and said with a shrug of his shoulders: "All sorts of things."

"The bicycle, too?" asked Peter.

"Yes," said the boy. He screwed up his eyes as though he were thinking hard about something, opened them again, and looked past Peter. His eyes were unnaturally large behind the glasses. Peter thought he looked just like a professor at some university.

"D'you want to make a deal?" the professor asked.

"Depends," said Peter. He noticed Adolf's horrified expression, but did not bother about it. The kid was always afraid. "What'll cost me?" he asked.

"Half a pack, whole pack," said the boy while he flicked the glowing end from the cigarette and carefully stowed away the butt. "Maybe more." And when Peter hesitated, the professor twisted his mouth into an encouraging smile. "Okay?" he asked.

10

The Black Market

The three of them rode along on the bike, Adolf on the crossbar, Peter on the luggage rack behind. They rode out of the town and along the riverbank on a narrow path to a place where the other boy said Peter had to do him a favor. The current had undermined the bank. The water was dark brown, like liquid manure.

Peter looked doubtfully at the froth floating past below him. "How deep is it?" he asked uncertainly. "Six feet, something like that," said the boy. With a slight shrug of his shoulders he added, "You don't have to do it, if you don't have the guts."

Peter began to unbutton his shirt. "Have you ever been down there?" he asked.

"No," said the boy. "I can't because of my glasses."

Peter stripped to his underpants and stretched a foot into

the water. It was cold. He slid in carefully, digging his fingers into the earth so that the current would not sweep him away. Then he took a deep breath, pushed off and dived under, head first, kicking his feet. He opened his eyes for a second but could not see anything in the brown muck. He reached the bottom, which felt slimy. The current carried him along fast, and his hands slid over a bottle, over branches and stones. He had to make a great effort to stay under. Then he ran out of breath. He surfaced some way downstream, climbed onto the bank, ran back, jackknifed in again. He let the current carry him along close to the bottom, dug into the mud with both hands, his fingers spread wide. Again he kept being pushed upward, he paddled wildly, kicking his legs, went down one more time, felt something sharp in his hand and grabbed it. As he surfaced again, he knew he had discovered something. He felt it with his fingers. It was a close-combat medal.

He forced himself to hide his joy from the others, forced himself to look indifferent as he threw the small decoration to the boy. "Not bad for a start," said the boy.

Peter plunged into the water again. He was feeling much more confident now. The boy had said that Knight's Crosses and Iron Crosses had been thrown into the river here, masses of decorations and medals. And he had said that the Yanks would pay a carton of cigarettes for a Knight's Cross. Two hundred cigarettes! If they went fifty-fifty, that was a hundred cigarettes for him. He groped his way through the mud holding his breath till his ears buzzed, surfaced, jumped back in, combed through the mud with his fingers. He swam down the same stretch at least a dozen times until his teeth were chattering with cold. The only other thing he found was a medal awarded to wounded soldiers.

The boy pulled his pack of cigarettes out of his pocket and placed ten cigarettes in Peter's hand. "Unfortunately, it's not worth more," he said. "I can get rid of the close-combat medal, but the others are a dime a dozen."

They ran along the path on the bank back to the road. Peter took the bicycle for a ride. Standing on the pedals, bent low over the handlebars, he raced between the mounds of rubble, the mudguards clattering. He had not ridden a bike for ages.

"How much does a bike like this cost?" he asked when he returned. The professor nodded and drawled, "I may be able to get you one." It sounded as though getting hold of a bike were the easiest thing in the world for him. But he did not say anything more, although Peter was eagerly waiting for an explanation.

The professor accompanied Peter and Adolf to the bombed alley where the black marketeers were, and helped them buy some bread. It was bad, black bread, soggy and as heavy as a rock, with a finger-thick, sticky, gooey layer at the bottom, potato-flour bread, maybe there was sawdust in it, too. But it cost only five cigarettes. They bought five eggs to go with it and set off for home. When they were saying goodbye, the boy told them he would be at the corner by the station next day at three, and they could come by if they did not have anything better to do.

Peter watched him ride away until Adolf tugged at his sleeve.

"Surely you don't believe that he's going to get you a bike," said Adolf.

Peter stared at him in surprise. He suddenly realized that the kid had hardly said a word the whole time. Something obviously was bothering him. Why was he making a fuss? "What do you know!" Peter said with annoyance and shook Adolf's hand off.

He decided to go alone next time. The little boy just got in his way.

It was getting dark by the time they got back to the garden. The gate to the street was locked and they had to call Billie to let them in. She was angry that they were so late, but her mood improved when they unpacked. They sat in front of the shed and ate potatoes with parsley. Each one also got a slice of bread and half an egg. Billie took the other three eggs over to Sophie. She maintained that you had to eat plenty of protein if you had dysentery, and no one dared contradict her, though Peter grumbled that it was a waste because the eggs would just go straight through the woman. But he did not say that until Billie was in the wagon and could not hear him.

Then, without warning, a strange woman appeared at the garden door. She was wearing a light gabardine coat, silk stockings, high-heeled shoes, and a soft felt hat with the brim turned down over her forehead. They did not recognize her until she spoke. It was the woman who had taken them in.

She was in a hurry and just said that Max had a concussion and a broken nose. He would be released in two days.

After that he would still need several days of rest, but they should not worry. She did not mind if they went on living in her garden, just as long as they kept it in order and looked after the rabbits. Before she left she told them where they could find Max. He was in the hospital where Adolf and Peter had been that afternoon.

The next day all four of them left for town early. They had to wait in the market place for two hours before they were allowed into the hospital. Max was lying on the first floor in a large room that held forty camp beds, side by side. All of them were occupied. They had to search before they found him. He had adhesive tape across his nose, and a white bandage around his head. His face was almost as white as the bandage. The nurse said they could pick him up the following evening, but he had to lie quietly till then.

Peter stayed in town when the other three started for home. He had been afraid that Adolf would stick with him, and had pondered for a long time how he could shake him off. But he did not need the excuse he had made up, after all. The kid had not wanted to stay with him.

Peter headed for the railroad station, then roamed through the rubble field. It was only eleven o'clock and there were not many dealers around. He began to get bored. When a woman with a large basket asked him to help her carry it, and promised in return to lead him to a monastery where there was free food, he went with her.

The monastery was on a hill overlooking the town. A monk gave him a portion of bean soup which he sipped from the plate because he did not have a spoon. Though he was still hungry, he did feel better after he had eaten. Earlier, when he had been climbing up the hill with the woman's heavy basket, he had been so hungry that he had become dizzy. He slowly walked back into the town and got to the meeting place a quarter of an hour early. He sat down on a smashed wall and waited.

He took the half-smoked cigarette out of the pack and placed it between his lips. As soon as he saw Karl approaching on his bicycle, he lit it. They nodded to each other like old friends, and Karl also lit a cigarette and casually asked between puffs: "You doin' anything this evening?"

Peter shook his head.

"Could be late," said Karl.

"So what!" said Peter, "I don't report to anyone. My friend is in the hospital and the others don't count." He tried to seem as indifferent as possible.

Karl pulled out a piece of gum and gave half to Peter. "Let's go," he said, and got on his bicycle. Karl rode down the street and Peter walked next to him. After the underpass they turned onto a rubble path that ran alongside the railroad tracks, and then into a road which led to the river through the middle of the rubble field. Before they reached the river Karl turned into a yard surrounded by high brick walls.

"You wanted a bicycle, didn't you?" said Karl. Peter nodded expectantly.

"Have you ever swiped a bike?" asked Karl.

Peter looked at him skeptically and hesitantly shook his head. Karl chewed for a long while on his gum, chewing with his mouth open.

"Okay, then listen," he said. "If you want to swipe a bike you first have to get the lock open. Then you have to take off with it. Third, you have to change it, so's no one'll recognize it. Understand?"

Peter nodded.

"Okay," Karl went on. "I'll take care of the locks. A guy with a workshop will repaint it. If you want to do the other, you can come in with us."

Peter was much too excited to answer right away. He chewed his gum hastily and almost choked in his desperate effort not to show his excitement. He had always been upset by the fact that he lost his composure so easily. He would have loved to be cool, callous, and hardened. But his feelings ran away with him every time. He had to forcibly pull himself together.

"And what do I get for it?" he asked. His voice sounded husky and he cleared his throat loudly so Karl would not notice.

"Every fifth bike belongs to you," said Karl, chewing indifferently.

Peter's thoughts turned somersaults. The whole town was full of bicycles. That morning the market place had teemed with cyclists. If they stole ten bikes, that would be two for him. And if they stole twenty, he'd have four. Four bikes! They could ride to Berlin on them. And then he could sell three of them. That would be a tremendous deal.

"Okay," he said quickly.

Karl pursed his lips, spat the chewing gum into the river, and crossed the road to the gate. "Remember this place," he said as he pulled the bike from behind the gate. "You bring the bikes here and leave them. Got it?"

"Got it!" said Peter. He felt the blood pulsing in his temples. No time to think. The fun had begun. He was in it now. He hurried to catch up with Karl who was pushing the bike along the towpath.

"If someone's chasing you, throw the bike behind the gate and scram through the ruins," said Karl. "You've got until evening to look around the place. You've got to know it like the back of your hand. Hiding places, paths, cellars. You've got to know it all. Got it?"

"Got it!" said Peter.

They turned into the road along which they had come. As they walked past the yard gate Karl said: "You can ride around the outside, or through the yard. If someone's chasing you, you go through the yard. You have to know the paths, every corner, every pothole. Remember you'll be riding without lights at night. Got it?"

"Got it!" said Peter.

They walked alongside the railroad tracks, through the underpass, then straight on toward the church and the market place. "That's the way you come," said Karl. "All at night, without lights. There's no streetlights. There's just a lamp in the market place and in the underpass."

"Got it!" said Peter.

They crossed the market place and turned into an alley that again led down to the railroad. Karl got onto the bike and let Peter sit on the back, and rode down the alley to a corner house, its upper floors burned out.

He rode through the gate into the backyard. Two jeeps were standing there and a few German cars with Yankee numbers. A soldier with a girl was standing in front of the door to the house. And children were crowding around.

Karl got off the bike. "I've still got some business to settle here. In the meantime you can take a look at the route so you'll know it by evening. Be back here at eight. Eight on the dot. Got it?"

Peter nodded. He was a bit disappointed. Laughter and shouting and loud American music were coming from the cellar window. There was something going on in there. He would have liked to stay with Karl, but Karl made no move to take Peter along.

Peter slunk away from the yard, walked back to the market place and down the road to the underpass and to the river. Little by little he forgot his disappointment and threw himself into his task with growing zeal.

By the time he returned to the yard around eight, he knew every foot of the road. He knew how he had to take the bend after the underpass so that he would not skid on the dust from the rubble. He had found a bombed cellar with two exits in which he could hide if necessary. He had walked along the route so often, he could have done it blindfolded.

He waited in the shadow of the house. Bright light streamed from the cellar windows. When he carefully peeked down he saw lounge chairs and armchairs around small round tables which had many bottles on them; a woman in a garish green turban hat, and two Yanks sprawled in the chairs. At the neighboring table were two women with peroxide-blond hair; a waiter in a black suit stood around stiffly. Two Yanks swayed in time to the music, and a bull-necked guy with short red hair sat with a girl in his lap.

He sat motionless and stared through the window. The longer he stared, the more everything blurred in a fog of smoke. The square of the cellar window suddenly seemed like a movie screen onto which was being projected a mysterious film with a plot he could not understand.

He jumped when he suddenly felt a hand on his shoulder. It took him a moment to realize that it was Karl standing next to him.

"Let's go," said Karl. And while he unchained his bike he added condescendingly: "I can take you down there sometime, if you want."

They walked up to the market place. The houses were dark. There were few lights burning behind the windows. The inn in which the Americans were sitting was the only place brightly lit. A jeep came out of the street next to the church, its headlights on high beam. An ox cart clattered over the cobblestones, and a few cyclists passed them.

They stopped near the church. A number of bicycles were chained to the bars of an iron grating next to the main door. Karl seemed to take no notice of them. They went on to the corner where the street entered the market place. There was a solitary bicycle chained to the metal post of a traffic sign. It was a new, shiny man's bike. The chain by which it was attached to the metal post had a padlock as large as a fist. It would be impossible to open it without tools. And Karl had no tools with him.

"You've got to get one thing straight," said Karl. "You

keep your trap shut! You don't tell a soul about this, not even your best friend. Got it?"

Peter nodded. "Got it!" he whispered hoarsely. "You can depend on it!"

They were standing in front of the traffic sign, and it seemed as if Karl was going to lean his bike next to the other one. He looked around calmly. There was no one in sight.

"Hold the chain so it won't rattle," he said quietly. Peter took hold of the chain which was wound around the crossbar of the bike. His fingers were stiff. He kept his eye on the square. Suddenly he saw Karl lift the upper part of the post. He pulled the chain away and Karl let the post down again, onto a pin in the lower part of the post. It slid down silently, as though greased, sat tight, as it had before — a solid metal post with a traffic sign on top.

"Scram!" Peter heard Karl's voice say. "Get going, man!" He had the bike in his hands, stood there paralyzed, saw Karl run off and swing up onto the saddle. Peter still stood motionless clenching his hands around the handlebars. Finally he started to run, then mounted the bike and started pedaling. He was sure that the shouting would start right away. Already he thought he could hear steps chasing him. He stood up in the pedals and raced down the street, the wind in his face. There was the underpass, and the yellow cone of light from the street lamp in it. He braked, rounded the bend, bent lower over the handlebars, and rode into the street leading to the river.

He had made it! He was safe; no one was behind him. And he had the bike. He let it coast and sat on the saddle which was so high that his feet could not reach the pedals.

The bicycle must have belonged to a giant. Now it belonged to him. To Karl and to him. He had stolen a bike. He had stolen a bike with Karl. A part of it belonged to him. The fifth would belong to him completely. And the tenth. And the fifteenth.

He pushed the bike under the gate by the wall, took a deep breath, stretched, and slowly walked across the road to the iron railing above the embankment. Just as he was about to sit down, the first shudder shot through him. He started to shiver, his hands shook, his teeth chattered. He desperately held on to the railing. He knew there was no sense in fighting it. He had to wait till it went away on its own — this shaking and shivering in which his fear, excitement and tension burned themselves out. He knew it well. He only hoped that Karl would not arrive at this moment. He must not see him like this.

He waited till the shivering subsided, sat down on the railing and kept a look-out for Karl. When Peter saw him coming along the towpath, he slowly went to meet him. He was not shivering any more.

It was almost midnight before Peter returned to the garden. It was too late to call the others. He would only have awakened the dog, and anyway, the garden gate was no obstacle to him. He climbed over it with ease. The way he was feeling, he could have climbed any fence.

The strong feeling was still with him the following morning. He took no notice of the fact that Billie and Adolf were watching him uneasily. He meaningfully shrugged his shoulders when they asked what he had been doing so late, put on a secretive and superior air, and casually counted out ten cigarettes into Adolf's hand.

Karl had given him a whole pack as a bonus for the bike, but why should he share everything with the others? He was being generous enough if he split it fifty-fifty. After all, it had been his deal. He had set it up. They were getting enough as it was. Let them dig in the garden and feed the rabbits and goat. He'd take care of them.

He lay in the sun all day long, just doing a few push-ups or kneebends from time to time to keep in shape. He also went for water. He could not expect Adolf to haul the heavy bucket; he might get a hernia.

Late in the afternoon all four set off to pick up Max. They waited in front of the hospital door till he came out. He stood on wobbly legs and blinked moodily into the sun hanging low between the gables of the houses. The head bandage had been replaced by a plaster which covered the bald spot on the back of his head. And there was a broad bluish bump on his nose. He seemed sullen and aloof.

Peter was glad when the others took Max between them and walked away with him. The way he looked, he was not up to much.

Peter stayed in the market place, loafed around, roamed around the church door, walked in ever smaller circles around the traffic sign. He had been thinking about the trick all day. He would copy it when he was back home in Berlin. He would make a profit out of it.

He leaned against the post and ran his fingers surreptitiously over the metal. You could hardly feel a thing. The post had been cleanly sawed through with a hacksaw. At an angle, so it would not twist round. He lifted it carefully about a finger's breadth. It was easy to lift. When he inspected the other traffic signs in the market place, he found two more posts sawed through the same way.

Peter waited impatiently for the time to pass. Long before eight he was at the meeting place and hung around the yard of the cellar bar.

Karl did not come until almost nine. Did not say hello, did not get off the bike, rode straight on. Peter had to run to keep up with him.

A bike was leaning against the post in front of the church, but it was a lady's bike, and when they came closer they saw that the chain was looped through the sprocket. They could unfasten it, but they could not ride away. There was nothing at either of the other posts in the market place.

"Shit!" said Karl. He was sitting on the saddle, keeping his balance with his toes. He smelled of beer and cigarette smoke, and had difficulty staying upright.

"We can wait, can't we?" said Peter hopefully.

"No sense in it," said Karl. His voice sounded as though his tongue were swollen.

"What about tomorrow?" asked Peter.

"Can't tomorrow. Got other plans," said Karl. Peter became uneasy. He had worked out that they would swipe two bikes this evening, and two more the following evening. He had hoped he would be able to take his first bike home at that time.

Karl surveyed him through half-closed eyes. "I've got something big planned for Friday," he said sluggishly. "You can be in on it if you want."

"What sort of thing?" asked Peter with renewed hope.

"I'll explain later," said Karl.

They made a date for Thursday evening in the yard of the cellar bar. "So long!" said Karl and rode away.

When Peter got up the following morning, Max and Adolf were gone. Billie said they had taken cigarettes to trade for ration cards and buy some bread. Peter did not wait for them to come back but took off for the town immediately. At noon he ate some soup in the monastery and then hung around the railroad station. He smoked a long butt which a Yank had thrown out of a jeep right at his feet, and managed to kill time till evening.

Karl was already waiting when he walked into the yard. He was talking to a Yank and resting his foot casually on the bumper of the jeep, chewing and smoking.

Peter stood in the farthest corner of the yard, not daring to draw attention to himself. He waited till the Yank had said goodbye to Karl and disappeared into the cellar.

Karl said "Hello!" when he saw him and shook his hand. He seemed to be in a good mood.

They made a round of the market place again. There was not a single bike leaning on any of the posts. They sat down on a stone bench against the church wall and watched the square. Karl rolled a cigarette, lit it, let Peter take a puff, and asked casually: "When're you planning to move on?"

"Why?" asked Peter, puzzled. "We don't know yet," he said, "it depends . . ." And then added hastily: "But I'll still be here for sure tomorrow."

Karl slowly blew the smoke out through his nose. "What about your friend, the one who was in hospital?" he asked.

Peter glanced up in surprise. He had once told Karl about Max. That had been right at the beginning of their friendship. "Why, what about him?" he asked back.

"You can bring him along tomorrow," said Karl.

Peter thought about it. He was not sure it would be a good idea. Max had changed somehow since he had been hit on the head with the stone. He had become dull, no longer the old Max. "I don't know whether he'd play along," he said hesitantly.

Karl straightened up, raising his eyebrows. "You don't know whether he'll play along?" he drawled.

"Man, d'you know how many would give their eyeteeth for me to let them join in? What're you thinking of! It's a tremendous deal I'm offering you! I'm not talking about a few measly cigarettes! This is for real dough. Gasoline, bacon, porcelain, dollars. Dollars! Y'understand?"

He smoked hastily, puffed the smoke out, tossed the butt away. "D'you think I want to rot in this stinkin' hole? I'm not nuts, man. As soon as I've got some money I'll get out. Nürnberg! Frankfurt! That's where you can make real money. And then to the States, man! There's nothin' doin' in Germany anymore, it's all crap!"

He suddenly pushed himself from the bench with both hands and stood up. "So tell your friend!" he said curtly, as he picked up his bike which was lying on the cobbles in front of the bench.

"I'll ask him this evening, you can count on it," said Peter, subdued. "He'll play along, that's for sure." Karl did not seem to be listening. He rolled up his pantlegs. Peter watched him with growing unease. He wanted to say something conciliatory, but could not think of anything.

Then he suddenly saw a cyclist stop at one of the traffic signs on the other side of the square. He jumped up, pulled at Karl's sleeve and nodded his head excitedly in that direction.

"Well, that's better!" said Karl. They watched the man chain his bike to the post and disappear behind a door three houses farther down.

Karl leaned his bike against the church wall, turned round grinning, and stuck his hands into his pants pockets. "Shall we draw for it — to see who goes 'n' gets it?" he asked. He had two matches in his hand and held them out to Peter. "Whoever gets the shorter one gets the bike. Okay?"

Peter stared at the two red sulfur heads clamped between Karl's thumb and forefinger. He suddenly felt fear rising in him. He grasped one of the matches and pulled it out with a jerk. It was the shorter one.

"It's all yours!" said Karl, still grinning. "Better get a move on, so you're gone before the guy comes out of the house again. I'll wait here, okay?"

Peter nodded and walked off, moving like a robot. He stayed close to the houses, keeping his eyes fixed on the door behind which the man had disappeared. He desperately hoped that it would open and the man would come out and ride way on the bike.

But the door did not open. And when he passed it, he did not hear a sound. No footsteps coming down the hall, no voices. He looked round. There was no one in the square, either. No one anywhere close, nothing which would provide him with an excuse. He had to do it. Karl was standing in front of the church, watching him.

The bike was chained around the crossbar, just like the first bike they had taken. Peter went toward it. His feet seemed to stick to the ground. He stared at the bike. He had to do it. His hands grasped the post, lifted it up, twisted it off the pin. He pulled the chain over the pin, holding the post in one hand. The effort made his arm shake. He replaced the post, pushed it back on the pin. It hit the bottom with a dull, metallic thud that echoed in his ears.

Suddenly there was another noise behind him. A door banged. He ran off with the bike, heard boots clattering on the cobbles, leaped onto the saddle. Someone was chasing him, was getting close. He heard him shout, heard the echo of the shout in the narrow alley into which he turned. Peter dashed down the alley. The footsteps were still behind him. If he fell now, he'd be done for. The alley was so dark, he could hardly see where he was going. At last it got lighter. He could make out the street in front of him, leading to the station. He braked, zoomed around the bend, and started pedaling again.

Just past the underpass he began to shiver so badly that he had to get off. He pushed the bike toward the railroad embankment, threw himself down next to it amid weeds and stinging nettles, and pressed himself against the ground.

He saw Karl ride by and held his hands against his mouth so his panting breath would not give him away. He waited till the shaking subsided. It stopped as suddenly as it had begun. The fear and the tension were gone as though nothing had happened. He got up and rode down to the river sitting up straight in the saddle.

Karl was perched on the railing. Peter sat down next to him and took the cigarette Karl offered him. He was filled with boundless pride. He felt the cool night wind on his hot face, and felt his limbs grow heavy as he inhaled the smoke from the cigarette. He was happy.

"If your friend is as good as you are, we can make a mint tomorrow," said Karl. "Pity you won't be staying any longer. We could get somethin' goin' together!"

Peter said nothing. He felt that he had never in his life been as happy as he was at this moment.

"Listen," said Karl. "I'll make a round of the bikes tomorrow and get the three we still need. Then, tomorrow evening you'll have your bike. Okay?" He slapped Peter on the shoulder, pinched the glowing end from his cigarette, and stood up.

"Where do we meet tomorrow?" asked Peter.

"Down here. At six," said Karl. They shook hands. "Got it?"

"Got it!" said Peter.

Peter felt tremendously strong next morning. He sat in front of the shed, stretched his legs in front of him, chewed on a piece of coarse bread, spat the grains out, and tore off the slimy bottom deposit, which he rolled into a ball and threw over the fence. Soon he would be able to afford something better for breakfast.

He watched the others. Tilli, who did not want to wash even though the dirt was becoming ingrained in her skin.

Billie, who was putting on airs as mother, and was giving orders all around. Adolf, who had become more quiet than usual, and Max in a bad mood. He wondered whether he should not let them go on alone while he himself stayed here and made a few more deals with Karl. The others could stay with Adolf's relatives till he caught up with them. Or maybe he should just cut out and go it alone. All he needed was a bit of extra cash. He could make it. The more he thought about it, the better he liked the idea.

Bored, he watched Billie and Max redividing the food. It was the same every day. Three slices of slimy bread per person, five potatoes per person. If they made the portions a bit smaller, maybe it would last an extra day. There was not much to share out anymore, particularly since they were feeding Sophie too. There was only half a loaf left and enough potatoes for one meal.

Peter imagined what he would eat when the deals began to pay off. Eggs and bacon, chocolate pudding with vanilla sauce, roasted meat, and bread with lots of butter — smeared thick with butter and with a double layer of sausage. The evening before he had seen a truck driver in the market place who had had a hunk of farm bread in one hand and a chunk of bacon in the other. And he had alternately taken a bite from the bread and then from the bacon. That's how he'd eat in the future.

At ten he went to the station with Max. Max wanted to find out whether they could jump a train. The tickets were too expensive; he had checked that out already.

They waited for two hours for a passenger train that was due at eleven. When it finally arrived it was so overcrowded that the people were being pushed out of the windows. They were sitting crowded together on the roofs of the cars, and standing shoulder to shoulder on the running boards outside, while a few hundred more were thronging on the platform, waiting to get on. There was no way they could get on. They'd have to stay.

On the way back Peter began to talk about the deal and about Karl. When they passed the market place he showed Max the sawed-through posts. It was easier to persuade Max than he had expected.

At half past five, Peter and Max set off, silently walking side by side into town and through the underpass to the river. They sat on the railing and waited until Karl came along the towpath on his bicycle. He stopped at the curb in front of them, remained sitting on the saddle and waved a casual greeting. He was dressed in black from top to toe: black sweater, black corduroy pants, black rubber boots. Behind his bicycle was a two-wheeled cart with balloon tires. An old, brown woolen carpet lay on it.

Peter got up and walked across to him. Max remained sitting on the rail.

"That your friend?" asked Karl. When Peter nodded Karl threw a skeptical glance at Max, but said, "Well, all right then. Come along."

They walked on the sidewalk next to him. They had to take long steps to keep up.

"I thought he was going to bring a bicycle for you," said Max scornfully. Peter threw him a venomous glance. "None of your damned business!" he said.

They walked along the river to the edge of town; then for at least half an hour along dirt roads to a village, and through the village to a railroad yard fenced in with barbed wire.

Karl got off his bike and told them to wait. He unlocked a door, pushed his bike through, and disappeared with it behind a row of burned-out freight cars. When he returned he had something on the cart that rattled with a hollow, tinny sound when he hit a pothole. They could not see what it was. The brown woolen carpet was thrown over it.

Karl rode along in front next to the tracks, made a wide detour around the hill on which the monastery stood, and on through a tall fir forest toward the town again. He stopped when they saw the first houses between the trees. He unhooked the cart and pushed the bike into a thicket and chained it to a tree trunk.

"Okay, now listen," he said, as he awkwardly lit a cigarette and jerked his thumb over his shoulder. "There's somethin' goin' on tonight in that house back there. A bunch of Yanks are comin' with a mass of cars. They're goin' to get smashed, with women and all, but that part's of no interest to us." He paused, took off his glasses and looked at them with eyes that were suddenly quite small and apprehensive: small, light-colored, child's eyes. "Have y'ever siphoned gas?" he asked as he put his glasses back on.

Peter shook his head.

"There's nothin' to it," said Karl casually. He pulled the woolen carpet off the cart. Four ten-gallon containers were standing on it with waste cotton stuffed carefully between them, and two large Yank cans with wire handles were wedged in on the side. Karl pulled out the two cans and threw one to each of them. "There's a piece of hose in each. You can get the gas out with that."

He began to explain how to put the hose into the tank, how to bend it downward carefully and suck the gas through. Max was not listening. He stood there with an indifferent expression on his face, holding the end of the five-foot-long hose in his hand like a whip and cracking it through the air with a flick of his wrist.

Karl fell silent and looked him up and down over the rim of his glasses. "What's with you?" he asked.

"I know how," said Max sullenly.

Karl sat down against a tree stump, stretched, closed his eyes, and said through his nose: "I couldn't care less. But it tastes awful if you get a mouthful of gas. Believe me!"

They waited. It began to get dark, and the sound of engines and laughter echoed from the edge of the woods. Pale light from the headlights flitted among the tree trunks. Karl sat calmly leaning against the tree and seemed to be asleep. He lazily opened his eyes, yawned, and said, "Don't get excited, we've got time. Let them get completely smashed first."

Gradually the noise between the houses at the woods' edge ebbed away. Now cars arrived only occasionally. The three boys dozed and waited in silence. A deep bell began to chime. Max counted. He counted to ten, but it could have been eleven. He had not started counting at the very beginning. Then the clear bell from the monastery began to chime. It was eleven.

Karl got up abruptly, and shook his legs as though they had fallen asleep. "I'll go check things out," he said. "You stay here. Understand?"

They listened to his quickly receding steps. He must have known the area well to be able to move so rapidly in the pitch-blackness of the woods.

He was back a few minutes later. He had a small box with him, which he put on the ground. "Here's some soot," he said. "Rub it on your faces and your hands. It's pretty light out there."

The soot felt soft and fluffy. Karl reached into the box and blackened his face as well. They watched as it disappeared under the soot in the darkness.

"Okay, let's go!" he said.

Karl turned onto the path, pulling the cart behind him. The wooden fence along the path ended at a stone pillar.

Karl pushed the cart up to the pillar and unloaded the containers, then pushed the cart back across the path into the woods. He pushed aside a broad plank that was hanging by only one nail at the top. The opening was just large enough for them to squeeze through. Karl handed them the containers, which they placed in a row behind the fence; then he climbed in last and pushed the plank back into place.

They groped their way after him through thick bushes along a wire net fence which separated two gardens. They could now hear soft music coming from the house. It got lighter. A lamp was on in front of the house, brightly lighting the entrance. They made out a wide driveway leading toward a stone balustrade with life-sized statues, and a portico with an arched roof. This was no house. This was a large villa.

"There's a guy keeping watch by the house," they heard Karl whisper. "He's sitting behind the pillar on the right." They could see the glow of the guard's cigarette in the shadows. "He's no problem," whispered Karl. "He's got to be drunk by now. He won't move from his spot."

He lifted the lower corner of the fence high enough for them to crawl under. "Now listen," he said quietly. "The tank is always at the back of the car. Only go to the cars standing with their hoods toward the house. Don't take any risks! It's a source we want to tap more often. Got it?"

They nodded in silence. Even Max was fully into it now. Karl did not seem to be the show-off he had thought him to be. This had all been organized perfectly.

"Okay," Karl continued. "One of you siphons, the other brings the full cans to the fence. I'll do the filling. Got it?"

"Got it!" they whispered back.

Max crawled under the fence. Peter followed close on his heels. They ran, stooping, along the wall of the garage up to the corner. From there they went on in the shadow of a row of bushes. That was not dangerous. Only the last ten yards between the bushes and the cars were difficult. They had to cross the lawn with no cover, and it was light there. The lamp over the entrance door illuminated everything like a floodlight.

Max dropped to the ground and crawled on his stomach through the grass. He stood up when he reached the shadow of the cars and set the can down. The first car was standing at an angle on the lawn, sideways to the house. The gas cap was at the back over the fender on his side. It could not have been better.

He unscrewed the cap and pushed the hose in. The smell of gas rose to his nose as he took the other end in his mouth and sucked at it. Without warning it was in his mouth. He spat and gagged, and suddenly noticed that it was flowing out of the hose onto the grass. He stuck the end of the hose into the can. It flowed as if it were coming from a faucet. The can filled quickly and he expected Peter to set his next to it. He turned round. Peter was not there. He was still standing over by the bushes. Why didn't he come, the bastard!

He clamped the hose shut, pushed it into the tank until only a short piece was sticking out, picked up the can, and crawled back. Crawl for one yard, push forward the can, crawl a bit farther, push the can along again.

"Give it here! Move it!" he hissed at Peter who was kneeling next to the last bush. He could not make out his face; he was probably scared stiff again, the ass.

He filled the second can, this time without getting a mouthful of gas. And as he crawled back on his stomach with the full can, he heard Peter coming back through the fence and took the empty can from him. It was running like clockwork.

Things were moving so fast that Peter could not keep up. "The third container is full," he whispered. And after a few more trips he said, "Let me siphon this time." Max showed him the next car, said that the hose was still in the tank, and ran to the fence with the full can.

There was no sign of Karl, and the containers were gone,

too. He became uneasy, stuck his head through the gap in the fence, and called in a whisper: "Hey!" And then, louder: "Hey, where are you?"

The answer came from the woods "Everything's okay!" Karl came over and took the can from him. "Stay there, I'll be right back," he said quietly, and when he returned he added, "I've stowed everything away already, we're almost full."

Peter was still sitting behind the car he was working on when Max came to the end of the line of bushes. What was taking him so long? Surely he must have had the can full long ago. Max crawled over on his stomach, then ran, stooping, along the row of cars. Peter had his hands at his throat. It looked as though he had swallowed the stuff. And the can was overflowing. Max put the empty one next to it, waited till it was full, and clamped the hose shut.

"I'm okay now," said Peter, subdued. He was still gagging.

Max picked up the two cans. "Wait here, I'll be right back," he hissed.

"Good work," said Karl when he brought back the empty cans. "These are the last ones."

Max dashed back. Suddenly he hesitated. His thoughts were racing. Something was wrong. Why two more cans? That was impossible. Earlier Peter had said that three containers were already full.

He crawled through the wire net fence. Peter was lying on his stomach at the end of the row of bushes, took the cans from him, and crawled on his stomach across the lawn. He seemed to have suddenly plucked up courage.

Max watched him. Abruptly he leaped up, and raced

back, not bothering about the branches slapping his face. The fourth large container *had* to be full already. Maybe Karl just wanted to get as much gasoline as possible — no point in going back with the smaller cans empty — but Max didn't believe it. Something was shady, something was foul, the swine was trying to steal from them. He searched the path with his eyes.

There was Karl. Max could just see him as a dark shadow under the trees. Already a good thirty yards away. A few seconds later, he would have been gone.

Max ran after him. "Stop, you bastard!" he yelled. Karl turned. He seemed to be quite calm and said, "Hey-hey-hey! Have you gone crazy?" Slowly he came toward Max and said, "Get lost, man, or you've had it!"

Max drew up his shoulders and hunched his back. A wild fury rose up in him. He let Karl come closer. He was almost a head taller, but Max was not afraid of him. He did not care.

Karl came toward him, arms outstretched, wanting to push him away the way one pushes away a child. He seemed quite confident, as if he did not expect Max to resist. When Max's fist hit him in the stomach, he did not even cry out in pain — he just crumpled up like a rag doll.

Max stood over him, breathing heavily, snorting out his fury. Then he turned Karl on his back, put his hand in the other boy's pockets, and pulled out two packs of cigarettes and a bundle of bills. He put everything in his own pockets.

He waited till Karl recovered. He watched him writhe on the ground, draw up his knees, gasp for air, then pull himself up, groaning, using the cart as support.

He heard Peter's voice behind him and called him to come over. He calmly said to Karl, "The gas costs two cartons. One each!"

"Two cartons!" screeched Karl. "You must be out of your mind!" He coughed and spat, and his voice sounded whining and choked.

"I know what those forty gallons are worth!" said Max.

"You don't know a thing, you half-wit! That's Yank gas. It's colored red. If they catch you with it, you're done for!"

Suddenly Peter was standing next to them, a can in each hand. "What's the matter?" he asked, flabbergasted.

"You shut up!" said Max roughly and, turning to Karl, he went on: "Two cartons, or I'll really give it to you!"

"I don't have two cartons here," said Karl. He was clutching his stomach with both hands. "You can have the bike."

Max watched him suspiciously. "Then bring it here!" he said and watched him disappear into the woods.

"What's happened?" Peter asked again. Max took the two cans from him and put them on top of the containers in the cart. He pulled a box of matches from his pocket.

"Have you gone nuts?" Peter shrieked.

Max snapped, "Get lost! Just get lost!" With horror Peter realized that Max was absolutely serious, and backed away, step by step. Max was capable of setting the gas on fire. He really would do it. Peter stood ten paces behind him and suddenly heard footsteps approaching through the woods. Karl was not alone: there was someone with him, someone who was walking with a firm step, who was not afraid.

Max grasped one of the gas cans and held it like a bucket,

as Karl came out of the woods with a man. Peter stood paralyzed with fear as Max swung the can forward. He saw the stream of gas hit the man directly in the chest with a splash, and heard the can crash to the ground. As it rolled to a stop he heard Max say in a peculiarly calm voice: "I've got a match in my hand!"

The man was standing some three yards from Max, his arms half outstretched, motionless, staring at the matchbox Max was holding and at the match he was pressing against the striking surface. Suddenly he was gone, he disappeared into the woods in a single bound. A flickering spark flew through the air and landed on the spot where he had been standing. Peter saw Max coming toward him, then a glaring blaze of light blinded him. He felt something grab his arm and spin him around. He began to run, and heard a piercing scream that would not stop. It pursued him and still echoed in his ears long after they had run down the street, past houses and fences, and down the steep road to the town.

Max and Peter ran till their heads were swimming. They were sick from hunger, and sick from running, and sick from the taste of gas in their mouths. They dropped down in the ditch in front of the garden gate.

Behind them, on the horizon, it was already beginning to grow light. They climbed over the gate and over the garden door, and woke Billie. When she saw them she put her hands in front of her face and screamed. Then they realized that their faces were still smeared with soot.

"We've got to get away!" said Max.

He pulled the cigarettes from his pocket and stared in

disbelief at the bundle of bills. He had four one hundreds and one fifty in his hands.

Billie asked no questions. They woke Sophie and the two little ones, packed their belongings, locked the goat in the wagon, locked everything else, too, and brought the key back.

At six they were standing by the side of the road leading north out of town.

Several dozen people were already sitting by the road, waiting for a ride. There were men, women, and children, with suitcases and handcarts and bicyles. There were girls lying on the slope, wrapped in blankets, and one-legged men who had taken off their artificial legs which they waved whenever a truck passed.

Around midday they finally found a man who promised to take them to Weissenbach for four hundred marks and a pack of cigarettes. The only reason he did it so cheaply was because his truck was falling apart. They had to get out every time they came to a steep hill.

Max and Peter slept standing and sitting. They slept every minute they rode. When the truck drove into Weissenbach that evening, shortly after dark, the others had to shake them awake.

They drove past two factories, over railroad tracks, and across an arched bridge. Suddenly Adolf knew where he was. He could remember the river and the bridge and the large, brightly lit house they could see from the bridge. It looked familiar. That had to be the house of his relatives.

When they got near to the house the others let Adolf go first. Only Tilli went with him, clutching his hand tightly.

He rang the bell. A maid in a white apron opened the door and told him to wait. They heard her call up the stairs: "M'lady, M'lady!" Doors slammed and steps thundered down the stairs. A lady appeared and ran toward Adolf, arms outstretched. Adolf stiffened; he thought she wanted to hug him. But she stopped inches away and clasped her hands in front of her breast and blurted out: "Oh Good Lord, you poor boy, your parents are dead. We only got the news two weeks ago. You must come live with us, you poor orphan."

Suddenly two more women appeared, and on the stairs behind them they saw three girls hanging over the railing, a boy inquisitively gaping at them, an old lady, and the maid. Tilli felt a hand stroking her hair. It seemed to her that someone was wiping his dirty hand on her head. She shook herself and shouted, "Let me go!" and hid behind Adolf who was still standing stiffly, not moving.

Adolf was embraced by his relatives and disappeared into a round of family activities. The gang was also welcomed to stay, so they settled down and got some good food and rest. Sophie, however, traveled on. She lived only twenty miles away, and wanted to get back to her home as soon as possible. The children took her to the railroad station. Just as she was about to leave, Tilli started wailing.

"I don't want to stay here with these old ladies. Take me with you, please. Please. I can be your friend, please!"

Sophie seemed as surprised as the others by this outburst,

but she knelt down and hugged the frantic little girl.

"Tilli, Tilli, calm yourself. It is better that you stay here. I don't know what awaits me. If everything is all right, you can come back and visit me. You can be happy here with Adolf's family. Try. Try."

But Tilli would not be comforted and screeched as the train carrying Sophie left the platform, "I'll run away; you'll see. I'm coming to be with you. You'll see!"

From that day Tilli had only one plan: to get to Sophie and to stay with her. She hurt Adolf's feelings terribly because it was now obvious that she would rather be with Sophie than with him. She was rude to Adolf's aunts and generally made life impossible for those around her. Finally, a month after Sophie had left, one of the old aunts gave Tilli and Billie train fare for a visit with Sophie.

Sophie met them at the train. It turned out that she also had aunts, two old ladies who seemed to live in order to supervise each other's lives. For some reason Tilli thought them splendid. Sophie also owned a foul-tempered goose that Tilli loved at once. The goose accepted the little girl's pats like a pet dog even though it usually bit anyone who approached it. The day was a complete success. The only way they could get Tilli to leave was to promise that she could come back soon.

On the way home Billie turned to the little girl. "Tilli, it's fine that you love Sophie, but what about Adolf? He cares for you. He offered to give you a home, and I know his aunts would keep you if he asked. He wants you to stay."

"Pooh, he can come visit me at Sophie's. I hate his aunts. They smell old." And the little girl wouldn't say any more about it. She couldn't understand Adolf's feelings. She had her own to consider.

Then after six weeks had passed, Max started to get restless. "It's time we tried to get home," he said.

"The Russians are fierce at the border," Peter commented. "They don't want hoards of refugees rushing into Berlin. At least that's what they say in the village."

"No matter. The three of us must try it. Otherwise we'll never get home," Max replied.

Billie asked, "But what about Tilli?"

"She can stay here or with Sophie. It's time we stopped being babysitters, and besides, who will look after her when we get to Berlin?"

Billie was going to answer sharply, but she saw the look in Max's eye and was silent. She, too, wanted to get home now.

11

The Russians

Billie woke up. She listened, holding her breath, but could hear nothing apart from the gentle rustling of the tree-tops above her. She sat up, leaning on her arms. The ground was damp with dew, her blanket was also damp, and her face felt ice-cold. She could see across a meadow through the low-hanging branches. The sky above was beginning to grow light.

Suddenly there was that sound again, quite close, behind her in the woods. That's what had woken her. A deep, bellowing, hoarse bleat, drawn out at first, then disjointed. Then she heard a voice next to her, a gruff man's voice, and for a moment she sat paralyzed with fear.

"That's just a deer, it got our scent," said the voice in broad, homey Saxon dialect. She took a deep breath. The Saxon. She had forgotten about him. "Well, I think we should be gettin' on our way," he continued. "It'll be light soon enough." She watched him sit up and stretch. He was small and chubby, and was wearing a pompom hat.

He had come toward them at night along the railroad embankment on his way to the border. He said that it was not smart to go along the tracks. Most illegal border-crossers tried there, and the Russians were wise to it and had sealed off everything.

They had joined him, stumbling across the fields. He had said they should be at least three miles away from the railroad tracks when they crossed the border. There was a river there, and if they were lucky, and were there early enough, they would be able to cross to the other side in the fog. But they had not got much farther at night; it had been too dark.

Now they had to hurry. Billie woke the two boys and rolled up her blanket. The Saxon had already put on his knapsack and had pulled a shoulder strap through the handle of his suitcase. "Move it, kids!" he said urgently.

The Saxon set the pace. Despite his short legs he moved fast and they had difficulty keeping up with him. They walked along the edge of the woods through the dew-wet grass. Within a very short time their shoes were soaked and squelched with every step.

Half an hour later a few houses emerged from the morning mist. A rooster crowed sleepily, and a dog started to bark and woke other dogs who answered it. Then suddenly they saw four figures scurrying across the meadows a few hundred yards in front of them. A lanky one with a walking stick in front, and three others laden like pack-mules behind.

"We seem to have company," said the Saxon, and he plowed straight ahead.

Far away they heard shots, a short, sharp, crackling *ratatatat*. It did not sound dangerous. The Saxon didn't seem uneasy, but maybe he had not heard it under his pompom hat.

For a quarter of an hour the path led straight through the woods, then it went diagonally down a moderately steep hill. The veils of mist became thicker and turned into a gray-white fog that laid itself on their faces, cold and damp, and made them shiver.

Two men with heavy suitcases came toward them.

"What's it look like?" asked the Saxon.

"You have to get across by five, that's when the relief guards come," the first man said without stopping.

The Saxon looked at his watch. "We'll make it," he said. He took off his watch and put it in his pocket. "Hide your watches; the guys over there are very keen on them," he said.

On the bank the people were standing in an orderly line, as if in front of a shop. Eleven people, all adults. The Saxon was the twelfth. Two more were in the middle of the river, standing with wobbling legs on a raft made of planks and logs and pulled across by ropes. Three more were standing on the opposite bank, pulling on the rope, and behind the three was another line.

Billie turned round and grinned. It looked like a ferry service, just as though there was no border and no border guards, as though none of this was dangerous.

The man in front of the Saxon suddenly began to talk. "Naturally, if you're caught, you'll have to say that you wanted to get over there, in other words here. And over here, if you're over there. If you're lucky, nothing'll happen to you 'cept that you'll be sent back, and then you're over there, d'you understand?"

Billie shrugged. What was he trying to say? She was confused.

"You've got to think of it this way: when you're over there, then over there is here, so you have to say you want to go over there, that's quite obvious. Then the Ruskies send you back, and you're where you wanted to go to, you're over there!"

The two women joined the line. They shivered with cold. Maybe with fear and impatience as well. It took a long time for the raft to be towed to and fro. There were still eight people in front of them, four more trips.

"To Siberia! All rumors! You'll be arrested for one, maybe two days, have to pay a fine. If worse comes to worst, you may lose your luggage. They may cut off the children's hair, because of the lice. That's all.

"Basically the Ivans are good-natured — the simple Ivans, that is. As long as they're not smashed. They're not familiar with civilization, that's all. Just listen to this: at Schering they gobbled up the laboratory guinea pigs, and croaked because of it." One of the women barked a rough laugh.

A little way downstream something was floating on the water, moving in the current as though it were alive. At first Billie thought that it was a piece of wood overgrown with moss. But it was not a piece of wood. It was a person in the water, a woman floating face down. A woman in a green coat, with long, black hair. Sometimes her hands came to the surface, whitish, bloated hands that moved gently.

One of the women behind them screamed suddenly and pressed her hands against her mouth, and the man said gruffly: "Don't look then, damnit!"

"Quiet you idiots!" someone called in a stifled voice. The body drifted past.

At last it was their turn. They held on to the rope and waited till the Saxon got off on the other side. Then they pulled back the empty raft and all three climbed on. It sank so deep that water sloshed into their shoes. It was pushed under by the current. They went down on their knees and held on tightly until it got back in balance.

And then, a machine gun started to fire, earsplittingly loud, out of the fog. A short spurt of gunfire, then another one.

They heard the bullets rip into the trees above their heads. The raft shot away with them in the current, turning and rocking in the waves. They heard loud shouts in a hard language. The Russians! Those were the Russians! The raft kept on increasing its speed.

They hit the bank, but it was the wrong bank, the Russian one. They had to get to the other one. Suddenly Peter jumped off. Splashed through the water, paddled wildly with his arms, caught hold of a branch hanging deep into the water, pulled himself up by it, crawled up the embankment, and ran off, his knapsack bouncing.

The raft drifted in circles in the middle of the river. Max tried to paddle with his hands. Then suddenly the rope floating behind them went taut, held the raft in the current, and let it bump gently against the bank. Max was able to grab a root and hold tight while Billie pulled them in. They landed and raced across the field toward the woods. There was no sign of Peter. They called him. No answer. They ran back through the woods to the path along which they had come, ran up the valley slope and called again. Still no answer. They ran all the way back through the woods to the edge opposite the village. There they finally found him.

He was hopping around, beating his arms against his chest and shivering with cold in his wet clothes. When they reached him he paused briefly and said, "Man, that was close, wasn't it!" He began to hop around again and beat his arms against his chest.

Max narrowed his eyes. "Get undressed!" he said grimly, threw his knapsack onto the ground, and fished out some things he had inherited from Adolf's cousin.

Billie was trembling with fury. All the food that Peter had in his knapsack was wet — the bread was soaked, the Yank cookies they had wanted to take home as a surprise were mush, and the flour was paste.

"What now?" she asked sullenly.

Max shrugged his shoulders. "We'll just have to find another place to cross."

"In broad daylight? You're nuts!" screeched Peter.

"You can stay here if you want!" said Max, furious.

"I will! That's just what I'll do! You can be sure of that!" Peter's voice almost broke. "I'm not crazy, I won't let them shoot me in broad daylight! Damn you, Max. I can make it myself without you. You bastard." He was standing in the field in front of them, waving his arms around, screeching. He would not stop screeching.

"Shut your trap, or I'll really give it to you!" Max snapped at him. Billie held on to his arm. "Stop it," she said. "Come on, both of you, stop it!"

A boy in short leather pants came out of the woods, carrying a school satchel on his back. He stopped, peered over at them, and came closer. Hesitantly he asked: "Did you come from over there?" And when Billie shook her head, he came a few paces closer and asked, "D'you want to get across?"

He was not much older than they were. He had a broad, open face, light eyes, tousled, brown, curly hair, and a firm way of walking, like a young tomcat. "You can't do it here right now," he said. "They've just caught a couple and all hell's broken loose. Hof's nearby. Do you know anyone there you can stay with?"

Max studied him attentively. He did not look like a schoolboy on his way to school.

"We do," he said. And after a pause he asked: "D'you know this area?"

The boy quickly pulled off his satchel. He seemed to be embarrassed that they had seen him like that. He grinned sheepishly. "I know my way round a bit," he said.

Adolf and Tilli sat next to each other on the running board of the car and let their legs dangle down. The sun shone warm on their faces, and the train moved so slowly that they could easily have jumped off if they had wanted.

Swallows were sitting on the telephone wires, side by side, like black notes on the staff lines in a song book. Tilli asked, "Why are the swallows sitting on the wires?" And Adolf said, "They're waiting till they're all together because they want to fly away to Africa." And Tilli asked, "But I want to know why they're sitting on the *wires?*" Adolf said, "Because they're *telephone wires,* and when someone telephones, it tickles their feet, and they like that." Tilli smiled. She could very well imagine what a beautiful feeling it must be to sit on a wire and feel it tickling your feet.

She giggled and clapped her hands, and every time she clapped, the swallows flew up and fluttered around excitedly before they settled down on the wires again.

She asked: "Do swallows know that they're swallows?" And Adolf thought for a while, and then he said, "Yes, they know." Because if he had said "no," Tilli would have asked why not, and it would have been much more difficult to find an answer for that.

He watched her out of the corner of his eye, clapping her hands, and calling to the swallows, and laughing joyfully. At that moment he felt happy, but at the same time a bit sad. He knew that the only reason she was so happy was because they were going to visit Sophie. That knowledge hurt. Since Sophie had appeared on the scene everything had changed between them.

They jumped off at the station in Hof and ran to the gate and had their tickets punched. Tilli proudly walked ahead of Adolf because she already knew the way, and the farther they went, the faster she walked. When they reached the street where Sophie lived, she was quite some distance ahead, and impatiently tried to make him hurry.

Tilli stopped by a garden gate and rang the bell. The piano playing above did not stop, and a loud voice scolded in time to the music. Behind the house someone was chopping wood. Tilli rang the bell again. With all the noise going on, perhaps no one had heard.

Then, suddenly, Billie appeared around the corner in an apron covered with white dust and with a scarf around her head. Adolf was so astonished that he could not speak. And Billie quickly said without pause: "It didn't work. Just don't say anything to the others; they're in a foul temper. But we've found someone who'll take us across next week. Just so you know."

The piano playing stopped abruptly and the loud voice said: "You haven't been practicing, Lisbeth. You haven't been practicing again!" As Adolf looked up, startled, Tilli said reassuringly: "That's only Auntie Selma, she's scolding Auntie Lisbeth again." And she pulled him along by his arm.

A man was standing next to a chopping block behind the house in the middle of a huge pile of logs. And Tilli said: "That's Rudel." Then she pointed to a younger man who was sitting with a drawing pad on his knees on a bench by the door, and said, "That's Hermann." A moment later she forgot everything — the men, and Billie and Adolf. A goose waddled from behind a woodpile and Tilli ran toward it crying "Elsa! Elsa!" She took it in her arms, tried to pick it up, and fell on her back because the goose was so much fatter than she was.

The house door crashed open and a woman dashed out, a small, sturdy old lady in a long, black dress with a delicate white pattern, and a sparse, braided white crown of hair on her head. She trotted energetically across the yard, past the woodpile towards a shed. Behind her came a second old lady, the spitting image of the first, except that she was a head taller and not as red in the face. She stopped in the doorway and said in a thin, tremulous voice, "But I did practice, Selma, why don't you believe me!"

Adolf and Billie were standing five paces away from her. Adolf thought she looked over at him, and he made a little awkward bow, and wanted to say hello, but Billie whispered close to his ear, "Forget it, she can't see you anyway. When she isn't wearing her glasses, she's as blind as a bat."

Sophie did not come until evening. She had cut her hair short and was wearing a blue dress with big, bright flowers. She was tanned, and her eyes laughed. When they were sitting in the kitchen at dinner, Adolf could not take his eyes off her because she looked so different from what he remembered: pale and nervous, with hair hanging down sadly, and terribly skinny. He sat there and stared at her. When she noticed and smiled at him, he turned red and began to hurriedly eat his soup.

Sophie said, "Next week we'll have to see whether we can dig out the cellar. When I went away last year there was a whole shelf of preserved food there. Perhaps we can still save some. It can't go bad under the rubble as long as the jars didn't break." With a sideways glance at Max she said, "D'you think you could start to dig around a bit tomorrow, maybe?"

Max calmly finished chewing and said grumpily, "I've already got something planned for tomorrow."

"With that boy you met on your way back here?" asked Sophie. When Max nodded she took a deep breath and said:

"Good Lord Max, you can't let a child take you across the border. You just can't do that! You've seen for yourselves what it's like!"

"Dieter knows what he's doing," said Max curtly. "He does it every week."

"At least wait till you hear from your parents," said Sophie. "Something could come any day!"

"What if the guy with the letters was caught?" asked Max. "Or if he never made it to Berlin?"

"In that case he'd hand them on, give them to someone else going in that direction," said Sophie. "It's done like that all the time. This isn't the first time! We don't even know whether your parents are still in Berlin! Maybe they were evacuated at the end of the war. Or they're living in a different district. What'll you do if you don't find anyone in Berlin?"

Max took his time before he answered. He looked at Sophie calmly and said casually, "We can go to relatives or neighbors."

Sophie rested her chin on her hands and stared at her plate.

They sat around the table in silence. Tilli took her plate in both hands, licked it clean, carried it to the kitchen cupboard and said, "You don't have to wash this one any more."

Then Aunt Selma came in through the door and said reproachfully, "Sophie, my child, would you please tell Rudel to repair the water pipes; the water's not running again!"

Sophie raised her eyebrows and answered softly, "I'm sure the water pipes are not broken, Aunt Selma. The water's just been shut off. It's been shut off in the whole town. I've written the times when it's shut off on a piece of paper and put it on the bathroom door."

Aunt Selma looked anxious and said, "Good heavens, in that case I'll have to apologize to Lisbeth. I was sure she had . . . I'll have to apologize." You could see how much she disliked the idea.

Max walked through the town with the handcart until he reached the railroad tracks that ran around the north end of the town. He followed the tracks westward to a rock Dieter had described to him in detail: a mighty stone slab that towered out of the ground at an angle and looked like a giant frog sitting next to the railroad embankment. He waited there for Dieter.

When Dieter arrived, he and Max went on together, keeping parallel to the embankment. About an hour later they came upon several men lying behind a hedge next to the tracks. They were at the foot of a hill around which the railroad wound in a narrow curve. Dieter and Max left their handcarts with the men and climbed up the hill to see whether a train was coming.

Dieter pointed to the light-colored, double-laned road that crossed the empty tracks some distance away. "That's the autobahn to Berlin," he said.

Max nodded. He had already noticed it. He watched a convoy driving along it northwards.

"Those are Yanks. They drive along there every day at this time. They're going to Berlin," said Dieter. The convoy was so far away that the roar of the engines was only a quiet hum.

"They'll be in Berlin in five hours," said Dieter.

"In five hours," murmured Max. "Just think of it!"

"Can't go along with them though," said Dieter.

There was still no sign of the train.

They walked down to the embankment again. At least thirty people had gathered there since they had left. There were many boys their own age among them, and also younger ones. Some were lying in the windbreak of the fir hedge, some sitting in the grass among handcarts and bicycles, passing around cigarettes. A couple were playing cards.

Dieter lit a butt, and after inhaling, passed it on to Max. They sat down on their handcarts. Max unbound his footcloths, rebound them tighter round his feet, and pulled his boots over them. He was wearing long black trousers with patches on the back and front, and new patches over the old ones, and a jacket with a herring-bone pattern, patched the same way as the trousers. They were workclothes Rudel had given him — just right for the job they had in mind.

Dieter took one last puff and casually said: "I can't go back across the border before next Sunday. You'll have to wait till then, or look for another way."

Max shook his head. "Those couple of days don't make any difference," he said.

They waited. The sun made them drowsy. Max fell asleep. He had no idea how much time had passed when someone suddenly shouted, "Get ready!" He got down from the handcart and a little later he heard a steam engine in the distance. It slowly puffed and pounded nearer as though it could barely haul its load.

They joined the others behind the fir hedge, each with a sack under his arm. When the engine had steamed past, the first men crawled through the hedge. Max and Dieter squeezed through the matted branches after them, and ran next to the train rattling slowly over the tracks. They threw their sacks onto a car and two men caught them under the armpits and lifted them up until they could reach the side. They hauled themselves up and climbed onto the mound of coal that filled the car. Dieter, still half lying on his stomach, began to throw coal briquets over the side. He turned onto his back, jammed the heels of his boots against the edge, and threw with both hands. They worked fast, in unison, four briquets at a time. They saw the men below disappear behind the fir bushes again. Thick, black-brown clouds of smoke wafted along above them.

"Hey, you!" called Dieter. "Tell me! That girl who's with you, who is she? Your sister?"

"Na!" Max called back. "We met her along the way. She's from Berlin, too." And since Dieter did not say anything else, he asked, "Why?"

"Just wanted to know," said Dieter.

They went on throwing briquets over the side and Max began to count: four, eight, twelve . . . forty, forty-four, forty-eight . . .

"He's coming!" someone from the next car shouted suddenly. Instantly Dieter was on his feet and said: "Let's go! Come on!" He scrambled like a spider forward across the coal, let himself down over the side onto the buffer between the cars, and jumped. Max jumped after him, and landed so hard on the gravel that his legs gave way. He rolled over, leaped up, and ran to Dieter who was waiting at the foot of the embankment.

They saw the others still on the freight cars jumping off, and saw the railroad policeman coming forward over the cars, waving his arms. He had a gun in his hands and was shouting as he rode by on the train: "Just wait till I catch you, you dirty bastards! Just wait till I catch you!" He threw a briquet at them which landed next to Max.

"Asshole!" shouted Dieter at the top of his lungs, and threw a stone at him. Max picked up the briquet and put it in his sack. Then they quickly set to work, because the others behind them were already beginning to pick up the coal.

12

The Border Crossing

Max and Dieter met Billie on the way home. They saw her walking along a hundred yards ahead of them, all arms and legs, her hair bouncing, twirling her cloth bag in her outstretched hand.

Max called to her and she waited till the two boys had caught up, laid her bag on Max's handcart, and walked along next to them.

Max said, "He can take us across next Sunday."

Billie studied Dieter. He was walking along next to her, staring straight ahead, as though they were not talking about him. He no longer looked like the schoolboy at the border. His hands were black with coal dust, his face was smeared black, and he had pushed his cap back on his head, so the visor stood straight up. He looked trustworthy.

"I'm with you," she said. "Whatever happens." And after

a pause she asked, "D'you actually live over there, not over here?"

"Over there," said Dieter tersely.

Billie waited in case he was going to say something more. But he did not, he just went on staring straight ahead.

"When you're over here, where do you stay?" she asked.

"I've got an uncle here," said Dieter curtly. He did not seem to want to be questioned.

Two small girls came toward them, rolling a bicycle wheel which rattled on the cobblestones. Billie waited till they had passed, then quietly said, "I've got a whole carton of Yank cigarettes."

The two boys stopped dead in their tracks and stared at her. Billie pointed to the handcart. "It's in the bag."

They looked in the bag, and Dieter asked, "Where d'you get it?" It was obvious he was very impressed.

"None of your business," Billie said, but soon relented — it was too good a story to keep to herself.

"I was sitting in a doorway — I was really tired, since I'd spent the whole morning going through the bombed-out area looking for scrap metal with no luck. Anyway, there was this Yank just sitting in his jeep on the other side of the street leering at all the girls who went by. Really disgusting, if you ask me! He was tossing this carton of cigarettes in the air and catching it. . . . Well, this really pretty girl came along and crossed the street right in front of the jeep. You should have seen the Yank — I thought his eyes would pop right out of his silly face. She was wearing this beautiful green dress; I haven't seen anything so stylish in ages — it had this little —"

"Forget the fashion show," Max interrupted; "how did you get the cigarettes?"

"I'm telling you, if you'll just keep quiet for a minute! The girl came right over to the doorway I was sitting in, and I said 'Excuse me' and moved so she could go through. I noticed the Yank was still staring at her and grinning like an idiot . . . and that gave me the idea." She paused dramatically.

"Okay," Dieter said after a moment, "I'll bite: what was this great idea?"

"Well, I waited until the girl was inside, and then I went over to the Yank. 'Excuse me, Captain,' I said — of course he was no more a captain than I am. . . . I'm really glad Sophie's been teaching me some English, you know — it's so much easier than having to point and pantomime everything, and hardly any of the Yanks can understand a word of German —"

"Please," Max almost howled. "The cigarettes! Get to the cigarettes!"

"This *is* getting to the cigarettes," Billie snapped. "As I was saying before I was interrupted" — she looked pointedly at Max — "I went up to the Yank and said, 'Excuse me, Captain, but my sister — the girl who just went inside — would be so pleased to make your acquaintance.' I said it as if I was about eight years old and not very bright. 'She's waiting for you right now.' Well, he put the carton of cigarettes under the seat and was out of that jeep faster than you can imagine. I waited until he had gone through the doorway, then I bent into the jeep, grabbed the carton, and ran like crazy."

"You're joking!" Max said, but he was clearly impressed.

"Look for yourself — there's the carton," Billie replied.

Dieter said, "For five packs I can get you a bottle of schnapps. You can get more for that over there than for cigarettes."

Billie shrugged. "I don't know," she said. "We have to give the people here something. After all, they've been feeding us the whole time."

"It was just a suggestion," said Dieter, embarrassed, and hunched his shoulders. "Because I can get it for a pretty good price. My uncle's just got in a new shipment."

They walked on to the station in silence. Dieter had to go farther along the tracks. They stopped.

Billie asked, "What d'you take across the border when you go?"

"Depends," said Dieter. "When I go from here, I usually have schnapps. When I come from over there, well . . . fabric, sometimes, dress fabric, leather. All sorts of things." And after a pause he added, "Last time it was ladies' stockings." He grinned sheepishly.

They watched him as he walked with swinging strides down the street next to the station.

"He's a hundred percent okay, you can be sure of it," said Max.

Billie said, "We can get the schnapps if he thinks it's the best thing."

Later, when they had turned into their street, she added,

"I think it'd be better if we didn't say anything about the carton to Sophie. She'd just worry." She took her bag from the handcart and hung it over her shoulder.

Adolf saw them come in through the garden gate. They looked like two people coming home from work. Drained and tired. Happy that the day was over, and that they were finally home. He was envious of them for that.

He watched how Tilli skipped over to them, greeted them effusively, and very proudly showed them her flower bed with the freshly raked-in manure. He waved to them and smiled, even though he did not feel at all like smiling, and quickly turned away.

Aunt Selma came out of the house and started to work in the garden. Aunt Selma was all right, but she was hard of hearing. You had to shout when you talked to her, and she shouted back even louder. Her voice sounded as though she were speaking into a megaphone.

She doggedly turned over soil in a flower bed and grumbled to herself: at the spade which did not want to go deep enough into the ground, at the stones that were hiding in the soil, and at the weeds, and at the flies, and at Tilli who was grubbing about in the earth and getting dirty, and was throwing small stones at her, and grumbling back in a high, trumpetlike voice.

"Now you've cut a worm in half!" Tilli shouted accusingly. And Aunt Selma bellowed, unmoved: "The earthworm doesn't mind, it'll just grow back!" And Tilli shouted, "Which one will grow back, this one or this one?" and held up the two halves of the earthworm. Aunt Selma bellowed,

"How should I know! The earthworm'll know!" And Tilli planted herself in front of her, angry and belligerent.

"Then I'll give it to Elsa!" she shouted. Aunt Selma bellowed after her, "Yes, give it to her! So she'll get even fatter. That fat goose will land up in the roasting pan soon anyway!"

Tilli whirled around and yelled, her face red. "You can't do that!"

Aunt Selma replied, "A goose is for roasting, it's not a plaything!"

Tilli yelled at the top of her lungs: "You're mean! You're mean! You're mean!" and threw a clump of earth at her. Aunt Selma shook the spade at her, ranted and roared and stamped her foot.

Adolf watched the two of them and wondered why Tilli, despite everything, still preferred this grumbling old Aunt Selma to his aunts, who cared about her, slipped her candies, were indulgent, patient, and friendly.

He hoped Sophie would come back soon because he had to be at the station at six, and he was afraid Tilli would not come with him if Sophie was not there. She certainly would not listen to him.

She only obeyed Sophie after long persuasion, after Sophie had promised that she could come again the next weekend, after Max and Billie promised to go to the station with her, and Aunt Selma had promised not to kill the goose.

Tilli cried all the way to the station, and would not shake hands with anyone when she got on the train, nor wave back when they waved goodbye.

"I'm really sorry for Adolf," said Max on the way home.

"If it hadn't been for him, she would have landed in an orphanage a long time ago. She owes him everything."

On both the following days Max went with Dieter to get coal again. In the afternoon he helped the other two dig out the bombed cellar in the neighboring garden. When they finally reached the shelf with the preserved food on Tuesday evening, they found every single glass broken.

On Wednesday Tilli arrived in the early morning. She had run away again. Max took her back on a bicycle. Afterward he rode through the villages with four packs of cigarettes and returned with a few pounds of apples, some potatoes, two pounds of flour, ten eggs, and a can of beef suet.

For two days, for lunch and dinner, they ate nothing but potatoes fried in beef suet. In spite of gulping it down so hot that it burned their tongues, the suet stuck to the roof of their mouths and coated their gums and throats with a furry layer. It felt as though they had a mass of feathers sticking in their throats.

Then finally Aunt Selma decided in a thunderous voice that it was time to kill the goose. "That's it! All over! Period!" They were just being ridiculous. The children were as skinny as rails, and the creature was getting fatter and fatter. Nothing was going to stop her. She laid the goose on the chopping block and held the ax in her hand. But she could not bring herself to do it. Nor could Sophie. Aunt Lisbeth had been against it anyway, and Rudel and Hermann were not there. The goose remained alive.

On Saturday Max and Billie set off early to meet Dieter. Three days earlier Sophie had got a job with the military government and she had raised their hopes that she could get transportation for them to Berlin through the Yanks. But nothing had come of it by Friday evening, and no message had come from Berlin, either.

Billie and Max met Dieter in a railway station restaurant near the border, and exchanged five packs of cigarettes for a bottle of schnapps. Dieter described the place where they were to meet Sunday night, and drew a detailed plan, so they could not miss him. They had definitely decided to cross the border with him. No one was going to stop them, not even Sophie.

It was dark by the time they returned. Sophie was not home yet. Peter and Adolf, who had brought the insistent Tilli for another visit, were sitting miserably in the kitchen. Aunt Selma was grumbling at the top of her voice, and Adolf whispered to them that Tilli was sitting in the bombed cellar and would not let anyone get near her.

The goose was gone.

Adolf had been searching the whole neighborhood and asking the neighbors ever since lunchtime. No one had seen it. It had disappeared without trace. Aunt Selma bellowed that they should leave her in peace. She had had enough — the dumb creature was gone, probably someone had stolen it, and that was that.

Tilli could not be coaxed from her hiding place. She thrashed around wildly when anyone tried to touch her, screaming and yelling. They had to leave her in the cellar and wait till Sophie got home. Maybe Sophie would be able to calm her down.

Sophie came around nine. She suddenly appeared in the

doorway with a mysterious smile on her face. When Peter started to tell her about the goose, she just put a finger on her lips and pushed him back in his chair. She pulled out three Yank cans from her bag and a six-pack of C-rations, placed everything on the table, and sat down with them. She looked at each one in turn, smiling, and said, "Children, tomorrow you're going home by Yank transport. You're leaving at nine, and you'll be in Berlin by two."

They sat around the kitchen table, holding their breath. Sophie went on quietly: "It's all been arranged, nothing can go wrong. It's one of those transports Max talked about, and you're going with it."

Max was suddenly suspicious. He thought about what Dieter had said about the Yank convoy on the autobahn. He had said no one could go along with it. Maybe Sophie was only trying to fool them so they would stay here, so they would not cross the border with Dieter. Maybe she was pretending so they would miss the chance to cross the border with Dieter. He stared at her and saw her open smile, and his suspicions vanished.

Maybe what she said was true. If it had only been a trick to keep them here, she would have had to say they would not be leaving until Monday. Otherwise — if things went wrong tomorrow morning — they could still go with Dieter. It had to be true. She had said at two o'clock. They would be in Berlin at two in the afternoon. Tomorrow at two!

He wanted to say something. He swallowed and stared at Sophie, who was still smiling. But before he could get a word out, a scream echoed throughout the house, a bloodcurdling scream from upstairs.

Instantly Sophie was in the hall and racing up the stairs. They stood at the bottom of the stairs and heard Aunt Lisbeth's voice, breaking in terror: "In there! It's moving! It's moving!"

Then they saw Sophie at the top of the stairs with the two old ladies trotting along behind her. Aunt Selma said in a troubled voice, "I don't understand it. I don't understand it. Eight pills, eight whole pills!" Sophie was carrying the goose. She brought it into the kitchen and there, in the light, they saw that the goose was naked, plucked clean except for a few feathers on its head and rump. It sat, naked, on the kitchen floor and groggily tried to get to its feet. It swayed its long, skinny, plucked neck, and sleepily fluttered its eyelids.

Aunt Selma kept repeating: "Eight pills! I thought it would be the kindest way. Not even I would have survived that! Who would have expected it!"

Billie ran to get Tilli from the cellar. The little girl came in, her eyes red and swollen from crying. She saw the goose, took it in her arms, rocked it, stroked it, and clutched it to her. And said, "She's freezing, she's got goose bumps!"

She took her cardigan off, and buttoned it around the goose.

They left at seven. It was cold, but they did not feel it. They were excited, full of expectation, and wide awake. They were so wound up, they were ready to burst. If everything went as Sophie had described it, they would arrive in Berlin this afternoon and would be home by evening. This evening. This very day they would be home!

Peter was pushing the bicycle on which they had hung their knapsacks, and Max and Billie were close behind. They were walking so fast that Sophie and the two little ones could barely keep up. No one said a word. There was nothing to say. When they closed their eyes they could imagine they were already walking through the streets of Berlin.

They walked past the trees along the road, past the bare fields on the other side of town, and then came to a signpost: AUTOBAHN BERLIN–MUNICH. There it was — *Berlin*. They were on their way. Just eight more hours. Less than eight hours. A few more minutes less.

Even Tilli seemed to sense some of the excitement that had seized the three in front. She had almost overslept this morning. The others had already decided to leave her at home, but she had got up, after all, and now her tiredness had all blown away. She walked along between Sophie and Adolf holding their hands, tried to keep in step with them, ran a little way because her legs were not long enough, and smiled proudly when she looked up at Adolf. For a moment Adolf had the feeling things were as they used to be. They were together on the trek. Tilli, Max and Peter and Billie and he, the gang, all five together. He clung to his thought, and felt as light as a feather. He was happy.

A good hour later they reached the autobahn. There was another signpost, a huge one, impossible to overlook: BERLIN. They turned onto the paved access road which led to the autobahn in a gentle curve. They walked in single file along the edge of the concrete surface.

The meeting place was behind the first bridge past the

access road, half a mile down the autobahn. They could not see it yet. The fog blocked their view.

They walked under the bridge, turned at the corner of the wall, and stopped behind it. Sophie looked at her watch. It was a quarter past eight. Another three-quarters of an hour and the convoy would be here. One of the trucks would slow down and stop very close to the wall. So close that the other trucks would not see them clamber under the tarp into the back of the truck. The driver would pretend he had to relieve himself, and Sophie would help them up. Then the truck would move off and rejoin the convoy. And five hours later, in Berlin, they would get out the same way. That's how Sophie had explained it to them. That's what she had arranged with the officer who rode in the jeep at the rear of the convoy.

Forty minutes to go. Sophie's watch seemed to have stopped. They stood right at the corner and listened into the fog. They could hear the few cars that passed them from quite a distance away, long before they raced through under the bridge. Maybe the convoy would come earlier than arranged. The earlier it came, the sooner they would be in Berlin. Half an hour to go.

"If they stop along the way, you mustn't make a sound," said Sophie. "If you're quiet, nothing will go wrong. The Yanks are never checked. They drive straight across the border. They only stop if one of them breaks down."

They took the knapsacks from the bicycle and held them ready. Adolf stood there, his head hanging. Then Max came over and punched him in a friendly way, put his arm around his shoulders and said, "Hey, kid, we've made it, damnit!"

Adolf smiled bravely, although he felt terribly sad.

Sophie said, "Write me as soon as you get home, promise me!"

They all answered in unison. "Of course, Sophie! You can be sure of that, Sophie! We'll write immediately, of course we will!"

Billie hugged the little girl, picked her up and kissed her cheek.

Tilli stayed quite still. She was so excited that she could not say a word. Suddenly she burst into tears, wriggled herself free, ran to Sophie and pressed against her, hiding her head under her coat. Billie asked softly, "Will she stay with you?" Sophie smiled and took Tilli's face in her hands and stroked her hair.

Then they heard the convoy, an almost inaudible hum at first that became louder and louder. They stood in the shadow of the ramp with their backs against the wall. Then the first jeep roared by, followed by two half-tracks, then the first truck, and the second. They counted: twelve, thirteen, fourteen, any moment now one would pull out and stop by the wall next to them. Maybe it would be the last one. Probably it would be the last one. The officer must have arranged it that way so the others ahead would not notice anything.

Max was standing right at the corner. He heard the deep drone of the truck engines swell to a thunderous roar as they came under the bridge. A surge of cold air hit his face, and the exhaust fumes rose to his nose when they drove out. Again and again in the same rhythm: the swelling deep drone, the thunderous roar under the bridge, the surge of air, and the stench of exhaust. Then suddenly it was over. Just one more jeep came along, the jeep that brought up the rear of the convoy. Each time he and Dieter had waited for the coal train, he had followed the convoy with his eyes from the hill. The jeep had always been the last car. Nothing came after it. He stared at the red glow of the rear lights quickly disappearing into the distance. This could not be true; Sophie had said it had all been arranged with the officer.

The stench of exhaust was still in the air, and the soft hum in the distance. Suddenly they felt the cold and shivered. They looked at Sophie, uncertain and questioning. Sophie was leaning rigidly against the wall, her eyes shut, her lips moving almost imperceptibly, and she was saying, "That bastard!" She stood there, her face white, leaning against the wall and said tonelessly, "The dirty bastard!"

Max pulled his knapsack over his shoulder, grasped the bike, and said, "So what? — we'll just cross the border with Dieter." He dragged the bike up the embankment and when he reached the top he turned around and said, "So we'll be home the day after tomorrow, so what!"

Sophie was the last to come up the slope. "Listen, Max ...," she began, but instantly fell silent when she saw Max smiling coldly at her, his eyes narrowed.

"Forget it," he said. "I'll go across with Dieter."

Peter stood next to him and pretended to do up his shoe-laces, and Billie said, "Don't worry, Sophie. So what if it didn't work."

They walked back along the road, one behind the other, Max in front. He knew the area. Before they came to the town, railroad tracks crossed the road, and they could follow them to a spot close to the meeting place they had arranged with Dieter. It was much too early and they could have gone back with Sophie. But he did not want to. They had already said their goodbyes. They were on their way. Everything had already been said.

They walked silently in single file, and when they reached the railroad underpass, they shook hands. Max pushed the bicycle toward Adolf and said: "Listen, Berlin's not that far away. After we're settled, you can visit. Don't forget!" Adolf nodded silently, felt the tears come into his eyes, lowered his head and pressed his lips tight shut.

From the top of the embankment they saw Sophie standing below with Tilli holding her hand and Adolf with the bicycle. Then they stepped over the tracks and walked along the ties in step with each other, Max in front, Billie behind him, and Peter bringing up the rear.

They walked for three hours along the tracks to the railroad restaurant where they had met Dieter. They asked for him there, but no one knew anything. They hung around in front of the station for a while longer, ate two slices of bread each, and kept a lookout for Dieter.

Around three o'clock they set off again, following the map Dieter had drawn for them. First, a bit farther along the tracks, then right at the first crossing, along a highway past two burned-out tanks, left at the next dirt road to a wood, two hundred yards into it, then right, then left, and there they found the hut in the middle of the forest, just as Dieter had described it.

It was a spacious wooden hut with a half-rotted plank floor. The door hung open on one hinge, but the roof was still watertight and there was a pile of old, dry hay in one corner. They could wait for night quite comfortably here.

They piled their knapsacks in one corner, pulled the door closed as far as they could, and settled down in the hay. There were crumpled packs of cigarettes and wax paper and empty cans and bottles. It looked as though they were not the first ones to wait here to be taken across the border.

After a while Billie commented: "We'd be home now if the thing with the Yanks had worked." But they did not want to think about it anymore. There was no sense in thinking about it. Dieter would get them across. He had never yet been caught; why should he be caught this time?

It was already getting dark when they heard voices. They strained their ears. Dieter had said he would not come until early morning. That was not Dieter. Those were adults. They heard a loud, strong, man's voice, and the voice of a woman. Dieter had said nothing about taking other people across the border. But they had to be border-crossers — who else would be wandering around at night?

"That's it," they heard the man say in a loud voice, and there they were, at the door. A tall, lean man in a heavy wool coat and a wide-brimmed felt hat. A woman in a fur coat and a thin, pale man in knickerbockers. Each man was carrying two heavy, bulging, leather suitcases.

"What are you doing here?" asked the tall one in the felt hat. "Don't tell me you want to get across, too!" And as he hauled the suitcases into the corner next to the door he said, "There, you see, Anne. Even children want to get across. It can't be that bad. Just sit down." And asked without pausing: "Where d'you want to go, young 'uns?"

When Billie said, "Berlin," he chattered on: "Berlin? D'you hear, Anne? Berlin! It's unbelievable." He pulled a flask out of his coat pocket. "Drink some schnapps, Anne, it'll perk you up," and he held the flask to the woman's lips so she had to drink, though she shook her head and pulled down the corners of her mouth. "Take a sip, it'll do you good!" He drank some himself, and handed the flask to the man in the knickerbockers. "Come on, Ziemann, that'll put some spirit in you! We could use it, it'll be a long night . . ." He talked nonstop. He sent them to collect wood, pulled out the boards behind the door and made a fire, drank from the flask, took two cans from his suitcase, and heated them over the fire.

They watched the three of them eating from the cans and were given half a can themselves. There was meat in it, just meat, red, stringy meat in gelled gravy. It tasted so good that they put the empty can in their knapsack so they could wipe it clean with bread later.

The man pulled a watch out of his pocket and said, "Ten past nine." He put the watch away again and said with a yawn, "When's the guy meant to come? At three? That's almost six hours. That's enough time for a good sleep!" He stretched out and pulled the hat over his face. Three minutes later he was fast asleep. His breath came regularly and when he breathed out he snored softly.

Max blinked into a bright beam of light that blinded him and forced him to squeeze his eyes shut. He heard the woman call fearfully, "Willi, Willi, wake up!" and then Billie's voice next to his ear: "Dieter's here!" But the dazzling, bright light was still in his eyes and he could not see anything. He heard the man who just woke up say, "My name is Korber; are you the expert who's going to take us across?"

At last he could make out something. Someone was standing in the doorway, a short, broad man with a strong nose, eyes hidden under the visor of a cap, and his collar turned up over his chin. He was holding a flashlight and shining it into their corner. "Do the children belong to you?" he asked. Max saw the tall man with the felt hat get up, supporting himself against the wooden wall, brush off his coat, and push the felt hat out of his eyes.

"Why?" he asked quietly. It sounded like a threat.

"I was told three adults. No one said anything about kids," said the man in the doorway. He talked jerkily, as though he could not say more than three words at one time. When he lowered the beam of the light to the floor Max saw that Dieter was standing behind the guide. Dieter stared at Max, his eyes wide, his hand up to his mouth and a finger on his lips, as if he were trying to tell him to keep his mouth shut.

"Listen," said the man with the felt hat. He took two paces toward the door so that Max could not see anything except the back of his coat with broad, straight shoulders, and the hat above. "I was guaranteed that you were the best guide in the area, and that you'll get me safely to the other side. So it shouldn't matter if children come along, too. Or isn't it all that safe?"

"If you want a hundred percent safety, then start looking again!" said the man in the doorway.

"I'll be satisfied with ninety-nine percent!" said the man in the felt hat. He turned around and called, "Okay, kids, move it! Come on! Let's go!" He began pulling the cases from the corner and the man in the doorway said sullenly, "You take them at your own risk!" The other man did not seem to hear. He was pushing his way through the door and said, "Considering the price I'm paying, I'm sure you can carry one of the cases, can't you?"

They groped their way outside, pulling on their knapsacks. The night was as black as pitch. They could not see a thing except the circle of light from the flashlight wandering across the ground ahead of them. They stumbled along behind the others, following the flashlight. Max suddenly felt a hand on his arm and heard Dieter whispering in his ear: "Damned shit! I'd thought you'd gone with the Yanks!"

"We wanted to, but it went wrong," Max whispered back. "How did you know?"

Dieter was breathing fast, as though he had been running. "The old bag told me. I was there this morning."

Max said softly, "We'd left by then," and asked: "Who's that up front?"

Dieter said, "My uncle. He doesn't know I guide people across myself. I had to go along with him. He's a shit."

"So what now?" asked Max. At that moment the beam of light from the flashlight shone straight at them, and the man up front, Dieter's uncle, called gruffly, "Boy! Come here!" Dieter added quickly, "Just don't let on that you know me!" and hurried forward.

They walked through the woods following the flashlight. The only thing they could hear was the soft sound of their steps on the forest floor, the creak of the leather straps, and the panting breath of the woman who seemed frightened stiff.

The forest seemed endless. They no longer had any idea how long they had been walking when Dieter's uncle suddenly stopped. He explained in his jerky way that they were just ten minutes from the border. From now on they would have to be absolutely quiet. He switched off the flashlight and they groped blindly forward, holding on to the knapsack of the one in front, trying to feel out the path with their feet. They breathed through their mouths so they could hear better and stared into the darkness, their eyes wide open, all their senses tense. They could hear nothing, see nothing, not a gleam of light, not a sound.

Then a whispered command came from ahead: "Halt!"

Now they could see the contours of the tree trunks. The edge of the woods seemed to be thirty, forty yards ahead.

"That's the border in front of us," they heard Dieter's uncle say. "Right at the edge of the forest. After that we go across fields for two hundred yards. That's the only place that's dangerous." He paused and they saw the luminous dial of a watch. Then he continued. "It's half past two. I'll see where the guards are. If I'm not back by three, go to the edge of the forest. If I haven't given you a sign by five past three, start running straight across the field. The boy will run first. Wait for me in the woods on the other side until I come. Then there'll be a second line of guards we've got to get through."

"What kind of sign will you give?" asked the man in the felt hat.

"The boy knows," Dieter's uncle answered. They listened to his footsteps moving away quickly. He seemed to have the eyes of an owl. He moved with such confidence through the pitch-black forest, it seemed that his feet had eyes.

Max was standing behind the man in the felt hat. He felt the suitcase against his knee and heard him quietly talking to the woman. Soothing words, so quiet that he could not understand them. Dieter was farther ahead, at the edge of the woods. Max wanted to go over to him, but did not dare move. Why didn't Dieter come over here, damnit! Why didn't he tell them what was happening!

He heard Dieter's voice. "It's time to go." Was it three already? It seemed as though only a few minutes had gone by. They stopped between the last trees.

"What kind of sign will he give?" asked the man in the felt hat.

"Sssh!" said Dieter as though he were listening for something that needed his complete attention. They listened with him. If no sign came, they would run across. Wasn't that it? Or did they have to wait for the sign? Good Lord, what was it he'd said?

"Let's go!" said Dieter in a hushed voice, and took off across the field. They scurried behind him through the tall grass, stooping low, their thumbs under the knapsack straps. The two men panted so loudly under the weight of the suitcases that Max was sure it could be heard miles away. It was suddenly very light in the field, and everything was wide open. There were no bushes for cover. Nothing. Everything level, absolutely flat. And the Russian guards had flare guns. Dieter had told them that. And powerful flashlights. At any moment a beam of light would catch them and nail them down. The Russians must be able to see them on the light field. They probably had their night glasses directed at them already, watching them. Waiting till they were far enough away from the woods. Till they were standing unprotected in the middle of the field.

But suddenly the forest was in front of them. Dieter had already disappeared into the darkness. So had the two men with the suitcases and the woman. A few steps more, and they would have made it. They had made it. They were across. They had crossed the border!

They followed the others a little way into the forest. It seemed to be lighter here than in the forest they had come from. Perhaps the trees were not so dense here. Maybe the day was dawning? No. It could not be that. It was only just after three.

"If you put your suitcases down here, there's a pit," said Dieter softly.

"Why?" asked the man, a slight suspicion in his voice.

"If a guard catches you with your luggage, it's gone for good." There was silence for a moment, the man seemed to be thinking about it.

"That sounds reasonable," he said and put his suitcase in the hole. "Come on, Ziemann, put the suitcases in here!" Turning to Dieter, he said, "You've done this often, haven't you? Hats off to you!"

Dieter said, "There are branches to cover them!"

And the man said: "Come on kids, hand over your knapsacks. Put them in, too."

Dieter quickly answered, "The knapsacks aren't necessary! Not the knapsacks!"

Then the man again: "Why not, d'you want them to lose all their belongings?" They laid their knapsacks next to the suitcases and pulled the branches over them. "It's all excellently organized," said the man. "Hats off. Hats off to you!"

Dieter said, "You'd best get a bit farther into the forest now." His voice sounded urgent, as if he were afraid.

"Okay, okay, okay," said the man. "Now don't go so fast, boy. What's your name, anyway?"

Dieter was running ahead. They could not hear what he said. They groped their way along behind him, arms outstretched, legs catching in the underbrush. It got darker again.

"Anne! Ziemann! Come here, we're over here! Find yourselves a spot, kids," called the man. Max dropped to the ground and felt for his two friends. They were next to him, sitting in the underbrush on the ground. It felt like blueberry bushes and scratchy raspberry plants.

They heard the man unscrew the top of his schnapps flask, heard it gurgling, and then his voice again. "Okay, Kurt, what do we do now? When's your father coming?" He had said "Kurt." Why had he said "Kurt"? Max lifted his head and listened, holding his breath.

"It could be right away. It could take some time," he heard Dieter say.

And then Billie's voice in his ear, softly, full of fear: "Did you hear that?"

Why had Dieter given a false name? For what reason? Max could not see him in the darkness, could not hear what he and the man were discussing. They were talking in whispers.

Then suddenly they heard Dieter come closer. His feet rustled through the underbrush. He did not answer when Max called him. He ran past him, toward the edge of the wood, a dark shadow between the black tree trunks. Then Max could see nothing, hear nothing — silence, not a sound, no rustling, no twigs snapping.

They waited. Waited for an eternity in the silence. They shivered in the cold, huddled together, pressing their arms against their chests and gritting their teeth. They could not stop shivering.

Suddenly they heard steps again, coming toward them quietly through the underbrush. Dieter was coming back; it had to be him. Max stretched out his arm, pulled Dieter down next to him, and asked in a whisper, "What's up?"

Dieter pushed something into his arms. It was his knapsack. "Take your knapsacks," he whispered. "Move it! Put them on!" He had brought all three.

"Hey, boy, Kurt! What's happening?" they heard the man call quietly. He came toward them. "Where are you, boy, say something! What's going on?" Max saw the man appear next to him. A huge, black shadow. He felt a hand grasping for him, felt it on his shoulder, on the knapsack on his back, felt the hand freeze on his knapsack, and grab him and pull him up. He heard the voice above him; it had taken on a dangerous tone.

"What does this mean? Where did the knapsacks come from?" The man was also holding on to Dieter. "Out with it, damn it all! What's going on here? Something's wrong!" Without letting go he called: "Ziemann, come here, we're going to get the suitcases! I suspected it! Filthy trick!" He pushed them away and stepped over them. The other man followed. They heard the two men trampling through the underbrush, sweeping the branches aside, then returning with the suitcases, swearing and panting.

In that instant a beam of light flashed through the trees. The sharp beam of a strong lamp, which jerked around, searching, caught the two men with the suitcases, held them fast, followed them. "Stop! Halt! Stop!" The Russians. But the two men with the suitcases did not stop. They rushed past them farther into the forest. The beam of light followed them.

"Let's go! Follow me!" called Dieter quietly and ran ahead, stooping low. They followed the sound of his steps. The beam of light was still flitting among the trees, but was not aimed at them. It pursued the men who were running into the forest. Dieter had set off in the opposite direction. He threw himself onto the ground into the brush. "Get down! Duck!" They crawled over to him and lay close to him on the ground.

The beam of light was far away now, deep in the forest. The Russian commands echoed over very indistinctly. Why didn't they shoot? The guards down at the river had shot at once. And why was it suddenly so quiet? No more shouting, no more lights. The two men with the suitcases could not have got away. They did not have a chance with those heavy suitcases.

"Shit! Shit! Shit!" said Dieter. It sounded as if he were about to burst into tears. There was still no sound from the forest. But the Russians had to be in there somewhere. Perhaps they were lying in ambush, waiting for something to move. They were bound to come back and search the forest with their flashlights.

"What are we going to do now?" asked Max.

"Shut up! Just stay down!" Dieter whispered back.

Now they could hear footsteps in the forest and a grouchy voice calling, "Dieter! Hey, Dieter! Where are you?" It was Dieter's uncle.

"Stay down!" Dieter hissed at them.

His uncle's voice called again, louder than before, and angrier: "Dieter, answer me! I know you're there!" He was in front of them, but so far away they were not afraid he would find them. "Come here, you bastard! Or you'll get a beating!" He searched around with the flashlight. He came almost to the edge of the woods. Then went back again. "You miserable brat! I'll beat you black and blue when I catch you!" Finally he gave up and ran out into the field.

Max began to understand. At the station in Weissenbach he had heard a refugee talk about guides who stole the luggage away from border-crossers and left them to fend for themselves. That was Dieter's uncle's game.

"Where are the Russians now?" Billie asked in a whisper. There was fear in her voice.

Dieter stood up. "Come with me," he said and took off.

They followed him to the edge of the woods, then hurried behind him in silence, along the edge of it.

A quarter of an hour later he stopped in front of a thicket and squeezed between some firs. When he came out again, he had his school satchel in his hand. He put it on and started down a narrow path leading into the forest. First they went through underbrush, then through forest, across an opening and through more forest, keeping away from the paths. Dieter seemed to know every inch and did not slow down once. They were trotting along with such concentration that they were startled when he stopped abruptly.

In the darkness in front of them lay a narrow valley with a stream running through it. The opposite side of the valley rose steeply, black to the sky.

"We have to go through the stream," said Dieter. "Take off your shoes." While they sat down to take off their shoes and socks and roll up their pants, he continued in a quiet voice. "The stream is the border. But that's not the dangerous part. The guards are up on the hill." He was sitting with his back to them and did not turn around. So that was it. The border was here.

"Let's go, but make it fast!" he said.

They ran through the tall grass down to the stream, and waded through the icy water. On the other side they ran to the edge of the forest at the foot of the valley side. They sat down to put their shoes back on.

"If one of them up there saw us through binoculars, we've had it," said Dieter gloomily. It sounded as if he had come to terms with their being caught and did not care. But then he added comfortingly, "I don't think they've seen us. It's pretty dark tonight."

The hillside was overgrown with young firs whose dry, thorny, entwined branches reached almost to the ground. They had to crawl the whole way on their stomachs. They were sweating from exertion when they finally reached the top.

The forest stopped at the summit. A deeply rutted path led along the edge of the wood. Beyond it were fields and meadows stretching to the horizon. And directly opposite was a path leading into the fields, with a hedge which they could use for cover.

Dieter was lying on his stomach at the edge of the path. He looked both ways to make sure it was safe, quickly scrambled across the path, and disappeared in the shadow of the bushes on the other side.

"Come over, one at a time!" they heard him call in a whisper. Peter went first, then Billie crawled across, finally Max.

They sat huddled together behind the hedge, listening into the darkness. Nothing moved.

"We've got that behind us," whispered Dieter. "We've got to hurry; it'll be light soon."

They walked single file through the fields using hedges and ridges as cover. The sky turned gray and fog rose and enveloped them. They felt safe under Dieter's guidance and strode along confidently. They came to railroad tracks and walked along the foot of the railroad embankment. It began to get light. Two seemingly endless coal trains went by.

Black signs hung on the cars and written on them in white chalk was BERLIN.

That woke them up, roused them from their trudging. Good Lord! If they could get onto a train like that, they would have made it. It would be just as good as the Yank convoy. No more stops till they got home.

How fast was the train traveling? Twenty miles per hour? Twenty-five? That would mean ten, twelve hours to Berlin. Add a few more hours for stops, and you have fifteen, twenty. Maybe one day. Certainly not more. They asked Dieter.

"No problem," he said, and added, astonished: "How'd you think you'd get there?"

A small town came into view, gray and inconspicuous, as though the smoke from the engine had laid itself over the houses.

"We'll stop off at the station first," said Dieter and led them toward it.

When they opened the station door they were hit by a stench of wet clothes, toilets, home-grown tobacco, and beet schnapps that made them gasp. The station hall was one big waiting room made of boards nailed together. It was full of people camping on the floor among their luggage. They looked as though they were at home there, as though they had been living there for weeks. No one looked up when they entered.

There was a small office opposite them, next to the door to the platforms. A Red Cross flag was hanging in front of it and Dieter headed for it.

He knocked on the door under the flag and went in without waiting for an answer. They followed and entered a tiny room hardly large enough for the four of them. There was a table in it, a metal locker, a campbed along the wall, and an iron stove in the corner by the window. In front of the stove was a nurse stirring a big pot. Her blue-and-white uniform and cap were freshly starched and when she turned around they saw an apron as white as snow.

"Oh, it's you, Dieter!" she said. "Whom have you brought this time?" When Dieter explained to her, she said, "Oh, Berlin CEC. You're not the first ones." She pushed a wooden spoon into his hand so he could stir, sat down at the table, got a block of forms from a drawer, and began to ask: "Name? age? address?" She banged a rubber stamp down on each form and said, "That's a permit authorizing you to travel on a passenger train. You can get home with it. You'll have to find out for yourselves which trains you have to take." She nodded at them and gave each of them a piece of paper. They stared at her as though she were a fairy godmother, then carefully folded the pieces of paper, and put them away.

Max asked cautiously, "How much does a ticket cost?"

She smiled in a friendly way and said, "It doesn't cost anything; you'll get through everywhere with that permit." Then she reached under the table and took out four large white mugs and asked, "Would you like some soup?"

They suddenly realized that their stomachs were growling with hunger and nodded shyly. The nurse dipped a large ladle into the pot and filled the mugs to the brim.

It was a thick, munchy bread soup that smelled strongly

of caraway seeds. They sat down next to each other on the camp bed, solemnly holding their mugs in their hands, and sniffed at the smell of bread and caraway over the rim of the mugs. They took tiny sips, felt the warmth running down inside, savored it, and chewed a long time before they swallowed. Never had they ever eaten such good soup before.

Later, at the ticket office, they asked about the trains and found out they first had to go to Plauen and might have to change trains on the way. In Plauen they would certainly have to change trains for Leipzig. The trains would be overcrowded, and they would be lucky to get a place. Then in Leipzig they would have to find out where to go from there. The next train in the direction of Plauen would leave sometime around midday, and the one after that sometime in the evening. They would just have to wait. All trains were running late, anyway.

They went back to an inn in town with Dieter. The curtains were still drawn in the restaurant, and the chairs were on the tables. Dieter cleared a table and they sat down. A little later a girl came in. She was tall and lanky, with her hair tied up and rubber boots on her feet. She opened the curtains and asked whether they wanted any coffee, then shuffled out. When she came back she was carrying a tray with five steaming cups.

Dieter asked, "Where's father?"

The girl put down the tray, pushed a cup toward each of them, and sat down with them. She sipped at the hot coffee with her elbows on the table and said casually, "They caught him yesterday."

"What did he get?" asked Dieter.

"Two days and twenty marks," she said.

"Oh well, he'll be back tomorrow," said Dieter.

Little by little they began to feel the strain of the sleepless night, the cold, the tension, and walking hour after hour. Their legs hurt, and their feet were so swollen that they could barely get their shoes off. When Dieter's sister kindled the fire in the stove and a blissful warmth slowly spread through the restaurant, their eyes began to close.

Something was shaking Max's arm, and someone was shouting in his ear. He wanted to keep on sleeping. But the shouting and shaking continued, and he slowly emerged from his deep sleep. It got lighter around him, and he could distinguish Billie's and Peter's and Dieter's voices quite close to him.

"Wake up, man! Come on, wake up!"

Max laboriously surfaced, opened his eyes, and saw the three of them indistinctly in front of him. "What time is it?" he asked.

"Half past five! The train's due!" said Billie urgently.

They got their knapsacks from the kitchen. "Come on, let's go," said Max.

They ran all the way to the station. When they came onto the platform, a passenger train was standing on the tracks and a man in a red cap was whistling and raised the signal light. It was the train to Plauen.

They raced to it and just reached the last car. A man helped them onto the running board, then onto the platform on the back.

They stood squashed between the others on the back platform, then pushed their way over to the rail. They saw Dieter standing on the platform.

He put his hands to his mouth. "I may come to Berlin some time!" he called after them.

Billie waved till they could not see him anymore.

And now, finally, they knew they would get to Berlin.

Afterword

*B*illie and Max spent two nights and two days on trains, on platforms, and in waiting rooms. They had absolutely nothing to eat. When they boarded the train, Peter got separated from Billie and Max. They looked for him in the station at Plauen and on the following day in the station at Leipzig. They looked through all the trains in which they rode. They did not find him.

On Wednesday, 10 October 1945, at 5 o'clock in the afternoon Billie and Max arrived by passenger train in the center of Berlin. There they parted. Max traveled to the suburb Pankow. Billie traveled north. They never saw each other again.

Billie found her family in the suburb of Frohnau, living with her aunt. All the members of her family, with the exception

of her brother who had fallen in Africa, had survived the
war.

Billie often thought about her journey with Max's gang and
fifteen years later she tried to locate Max Milk in East Berlin. She only found his eldest brother. She wrote the following letter to her family about the meeting.

Berlin 10/10/1960
Today I finally met Max Milk's brother. He told me
what had happened when Max came home on October
10, 1945. I will try to repeat his description as accurately
as possible:

The family was just sitting down to dinner in the
kitchen when Max arrived. His brother opened the
apartment door. He did not recognize Max, but Max
entered and hung his knapsack on the door. His mother
said, "Thank God, boy, that you're back again!" She
set another plate on the table and his brothers and sisters
moved to make room for Max. They were all very
curious, but no one dared ask anything.

Then his father looked up from his plate and asked
Max whether he's brought "the boots" with him. Max
said the Americans took them away from him.

Whereupon he got slapped for the first time. "The
Americans don't take things away from small chil-
dren!" said his father.

When his father asked about the boots again, Max
maintained that the Russians on the border took them

away. This answer made his father even more furious. "The Russians are the last people who'd do something like that!" said Max's father, an old communist.

The father then slapped Max again, so hard that he crashed off his chair.

Thereupon, said the brother, Max got up without a word, took his knapsack from the hook, and left the house. They never heard from him again. Even the inquiries which the mother made through the Red Cross Tracing Service brought no results.

Poor Max — I hope he's all right. After all we went through, he deserves a bit of happiness, doesn't he?